Praise for *Ghost on Black Mountain*

"Pull up a rocker and gaze into the hills at sundown. Old-time front porch storytelling unfolds in this dark, twisted tale where hardscrabble lives, murderous secrets, and ghosts intersect on a mysterious mountain."

—Beth Hoffman, *New York Times* bestselling author
of *Saving CeeCee Honeycutt*

"Ann Hite's *Ghost on Black Mountain* is an eerie page-turner told in authentic mountain voices that stick with the reader long after the last page is turned."

—Amy Greene, author of *Bloodroot*

"Haunting, dark and unnerving, Hite's brilliant modern gothic casts an unbreakable spell."

—Caroline Leavitt, *New York Times* bestselling author
of *Pictures of You*

"The authentic voice of Nellie Pritchard, who comes to Black Mountain as a new bride, wraps around you and pulls you deep into this haunted story. Ann Hite delivers an eerie page-turner that I couldn't put down."

—Joshilyn Jackson, *New York Times* bestselling author
of *Gods in Alabama* and *Backseat Saints*

Ghost on Black Mountain

ANN HITE

GALLERY BOOKS

New York   London   Toronto   Sydney   New Delhi

G

Gallery Books

A Division of Simon & Schuster, Inc.

1230 Avenue of the Americas

New York, NY 10020

First Gallery Books trade paperback edition September 2011

GALLERY BOOKS and colophon are trademarks of Simon & Schuster, Inc.

For information about special discounts for bulk purchases,
please contact Simon & Schuster Special Sales at 1-866-506-1949
or business@simonandschuster.com.

The Simon & Schuster Speakers Bureau can bring authors to your
live event. For more information or to book an event, contact the
Simon & Schuster Speakers Bureau at 1-866-248-3049
or visit our website at www.simonspeakers.com.

Designed by Davina Mock-Maniscalco
Map by Jerry Clifford Hite

Manufactured in the United States of America

10 9 8 7 6 5 4 3 2 1

Library of Congress Cataloging-in-Publication Data

Hite, Ann.
    Ghost on Black Mountain / Ann Hite.—1st Gallery Books trade pbk. ed.
        p. cm.
      1. Women—Southern States—Fiction. 2. Country life—Southern
    States—Fiction. 3. Murder—Fiction. I. Title.
    PS3608.I845G56 2011
    813'.6—dc22

                                                        2011000242

ISBN 978-1-4516-0642-3
ISBN 978-1-4516-0643-0 (ebook)

For Jack and Ella,
who are the very essence of this book,
my heart and soul.

Granny, your voice still lives.

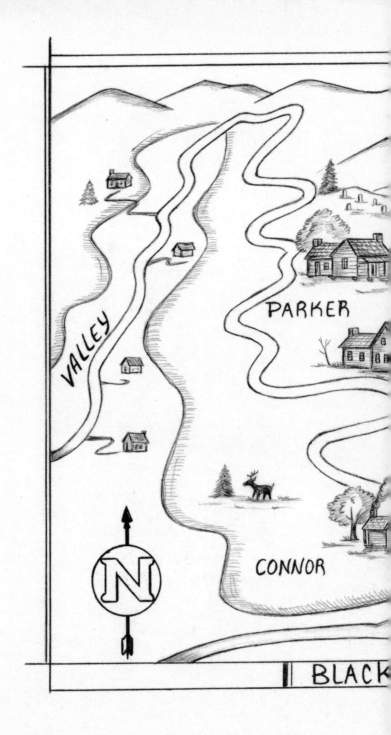

Part One

Nellie Pritchard

One

Mama warned me against marrying Hobbs Pritchard. She saw my future in her tea leaves: death. I was young, only seventeen, and thought I knew all there was to know about life. Nobody could tell me different. Mama and me lived on the edge of Asheville, not the rich part of town but not the worst either. We attended Hope in Christ Church. It was our place to go on Sundays to pray for those worse off than ourselves. The Depression brought hard times on everyone. The church did its part by serving one meal a day. People lined up at the door hours before time to eat. We could only take one hundred people for each meal. And I was there standing behind the counter ready to serve. Folks would fight over the places in line. It nearly turned my heart inside out. One afternoon Hobbs Pritchard came walking up to me all cocky and sure of himself.

"What are you doing here in a place like this? You're way too pretty." He smiled and opened his hands like he was some angel sent from God to ask me that very question. I never stopped to wonder what brought him into a soup kitchen.

He showed up right at a time when I thought I couldn't scoop one more ladle of weak chicken broth. I really hated that mess. The smell got in my nose and stayed with me all night.

"I'm helping those in a bad way."

He folded his arms across his chest, tucking each of his hands under a armpit. "Why?"

Now, that was a question I'd never even thought on. I did what I did because Mama said it was a privilege to work the food line, because the church needed me, because there were people out there starving with no homes, living in cardboard boxes. "I really don't know." I looked into his crystal-clear blue eyes that reminded me of a winter sky. Those eyes made me see life his way in an instant.

In the first days of sweet romance, if Hobbs had asked me to jump off a cliff, I would have with a smile on my face. Mama always said, "Nellie, don't love a man too much. A woman should save some feelings back to care for herself." And Mama should have known, seeing how she loved my daddy with every bone in her body. When he died—a horrible accident in the stone quarry where he worked—part of her soul faded away. One day she was something else to look at in full bloom, and the next she was dropping one beautiful petal at a time until all her heart was gone like a bunch of spent tulips. Maybe it was this story that made me fall for Hobbs as hard as I did. The last thing I wanted was to be used up before I was old with no man to love me.

One night Hobbs took me out of town to look at the stars. We stretched out in the bed of his old truck. Now, I knew I was playing with fire, but I didn't care one bit. I thought I could handle anything thrown at me.

"You done changed me, Nellie."

I kept real still, afraid all the beauty of the night would disappear. This man was making me believe I might just be something special.

"I got me a decent place up on Black Mountain. I'm not some poor hobo standing in your soup line. I'm a man to be reckoned with." He leaned over and kissed me, running his hand clean down the front of my dress. My whole body heated. He laughed at the little shiver I gave.

"We're going to get married, Nellie girl. How about tomorrow?" And the deal was sealed without a question asked.

Mama refused to come. "It's too soon, Nellie. You don't even know this boy. He could be the worst man alive."

The ceremony wasn't much to speak of, just the Baptist preacher, a Bible, and words that bound me until death did part us. When Hobbs kissed me, the preacher puffed up like some old bullfrog. Out of my side vision I saw a girl, pretty in a rugged way—like she'd been pulled from pillar to bedpost, roaming the streets too early in life. I'd seen lots like her in the soup line. She stood in the door of that small church, casting a shadow up the aisle, and looked me dead in the eyes. Then she left. Chills walked up my arms, but I pushed them away. I loved Hobbs Pritchard with all my heart and soul, and he loved me.

Our honeymoon consisted of one night in the back room of Mr. Hamby's mercantile. Hobbs paid real good money for the privilege. He tore at the pretty buttons on my white dress. I'd made it for Easter the spring before. I watched each one of those tiny fake pearls pop off and hit that cold hard floor, bouncing like little balls.

"It's time for me to get what I got coming to me."

He pushed me on the old musty cot. I wanted to slow him down, but his desires just couldn't be contained. He hammered me with his body, drinking that love I offered in one sloppy gulp. When he finished his business, he stood and dressed.

"I got to go out for a while. You stay put." And he left, no kiss or hug. I was right hurt, but then I remembered he wasn't big on affection unless it suited him. This much I already knew. Mama always said there wasn't no moving Daddy out of a mood when he got into one. I had to get used to Hobbs's ways. I looked up at the dirty ceiling, tracing a water stain that looked like the state of Georgia. Somehow I had to soften him.

Hobbs moved me straight up to Black Mountain the very next day. He waited in the truck while I visited with Mama and packed a few things. He said I didn't need my old stuff, but I told him I couldn't go to my new home empty-handed.

"You can't just leave, Nellie. This ain't the right thing to do." Mama followed me from the kitchen to my tiny bedroom.

"He's my husband, Mama. I love him."

"He's no good." Mama stamped her foot as if she could force me back into my innocent ways.

"You've not seen his soft side. It shows when he looks at me. You don't even know him either." I gathered my few dresses.

"I've heard stories about him, Nellie. Tony down at the bakery told me just this morning that he's killed at least one man."

I held my hands over my ears. "Don't. He's my husband. I'm going to his home on Black Mountain. You even said yourself you might like to live up there one day."

"That's just pie-in-the-sky dreaming. You can't go there, not with him." She touched my arm, and I nearly broke in half at the thought of not feeling her touch whenever I wanted.

"I got to go. I love you." I buried my face in her neck and breathed in the smell of her cold cream that she smeared on her face each night.

"Please listen to me, Nellie." She wrapped her arms around me. "You'll be too far away. I won't be able to help you." She stroked my blond hair like she did when I was a little girl. I almost gave in and stayed, but that was giving up before I even tried. Didn't she understand? Hadn't she ever noticed? Not one boy had given me the time of day. If I didn't love Hobbs with my whole heart, I might lose my chance to be loved by a man.

The horn on the truck interrupted us. "I got to go." I pulled away and left the only home I'd ever known with a feed sack of clothes, a few trinkets, and a childhood of memories.

Mama stood in the door, twisting the tail of her skirt in her weathered fingers, and cried like a baby. "Nothing in this world, Nellie, will ever be the same. You'll never come back here. I've seen it all in the tea leaves: death."

Mama was just desperate to keep me home. There wasn't nothing bad going to happen. I didn't much believe in tea leaves anyway.

Two

The leaves had turned the mountain into orange, red, and yellow flames that shot into the sky. I sat next to my husband in his truck, knowing I was the luckiest girl in all the world. We passed little cabins that looked like they might slide down the side of the steep drop-offs. And always the river flashed into view, twisting and turning, sometimes next to the road, sometimes just loud churning music.

As we passed, folks threw up a hand here and there like someone was forcing them to be nice, keeping busy with whatever chore they was working on. I expected more of a welcome with Hobbs living in such a small place. That's when I seen a whole gaggle of boys—their height resembling doorsteps—playing in the front of one cabin that sat in a sunny clearing all fresh and clean. One of the boys looked to be a couple of years older than me and watched me close, even though he was trying to act like he wasn't paying us no mind. His mama stood in the door, wearing a faded dress that hung on her slight figure. Her face, strong and creased, reminded me of a map that had been studied by many on their way to different places.

"Who is that family, Hobbs?"

Hobbs had been real quiet on the trip. Daddy used to draw inside himself just like that when me or Mama did something to get under his skin. What had I done to make Hobbs mad?

"That's the Connors, poor as dirt. High and mighty too. The Depression put them under. Take a good look. That's what this mountain can do to a soul if they don't stand against it. The Connors turned their God-loving hearts away from my help. Won't accept any offers." He threw his hand out the window in a half wave. The woman only stared. "She's the worst. Ain't nothing like a woman with some kind of attitude." His laugh turned mean around the edges.

I looked out the back window and hoped to study on the woman a little longer, but she was gone and so was the boy that had stared at me. The rest of his brothers scrambled in the yard like a bunch of ants eating on a sugar cookie.

We stopped at the next house, larger than the others, and my stomach flipped to think I'd have that much room to wander around.

Hobbs grinded the truck gears metal to metal. "This ain't ours. Don't worry. Ours is bigger. This here is where Aunt Ida and my stepbrother Jack live. I'm sure they are dying to meet you. And Aunt Ida would beat me with a stick if I passed by here without stopping."

I married a man without even meeting his family first. That just wasn't proper. But not much about Hobbs and me had been proper. My whole insides froze up at the thought of meeting them.

Hobbs jumped out of the truck; a flash of his bare chest showed through his unbuttoned collar. "Come on, girl. Don't get all shy now." He kind of smiled, and I knew he was playing with me. If I closed my eyes, I could see us with our own babies like a real family.

I slid out of the truck. "What if they don't like me, Hobbs?"

"That's just tough shit, ain't it, Nellie." He grabbed my hand and pulled me along. His excitement spread through my fingers. We were going to be the happiest couple on the mountain, maybe even in the South.

A woman met us on the front porch. A deep frown creased her forehead. "Hobbs, where have you been? We got trouble with that Connor bunch. They won't pay the rent on the land. We can't keep holding them up. It ain't theirs no more. That wife of his runs the whole show and tells Connor what to do. It's just plain sinful and unnatural. Where's his backbone?" She looked over and sized me up. I knew I'd failed some test. "Who you got here, Hobbs? She's just a baby."

Was she making fun of me or did I look that young?

"You're too old for her."

Hobbs was twenty-five to my seventeen going on eighteen. That wasn't so bad.

Hobbs looked at me and shrugged with a little-boy grin. "This here is my wife, Aunt Ida."

"Are you telling me a whopper, boy?" Aunt Ida's face seemed to melt into one huge disappointment.

"I ain't a boy. And this is my wife. I found her serving folks in a soup kitchen in Asheville. If that ain't a real woman, I don't know what is." He wrapped his arm around my shoulders, pulling me next to his body that gave off heat on that chilly day. I was snug, protected.

"You done married some little girl from Asheville without telling me?" The news was starting to sink in to this woman's head. I thought she might pop from anger, but Hobbs didn't seem to notice. "Jack, come on out here. Jack?" She yelled at the top of her lungs, staring straight at me like she could drive a hammer through my skull.

A tall man ambled out of the barn to the side of the house. He wore a big straw hat that reminded me of that book I read, *Huckleberry Finn*, except this was a mighty fine looking man, almost as cute as Hobbs.

Hobbs looked at Jack and a small shadow passed over his face. Funny how I didn't even know Hobbs, but his dislikes and moods were starting to make their mark on my memory. Our love was that strong.

Hobbs gave me a little squeeze. "This here is Nellie Pritchard, my new wife. We got married yesterday." He looked at Jack.

"Nice to meet you, Nellie. I reckon we need a young woman in this family." His voice was softer than the wind slipping through the leaves.

A thought scooted through my mind. Had I seen him first, things might have turned out different when it came to marrying Hobbs. "It's nice to meet you."

Hobbs stiffened. "I'm going to get Nellie on up to have a look at our place. You come up and visit us, Brother." But I couldn't hear the invitation in his tone, not for the life of me.

"Now, Hobbs, what are you going to do up there in that dirty old house? You need proper things like linens and dishes. I've got some things here I've been saving that belonged to your mama. It's been over a year since your sister left, so I don't reckon she's coming back. Maybe you and your new bride might want them?" She smiled pretty at me, too pretty. "You know that AzLeigh, Hobbs's sister, up and left about a year ago. Poor thing, her husband and baby died with barely two weeks passing between them. It was right sad. I think she must've lost her mind, leaving like she did. Nothing, not a thing did she take. You know what they say about this mountain? Once you leave there ain't no coming back, not really, but you'll long for it. It never gets out of your blood."

"AzLeigh ain't crazy." Both Hobbs and Jack said this almost at the same time, and both frowned at each other for having done it.

"She's about as smart as one woman can be." Jack's words were soft.

"I don't reckon any of us knows AzLeigh better than her own blood brother." Hobbs shot a look at me. "You want Mama's things?"

My words stuck in my mouth. I didn't know how to answer.

"Sure we do, Aunt Ida." He looked away from me like my not answering didn't mean a thing.

"Good, come on in here and take a look. Jack, you need to see if there's anything you want to take."

I felt Hobbs's arm stiffen around my shoulders.

"No. I don't want nothing. I don't have a claim to it."

Hobbs relaxed just a bit. "Let's get this mess and head on home. Me and Nellie here has some unfinished business." He winked at me, and for a second I couldn't imagine what he was talking about until I looked at the sly smile on Aunt Ida's face, and my cheeks heated like they was on fire. I looked at the ground.

"Look now, how you've shamed that poor child. You got to remember she's a proper young lady, Hobbs. She ain't used to the likes of you. Take that other girl down in Asheville . . ." Aunt Ida rambled on.

"Aunt Ida, let's get them things." Hobbs pulled me into the house.

I was too busy trying to cool down the heat in my face to give anything else much thought, and that was bad on my part. Anyway, I never thought he was some kind of saint. I knew he had to have had some girlfriends, being older than me by eight years. But what came before me was before me and it didn't matter.

"Hobbs, you should let me send some help for your new wife. That big dirty house is a sight and you know it." Aunt Ida had a stern look on her face.

"I don't want nobody underfoot, Aunt Ida."

"I bet there's ten years' worth of dust, not to mention them floors. The little colored gal that works for the preacher could do it."

I opened my mouth to say no thank you, but Aunt Ida cut a glare at me that hushed me up.

"I better not even see that girl's face," Hobbs threatened.

Aunt Ida smiled. "I'll send her tomorrow."

"That's nice, ma'am." What was I going to say?

"You can call me Aunt Ida." She cocked her eyebrow at me.

The things Aunt Ida gave us were as lacy and dainty as a fine woman in her flower garden, like the linens Mama washed with her dried cracked fingers for the rich women of Asheville. I touched the sheets and thought of Hobbs and me wrapped in them quiet, not all hurried like our first time. I stole me a glance at him and he caught it with his crooked smile. Hobbs didn't know a thing about slowing down.

The lace was soft under my touch, not the scratchy dime-store stuff. How would I fit in with such nice things? The closest I ever came to fine things was a bar of lavender soap, a washtub, and a scrub board.

Hobbs's house looked the same as the rich houses in Asheville. It had a whopper of a porch, the kind that wrapped around the house, the kind I used to imagine I could roller-skate on all afternoon without one chore waiting on me.

"Nice, ain't it?"

I was without one little word. At home me and Mama could hear each other breathe at night.

"My daddy built it for my mama when he brought her here from Asheville. She came from a rich family and was used to the finer things in life. Daddy loved her. We all did. She made a room glow when she entered." He looked so far off I was afraid he might not come back.

"I ain't never been past the front hall of a house that big." I whispered the words.

"Let's go in, Mrs. Hobbs Pritchard. Mama would approve of you."

The house was musty with age and lack of love. Cobwebs hung here and there. The windows were filthy. I was proud someone was coming to help because we had our work cut out for us. Lordy be, Mama would die. Hobbs loved me enough to marry me and bring me to such a fine home. I was the luckiest girl in the state of North Carolina. I threw my arms around his neck.

"Whoa, girl." He laughed as he lost his balance and fell backwards on the sofa that was covered with a dusty sheet. His kisses reminded me of soft peppermint sticks and were just as dangerous as sugar was to teeth. Maybe one day I could teach him how to slow down. We had a whole lifetime ahead. Mama was so wrong. I'd have to write her a letter and tell her about my new home. Maybe Hobbs would get over being hurt and let her come visit. Outside the big window in the front room was the perfect place for a garden. The sun caught on the river that twisted off in the woods. The sound would sing me to sleep every night.

Hobbs kissed me some more. Aunt Ida mentioning that girl shouldn't have bothered me a bit. Was she someone recent? All those silly thoughts kept pricking me as sharp as a needle sewing through thick cloth.

Three

That night as Hobbs slept tangled in his mother's fine linens, I stood in the window, overlooking the front yard, watching the mountain breathe. *Nellie.* The name floated over the sound of the river. I was thinking on my marriage to Hobbs. Wishing somehow things could have been different. Mama was an ache in my chest. A big old harvest moon hung in the sky, bathing the clearing with a ghost light.

The man stood at the edge of the woods just like he belonged there, like a brown tin photo from time gone by. He stared out at the house. Was he the mountain come alive? That was silly. He was a living, breathing trespasser. I turned to call Hobbs from the bed, but when I glanced back the man was gone. Had he seen me and run? Or was he part of my dreams?

That morning after breakfast someone knocked on the kitchen door. Hobbs was out at the barn.

A little colored girl dressed in a faded blue shift nodded. "I be Shelly. Mrs. Dobbins told me I had to come over and help you." It was clear she was not happy to be on our doorstep.

I guessed her age to be fourteen. "Nice to meet you, Shelly."

She gave me a long look. "You tell me what to do, and I'll do it."

"Come on in, and we'll get started." I stepped out of the door.

"Yes ma'am."

"My husband was born here." I looked around the room.

"Everybody knows that, ma'am." She watched me.

"Well, it's a mess."

"Yes ma'am."

I looked out the window just in time to see Hobbs leave the barn and climb into his truck. "You stay here." I went out on the porch. "Hey Hobbs."

He looked over at me with a frown and stopped the truck. "I'm going to take care of business."

I ran up to the passenger side. "That girl is here to help."

"Well, get her to work. I don't want to pay good money for her standing around. I can't see why you couldn't do the work yourself."

I opened my mouth to remind him how I never asked for no help, but he kept talking.

"I ain't going to be bothered with woman's work, Nellie. You go take care of that. I'll see you tonight." He shifted the truck into gear and stepped on the gas.

"I love you." But I was shouting at the back of the truck.

"Mrs. Pritchard." Shelly stood in the door.

"Nellie, call me Nellie."

"My mama would tan my hide for that. No ma'am, it ain't proper." She had her hand on her hip.

"I'm closer to your age than your mama's."

"I'll be fourteen on Christmas."

"Eighteen in the spring."

Shelly shook her head. "Mama was right."

"What?" I followed her back into the kitchen.

"She said that anyone that would marry Hobbs Pritchard was either crazy in the head or so young she had no sense." She looked at me as I filled a pot with water. "I guess you be the last one. I ain't got a bit of use for Hobbs Pritchard, ma'am. Most on this mountain don't. Mama would whip me for saying that, but I'm warning you. He ain't liked." She took the pot from me and put it on the wood stove.

I stoked the fire.

"You want to start with washing these walls and windows? Ain't nobody cared for this house in a passel of years." Shelly waited for my answer.

"Why don't you like Hobbs?"

"I ain't going to talk about it. Don't ask me no more."

"Shoot. I don't have any soap. How can we clean?" I looked in the cupboard.

"I got some stuff Mama sent. She figured you'd be lacking in this house." Shelly went to the door and picked up a feed bag. "The only reason Mrs. Dobbins is doing this, letting me work here today, is to get Hobbs's old aunt to come to church. Miss Ida Pritchard snubbing the church has crawled right under Mrs. Dobbins's skin." She pulled some bottles out of the bag. "One more thing."

If I kept my mouth shut, Shelly would end up answering all my questions.

"This house has a ghost roaming the rooms because of you."

For a minute I couldn't speak. A cold prickle ran up my scalp. "What do you mean?" A pressure built in my stomach and worked into my chest.

She shrugged. "I got sight. Them spirits stuck here on this mountain always come to bother me."

"Mama said ghosts just aren't so." I moved to the other side of the kitchen and pushed the memory of the man standing in the yard from my mind. There wasn't no such thing as ghosts.

"No disrespect, ma'am, but your mama lies." She lined up her cleaning supplies on the table. "Just be careful is all."

"I think the walls and windows will do fine." This strange girl and me had a lot of work to do. "There will be some ghosts around here if Hobbs comes home and we ain't working."

Shelly looked at me sharp. "It ain't no joking matter, Miss Pritchard."

No, it sure isn't.

Four

The days turned chilly. The beauty of the leaves, the view of the valley, and the happiness rushing around my insides made me know I was in the best place in the world. The house showed a little order after Shelly and me got a hold of it. We got the rooms where me and Hobbs spent most of our time. We scrubbed, polished, washed, and ironed until I thought I might fall flat on my face. Shelly came two times a week. We didn't talk too much after that first day and I sure didn't see any ghosts. Us working together filled up what would have been empty hours.

I found me a lavender bush out beside the kitchen door. Lord, I guessed Hobbs hadn't even paid it no mind. It was probably growing wild from back when his mama planted it. Come late spring the lavender added to water and sprinkled throughout the rooms would give the place a fresh smell. Just like home.

Hobbs and me visited with Aunt Ida nearly every day. Some days it was the last place I wanted to be. I tried and tried to talk to that woman. I smiled. I even searched my heart for goodwill, but Aunt Ida ruined everything I did with her sharp words and disgusted looks. But shame always built in my heart, and I went with a smile on my face, being how Hobbs loved his family so much. I couldn't fault him that. Jack kept out of sight—only showing up when we stayed for supper—quiet and brooding like a thunderstorm in the distance. That was too bad. The truth was I wanted to know more about Jack.

One evening Hobbs and me stood in the kitchen with Aunt Ida. Hobbs had a way of saying what was on his mind, no matter how bad it came out. "Aunt Ida, you got to teach Nellie to cook." He threw one of his "I know everything" looks at me. "Her food tastes like that soup kitchen she worked in." He laughed at his own joke, but Aunt Ida only stared at me with a smug look on her face.

I didn't take no offense to Hobbs's remark. Shoot, he talked like that all the time. It was just his way. I didn't come from a family like his. Mama and me were plain people with simple ideas. "When can I come for a cooking lesson, Aunt Ida?" I turned on my smile.

Hobbs laughed like he won some contest. "You can try and teach her. I'm not sure it'll help." He went outside.

Aunt Ida gave me a long, slow look. "You come on down here tomorrow. I'll show you his favorite dinner."

"What is his favorite?" Her biscuits were soft and fluffy just like Mama's. Come to think of it, my biscuits were like Mama's. Maybe Hobbs hadn't noticed how good they were. He was always thinking on something else.

"Chicken pot pie. His mama made it when she was alive."

"He loved his mama."

Aunt Ida placed fat pieces of fried chicken on a platter. One piece of that chicken would have fed two adults in the soup line.

"Lord, child, he was too close to her. She ruined him and then died. Took the wind right out of him. He was seventeen. Too young to be the man of the house."

"Where was his daddy?"

"Oh, he was a walking dead man until he up and married Jack's mama six months later. Hobbs never forgave him, or Jack for that matter." She leveled a serious stare at me. "You've seen Jack. He's calm where Hobbs is loud. He's sweet where Hobbs has a mean streak. You think he ain't mean, but girlie, you're wrong. You best watch yourself and maybe you'll be okay. Hobbs dug deeper into that pit of mean when his mama died. AzLeigh, his sister, loved Bess—their stepmother—better than anything. She loved Jack too. Hobbs saw it as betrayal even though he never talked about it. See, he loved AzLeigh and his mama with his whole heart. Something can be said for not loving a person like that." She cocked her eyebrow at me.

"I got so much to learn about him, but we got a lifetime." I gave her my brightest tone of voice.

"Maybe so."

Her words sent chills up my neck. She was only jealous of me and Hobbs. Anyone could see she loved him like he was her own. Sometimes people turned mean and afraid when a new person came into the picture. Daddy was like that when Mama tried to do anything new. He got downright ugly with her. It was the only time I ever disliked him; that side of him was hard to swallow.

"Let's get this supper on the table. I can't imagine your mama never taught you to cook." She smiled. "Hobbs didn't mean to hurt you."

"Oh, he's right. I'm a terrible cook." I picked up the platter of chicken and went to the dining room; imagine, a dining room. I had moved into high society. The table was covered with lace and there were plates with gold rims. In the large mirror over the fireplace was a girl as plain as plain could be. She was a girl who told lies on herself. Because she was a good cook. That was a fact.

"You go out and call Hobbs to eat. Maybe you shouldn't worry so much on how you look." Aunt Ida met my stare in the reflection.

I wandered out to the barn instead of standing on the back porch screaming my lungs out.

Hobbs's voice was mean. "We got to get the Connors to give in, Jack!"

"I ain't going to help with your business, Hobbs. I told you that when Clyde Parker got himself killed. And I made it real clear when you ran AzLeigh off. That was it for me." Jack's voice was as calm as a pretty little pond in the woods.

"AzLeigh wouldn't listen. She brought trouble on herself. Clyde was a accident and you dern well know it. The Connors are too high and mighty. They'll listen to your reasoning."

"Like AzLeigh? You tricked me into thinking you cared about her loss too." Jack's voice never got a bit louder, but the words cut the air.

I should've stepped into the door, instead of hiding like some sneak, but I didn't. I just listened.

"AzLeigh ain't nothing to you."

I could imagine the mean look on Hobbs's face.

"Neither is the Connors."

"We need them to play along."

"Why? You afraid the whole mountain will turn against you? The Depression won't last forever and these good folks will get back on their feet. Where will that leave you?"

"They can't get their land unless I sell it back."

"You can't resist making the money. They'll get their land back."

Hobbs laughed.

"What'd you tell that girl in Asheville when you married your little wife?"

My heart started beating in my ears, and I stepped in the doorway. "You boys come eat. Orders from Aunt Ida." My face burned hot.

Jack smiled. I got the feeling he'd known I was there all along. "Let's go eat, Brother." If he had been writing the word "brother" on a piece of paper, it would have been big and bold.

Hobbs cut a look at me. I was learning each expression meant something different. I looked at the ground. He was daring me to ask one little question. I knew to keep my mouth shut.

Five

Shelly knocked on the door the next morning just after Hobbs left out. He never told me about anything he did, and most of the time I couldn't find the nerve to ask. He got so cranky.

"I thought we'd work upstairs today."

"Yes ma'am." She held on to the words, drawing them out with a sigh.

"Would you rather work in the dining room? We could go through that sideboard." I didn't much feel like working either. "How about we take us a walk first. I need to get out."

Shelly's face lit up. "Yes ma'am. That sounds real good."

The sky was so clear and blue that I felt like crying. I was missing Mama. If I brought the subject up with Hobbs, he still growled how he had no use for the "woman."

Me and Shelly walked into the woods near the hollow tree. We didn't even speak for the longest time—the river was loud—and we probably wouldn't have spoken at all if not for seeing that man again, the one I saw in the night. He was standing way down the path.

"Lordy be, I didn't dream him."

Shelly straightened her shoulders and looked at me.

"Sir!" I yelled. "Can I help you? Why are you here on my husband's land?"

Shelly touched my arm. "You see him?" She seemed shocked.

"Who is he?"

The man wore glasses, but he was so far away I couldn't make out any other details.

Shelly had stopped walking. "He be someone you don't want to know, ma'am."

The man stood stock still.

"I want a better look." I walked toward him.

He moved in the direction of the river.

"I saw you the other night!" I yelled, but he was gone, just like that.

"It's best we not go to the river, Mrs. Pritchard. It can be dangerous being so high because of the rain."

I studied her face. "Shelly, you're afraid of him."

"Not me." She didn't look me in the eye.

"And don't call me Mrs. Pritchard!"

Shelly gave me a mean look. "I'm not getting my tail whipped because of you."

"Then call me Miss Nellie."

She looked around. "I reckon."

"Good." I walked closer. "Now, tell me why that man is here."

"Well, I guess because he had a falling-out with Hobbs, or that's what folks claim."

"So you know him?"

She didn't look at me. "No, can't say I ever spoke to him."

"What kind of falling-out did him and Hobbs have?"

This time she met my stare. "I ain't going to talk about

Hobbs Pritchard behind his back. I ain't stupid. No disrespect intended."

"Hobbs wouldn't hurt you, Shelly." We were walking side by side.

She looked at me like I lost my mind. "Don't take no hurt on this, but there's a lot you don't know about your husband." She let this sink in. "I reckon you better take me on back to that dern house so you can work me some. I ain't a good liar."

I studied her for a minute. I bet she knew about that girl in Asheville. "I know folks have a quarrel with him."

"Yes ma'am." Shelly grinned and broke into a run. "If you is so young like me why don't you race me to the house?"

I broke into a run, giggling like a schoolgirl. The world passed by me in a blur. Wonder if I could run right off that mountain? Then I thought of the man we seen in the woods. What did Hobbs do to him? What kind of husband had folks roaming on his farm looking for him, anyway?

Six

Hobbs had two boys come to the house and chop wood for the winter. The job should have been done in the summer so the wood could cure, but seeing how Hobbs had no idea we'd be marrying and moving in the house, he could be forgiven. But I was a little nervous about a mountain winter without plenty of wood.

"Don't be silly, Nellie. I can get all the cured wood I want. You won't be cold this winter." He was knocking around the kitchen while I cooked bacon and eggs for breakfast. I wanted to ask him why he didn't just buy all the wood and not bother with them boys, but I kept them thoughts tight in my head. Wasn't no use to cause trouble. Like Aunt Ida said, he had his ways. I'd seen them that very morning when he found where Shelly left a cleaning rag in the dining room and promised to beat her. I told him it was my rag and for a minute I thought he'd slap my nose off my face.

"Where did them boys come from?" The bacon popped grease on my arm. I dearly hated bacon. The boys were

Connors, but I wanted to hear Hobbs's answer. I was still thinking on all Shelly had said or hadn't said.

"The tall one is Maynard and the short one is Oshie. Both of them are Connors. At least they see some reason, but their daddy don't. He'd beat them if he knew they were here. I can't figure why they agreed to come."

"How much is their pay?" I placed the platter of bacon on the table.

Hobbs threw his head back in a big laugh like I'd told some kind of joke. "I don't pay for work, Nellie. People pay me. You're dumber than a mule."

The words stung like one of those switches Daddy used on my bare legs when I was young and did something wrong. He'd send me out into the yard to find a switch that had a good snap to it. "I just thought since they're working for us . . ."

"Well, I didn't marry you to think, now did I?" He pulled me to him, and I nearly dropped the basket of raw eggs. "You're funny, Nellie. Just keep entertaining me and I'll stay around."

"What do you mean? Are you going somewhere?" Heat moved through my face.

His grin made him hard to figure. "I got to work sometime, Nellie."

Now he had a good point. "What kind of work, Hobbs?" That was a stupid question for a wife to ask her husband. "You don't farm."

Again he threw back his head and laughed in a mean way. "I'd rather die. I'm a businessman. It's tough to do business up here, so I travel around. You're going to have to get used to that now, sweetie. I just can't sit here all the time."

He hadn't sat at home. A big lump got stuck in my throat. I counted the eggs in the bowl. Hobbs had brought them home from someone who owed him money. He was smart like that. Mama would call him slick. "I thought maybe we could have

Mama come visit." I drew in my breath and cracked each one of the eggs into the cast-iron skillet.

"That woman wouldn't even come to our wedding. I can't tolerate her. You don't need to be talking to her." He piled a bunch of bacon on his plate. "You got all you need right here on this mountain. Just put that nonsense out of your head. You don't need your mama like some baby girl."

The eggs went to bubbling in the pan. I kept my mouth closed tight. What was I thinking? Mama hurt him, and who could blame him for being upset? Some folks weren't as easy to forgive as me. I looked at the side of his face. How in the world had I got such a fine man to notice me? He could have had any number of girls with his charms. If Hobbs hadn't come along, who would have? He was mine.

"When you leaving?" I scraped the eggs onto a plate.

"Now, don't go worrying on that. I'll let you know in plenty of time. Is that why you want your mama? You're going to miss old Hobbs too much? You need him to protect you." Little bits of bacon flew out of his mouth as he pulled me on his lap. "I picked you cause you're strong. You'll be fine when I go away." He pinched my leg. I looked away to hide the tears.

"Now, let's eat. I got to visit the Connor farm and I ain't relishing the idea. Will you be okay here with them boys?"

"Why wouldn't I?" All them mixed-up thoughts rushed out with a attitude.

But Hobbs didn't notice. "Those boys don't like me much, but they listen to reason."

"I can't see they would cause anyone a bit of harm."

He looked at me a little sharp. "Whether you've noticed or not, folks up here don't care for me. So you got to be careful, Nellie. They're jealous cause I've made something out of myself. I can't help I got some sense."

"Why are they jealous?"

"Ain't nothing for you to trouble your little mind over." He slapped me on the bottom.

After breakfast Hobbs took out of the house like it was going to fall in on him, but not before he warned me to stay away from the Connor boys. I stood in the kitchen window and watched them work their fool heads off. They weren't talking or even looking at each other like most brothers would when saddled with a day's work. It looked to me like they needed some cheering up. And I was a grown-up woman with just as much sense as Hobbs. I could take care of myself.

Them boys stopped their chopping and watched me pick my way across the yard, balancing overloaded plates of eggs and bacon. Didn't their mama teach them any manners? "I have some breakfast for you."

Both looked at me like I was some kind of ghost.

"I have plenty of milk too, but my hands are so full I couldn't tote it." They stood there like a couple of dummies.

The oldest boy took off his hat. "I'm Maynard Connor, ma'am, and this here is my brother without a stitch of manners, Oshie." He grabbed the cap off of Oshie's head and slapped it at him. "I mean no disrespect, ma'am, but we can't eat your food."

"I'm a good cook. Don't you believe a thing my husband says. He likes to joke. You have to get used to his ways."

Oshie gave me a disgusted look. "We know all about Hobbs Pritchard's ways, ma'am."

"My name is Nellie. I come from Asheville."

Maynard nodded. "We know, but you need to get back in that house with your food before Hobbs catches you."

"That's no way to act." The words popped out of my mouth. "He don't care if you eat his food."

Oshie laughed mean-like. "He'd rather feed that food to some old hogs than give it to us."

Maynard nodded and spoke gentle as if my mind was

unhinged. "We're beholding to the thought, ma'am, but it's best you go on back in that house and not talk to us no more."

"Yeah, if you don't care nothing about yourself, at least think of us. Hobbs would kill us dead for talking to you." Oshie looked at me like I had some kind of disease.

I opened my mouth to argue with them about how Hobbs wasn't and couldn't be like they said, but I saw in them boys a truth that couldn't be denied. I nodded and turned, but something stopped me dead in my tracks, and I whipped back around.

"I ain't like that. My mama taught me manners and how to treat folks when they offered me good Christian thoughts."

Oshie puffed up. "We don't need your Christian thoughts."

Tears stung the back of my throat.

Maynard took a step forward. "It ain't got a thing to do with you, Mrs. Pritchard."

And there it was, the Mrs. part. I was changed whether I wanted to be or not. I only nodded and went back to the house, where I dumped the food in the trash. It was a pure sin with so many souls hungry, but them boys were too proud and stubborn to take my kindness.

Seven

Hobbs was in the habit of sleeping a big part of Saturday and Sunday. This was probably caused from his late hours. The weekend seemed to always bring some emergency that called him away to a neighboring farm. And so I wasn't a bit surprised to see a man standing outside one chilly Saturday at dusk.

"Who is that out in the drive, Hobbs?"

Hobbs stood behind me to look out the window. He smelled like pine trees. I leaned back against him. For a second, he relaxed into me. "That's Harper Wallace. He works for me. There must be some kind of trouble." He pushed me away with a light touch.

"What kind of trouble is it this time?" My words had a tired, run-down sound.

Hobbs's look turned dark and he wrapped his large hand around my wrist, pulling me close to his face. "You got some kind of attitude? My business ain't your problem. I told you there was trouble. That's all I need to say."

My throat closed. Why couldn't I keep my mouth shut?

His grip tightened. He could snap my bone without much effort. "I work while you sit around this house doing nothing much, some little colored girl cleaning. Just shut up and leave me alone." His fingers left prints on my skin.

Part of me wanted to tell him that he could go to hell. The other part wanted him to be the man I met in Asheville, the one who saved me from a life of serving.

"Now, don't go getting your feelings hurt, or I'll have to stay here and love on you. My work will go down the drain. We got to have money."

"Go on and look after things." In that instant, I wanted him to leave and not come back.

"Don't worry, now. I'll be back before sunup and I'll wake you."

And he was true to his word.

Hobbs crawled into bed around dawn, giving me whiskey kisses. I tolerated it until he turned over on his back and snored louder than ever. Men drank and women turned their heads. Mama and Daddy taught me that.

That's when I decided I would go visit the First Episcopal Church of Black Mountain. I thought it was funny that such a small town would have a first anything since they didn't even have a second. I was missing that old soup line back at home something terrible. See, when I was there I had a purpose, a reason to put my feet on the floor each morning. Shoot, on most days on the mountain, I could have crawled back in the bed after Hobbs left and stayed all day. Nobody cared. All I did was wander around that big house all day, dusting a few trinkets, sweeping a floor, and cooking supper. There wasn't even any mending to be done or a book to read.

The icy air bit my arms through my thin sweater. But walking helped warm me. When I reached the church, folks had begun to stroll through the door. The sound of the bell up in the tower vibrated through my body, *bong, bong, bong.* The boy ringing it swung into the air with each pull on the rope. I closed my eyes so tight my church back home appeared. *Bong, bong, bong.*

"What are you smiling at, Mrs. Pritchard?"

My eyes fluttered open and Jack stood before me, grinning.

"I like the bell." I didn't even know his last name.

"I wondered how long it would take you to visit our little church."

"How'd you know I'd come?" I tried not to look into his green stare.

"You struck me as a churchgoer the first day I met you." He took off his wide hat. His hair was sparse in the front, which made him look older than Hobbs. "Hobbs ain't going to take to you visiting the church." He winked. "But I'm sure he's still sleeping off his work emergency, right?" He looked at the people passing us. "You don't have to worry about these folks. They'll keep your secret."

Again my cheeks went red. "I'm not going to hide my churchgoing."

Jack laughed. "Mrs. Pritchard, you got some guts." He guided me through the door. He smelled like fresh soap.

Folks turned their heads as we scooted into one of the shiny pews. "These are nice." I ran my hand along the silky wood.

The church was filled slap full of people. Most I recognized from riding with Hobbs on rent-collection day. If they looked at me—most of them avoided that—it was with a frown on their face. One of the women was dressed better than the others. She held her back straight and her head high. Her dress was store-bought from a city bigger than Asheville. Her daughter could have worn rags and still been beautiful.

"That's the preacher's wife. She fancies herself a writer.

Never read anything she's put on paper. She don't fit in too good," Jack whispered. My ear tingled with his breath.

The choir began to sing, and I lost myself in the words of those old hymns that I'd been hearing every Sunday since I could remember. The pastor stood at the pulpit, handsome in a city sort of way, and began to preach. Though he screamed with passion, his sermon was as dry as three-day-old bread. That was a true shame because he was telling my favorite story about Lot's wife looking back and turning into a pillar of salt. Mama always said that woman should have looked into the future and not back over her shoulder into what was gone for good.

At the end of the service I accepted the offered ride from Jack and stepped out the back door. Maynard Connor stood next to a small rise. For a minute we looked at a stream of clear water shooting from a small pipe. Folks were talking, going on about their after-church socializing.

Maynard picked up a beaten tin cup and let the water splash into it. He held it between us, and for a second I thought he would place the rim to my lips. This was one of those moments Mama had talked about, where time stood quiet and glowed gold around the edges. But then he placed the cup to his own mouth and drank deep. The spring water splashed from the pipe. When Maynard was finished, he wiped his mouth on his shirtsleeve.

"This here is a special spring. I'm sure Hobbs ain't never told you about it." The water sent ripples in the small puddle on the ground. "It's blessed by God." His face was calm and handsome.

He placed the cup back where it belonged. "Even Pastor Dobbins has to admit the miracle he saw."

"What miracle?"

"Shelly Parker. Ask her sometime." The water sparkled in the sun.

"Why are you drinking from this spring?"

He looked older than the first time I saw him. "You'll know before too long, Mrs. Pritchard. You'll understand and remember sometimes to do good a person has to do something bad. It can't be helped."

Oshie ran out from beside the church and stopped dead still. "You got to come on, Daddy said so." He tipped his hat to me. "Is Hobbs with you?"

Jack laughed from behind me. "That'll be the day."

Oshie relaxed.

Maynard gave me a sideways glance. "Got to go, Mrs. Pritchard."

"It was good talking to you, Mr. Connor."

I watched the brothers walk off.

"What was that all about?" Jack touched my arm.

Maynard's words floated in my thoughts. "I think Maynard would be a good friend if he could."

Jack raised an eyebrow. "When did you meet him?"

"Him and his rude brother were cutting wood for Hobbs the other day."

"I bet their daddy don't know about that." He looked down at me. "Stay clear of Hobbs's business, Nellie." We walked to the truck.

Hobbs was sitting at the kitchen table when I got home. "Where you been?"

"I went to church."

"I don't like my wife sneaking around." He stared a hole through me.

"Going to church ain't sneaking, Hobbs. Everybody on this mountain was there."

"Not me."

"No, not you." I wanted to laugh at him but he'd only take offense and get mad.

"What did you think?" His voice was calm.

"I nearly jumped out of my seat with all the screaming. It was one of the worst sermons I've sat through."

Hobbs smiled with pure pleasure. "Ain't that what all good Bible-thumping folks want, cleaning of the soul?"

"I believe in God and going to church. Remember, you found me in a soup kitchen."

"You left quick enough."

He was right about that.

"Hobbs! Hobbs!" A racket came from the yard.

Hobbs pushed past me and threw open the kitchen door. "What in the hell is wrong with you, Harper, coming on Sunday?"

"Someone set"—he looked at me—"the barn on fire."

"What barn?" Our barn was fine.

"Shit." Hobbs jumped off the back porch in a run. "Go in the house and lock up, Nellie. Don't open the door unless it's me or Jack. Now!"

I shut the door and turned the skeleton key for the first time since I'd been living there. I stared out the kitchen window. What was Hobbs up to now? The man I'd seen before was standing on the edge of the woods. He wore little round spectacles like a person would have worn a long time before. He stared right at me, into me. Shelly had said I didn't want to know him. Maybe he set the fire Hobbs was running to. I looked away, and when I looked back, the man was gone. The grass stood tall, not mashed down like it should have been. I stood in front of the window for the longest time, but he didn't come back. Finally I made some coffee and went to sit in the rocker. The light was dimming. The days were so short in the mountains. Dark found us at five thirty.

I tried not to think about how life wasn't exactly like I

thought it would be. The whole front room turned cold. My breath came out in little clouds. The fire had gone out. A woman, tall and big boned, moved down the staircase one step at a time. Her skin had a grayish tint. She wore a plain black dress and was shoeless. All I could do was stare. Fifty things went through my mind to say. How in the world did she get in the house? But I couldn't open my mouth. On the last stair, the woman turned and smiled as if she had always known me.

I closed my eyes tight until little dots danced around. When I finally found the nerve to look, the woman was gone. The room was warmer.

"Mama, you said there weren't no ghosts, but I think you're wrong." My words danced around the room. I sat down in the rocker and stayed there for what seemed forever, until a truck barreled down the drive. I threw open the door and ran out into the yard almost crazy with fear and worry. Jack climbed out. One long breath escaped my chest. But, before he could say a word, Hobbs's truck came up the drive. I sobbed and that wasn't like me at all.

Hobbs jumped from the cab and came at me yelling. "What the hell happened? Did he come here? Did he?"

"Yes, he was standing on the edge of the woods just as you left earlier. It's the third time I've caught him on this land."

Jack came closer. "Did you know the man, Nellie?"

"I ain't never seen him anywhere but in the woods and this yard. He dresses in clothes my grandpa would have worn."

Hobbs looked surprised and his friend Harper looked downright scared. "You didn't see Maynard Connor!" Hobbs shouted at me. "Did you really see a man?"

"Yes. I ain't crazy!" I shouted.

"We know that, Nellie. You're scaring her worse, Hobbs." Jack spoke with a softness Hobbs couldn't even get close to.

"Shut the blubbering up." Hobbs looked like he could run through me.

"She sure saw something." Harper gave a little shiver.

I gained some control.

"It sounds like Hocket to me, boss."

"Shut the hell up, Harper. I ain't in the mood for some stupid mountain tale." Hobbs looked over at Jack. "Take her inside. I'll go have a look. I'm going to kill Maynard Connor when I find him."

I gave Jack a long look. Lots of people said stuff like that when they were angry.

"Come on." Jack motioned me to the kitchen door.

I stopped on the porch to gather some firewood and Jack took it from me. "I'll take care of the fire. You go rest."

I nodded.

Hobbs was sound asleep and the whole house was quiet. At first I thought I was dreaming. *Nellie. Nellie.* I sat up with a cold chill working down my backbone. He stood in the same place he had been early that evening. The half moon showed on him in a milky-white kind of way. I ran down the stairs and out of the house. I didn't want him to disappear this time. But he never moved.

"You'll die too." The man spoke soft but loud enough for me to hear him over the river in the distance.

"Why are you here? Why do you keep coming on my husband's land?"

The man stepped forward. "The question is, what did your husband do to me, ma'am?"

"I don't . . ."

He turned and walked into the woods but not before he threw me a warning over his shoulder. "You're in too deep to leave." These words floated on the air after he disappeared into the black dark.

Eight

I'd been on the mountain for two months. The only person I really talked to was Shelly, who hardly ever talked back but listened to every word. The work on the house was pretty much finished, but I didn't want her to stop coming. So we worked on some rooms twice; me rattling on about Asheville, and her smiling and nodding.

A week or so before Thanksgiving, Hobbs came home one chilly afternoon with some news. "I got to go away on business. That fire set me back too far." His expression told me not to mess with him.

"How long?" My shoulders slumped.

"Hell, I don't know. Don't start asking me a thousand and one questions."

"I just wanted to get an idea—"

He grabbed the front of my dress and pulled me near his face. "It ain't none of your business." Then he pushed me back.

I bit back the words I wanted to say: Why you got to be so mean?

"Be a good wife while I'm gone. You stay right here in this house. Don't be out and about. I got my people watching." He laughed and went upstairs.

Good Lord, what did he expect me to do? I had been the wife he wanted. I never asked for one thing except Mama. He came back down the stairs with a shadow across his face. He wouldn't be home anytime soon. That was clear.

The day before Thanksgiving, Jack brought me a turkey all ready to go in the oven. "Aunt Ida sure is grumbling about having dinner up here. But it's good for her. She does too much and bosses everyone."

"Maybe Hobbs will make it home for our first Thanksgiving as a family. It looks like we could have the whole mountain up here for dinner." I patted the turkey.

"We may just have to do that." Jack tipped his hat.

"Tell Aunt Ida not to worry about a thing. I've got it under control. I'm going to cook like my mama does every holiday." The ache started in my chest real sharp like. Was she cooking since I wasn't there? Knowing her, she was and feeding the whole dern soup line.

Jack gave a easy laugh. "Oh, Aunt Ida will cook. You couldn't stop her. We may just have to feed the mountain."

"What about the Connors?" The name hung in the air.

"What about them?" He looked away.

"Will Maynard come home?"

"They'll make do like every year since this Depression began. But they won't have Maynard. It's too risky."

"Where'd he go?" A lump formed in my throat.

"After that night, he left, went off the mountain. Who knows? He was stupid."

See, what Jack or nobody, especially Hobbs, knew was I

saw Maynard early the morning after the fire. He was making his way down the mountain, hugging the side of the road. I was walking up the drive. I couldn't sit in that house and went out for fresh air.

For a second, he looked like a deer about to be shot, but his shoulders relaxed. "Mrs. Pritchard." He tipped his hat.

"Mr. Connor." I nodded.

"It was mighty fine knowing you." He pulled on his brim.

"Yes sir, it was a pleasure to know you."

He walked on by and that was the end of that. I prayed that he'd get far away and never be caught by Hobbs.

"You know what the old folks say about leaving?" Jack's words pulled me back to the kitchen.

If I told him about Maynard, he'd keep my secret. "No."

"Once a person leaves the mountain, they never come back, not really. They're lost forever." And somehow I knew that to be the truth.

The work in the kitchen filled my time. I made sweet potato pies, ash potato salad, cornbread dressing, and even some collard greens. On toward evening, clouds moved in across the western sky. A thought took a hold of me. I wrapped one of those pies in a pretty tea towel and set out down the road.

The Connor cabin was quiet, but I knew many pairs of eyes were watching me as I walked across their yard. The door opened as I reached out to knock.

The woman looked much older up close. Her forehead was covered in a mess of wrinkles. "Can I help you?" The proper words sliced the air.

"I brought you a pie for Thanksgiving."

The woman looked at the plate like it was death itself. "Why?"

I took a step back. Why indeed? This wasn't how I imagined the visit would go. "I wanted to share, be neighborly for the holiday."

The woman watched me like I might bare teeth and bite her.

"I miss my mama," I blurted like some kind of kid. "She always shared a pie with a neighbor on Thanksgiving. I'm sorry if I bothered you." I turned to leave.

"Don't go away hurt." The woman's voice was a tad softer. "But child, you got yourself in one situation when you married Hobbs Pritchard. Don't you know that? I think you must be a smart girl. You can't come up this mountain married to the meanest man and expect folks to like you. I bet your mama didn't want you to marry him."

"I just wanted to know if Maynard is okay."

The woman's face turned sad. "It's your husband that ran my boy off."

"What happened?" All of a sudden I needed to know what Maynard did that was so bad.

"Don't play dumb."

"I don't know nothing. Hobbs keeps it from me."

"He's a moonshiner, girl, and a thief. It's the thieving part that makes us hate him. Maynard gave Hobbs something to think on by burning his still. He was looking out for his family." Her voice grew loud and angry. "I don't want your pie or nothing Hobbs owns, Missy Mae." She turned a mean look on me. "You want to know what all he's done? I don't think you do, young lady. It's much easier for you to play dumb. You need to go home before he kills you. He killed his own stepmama even though they couldn't prove it. Her ghost prowls that house. I've seen her looking out the window myself. God rest her good soul. Won't one soul blame you for leaving the likes of Hobbs Pritchard. Go on home." She shut the door in my face.

I stood there for a minute staring at the wood. Then I

turned and walked. I walked back down that road as the light turned gray and the sky spit snow. When I was out of sight, I threw that pie, towel and all, as hard as I could into the woods. I thought on that moonshine still and Hobbs killing his stepmama. It was dark when I let myself in the house. There stood the woman I saw before. She smiled and walked right through the wall before I could say a word to her.

Nellie; again death was whispering in my ear. I jumped out of bed. The world outside was alive with light caused by a thick blanket of snow. Even the sound of the river was muffled. Winter had come sooner than later. The man stood closer to the house this time and looked at me. He took off his cap, gave a little nod, and walked toward the house until I couldn't see him. I waited, thinking he would knock. But he never did. I went downstairs and the porch was empty. I was seeing things.

Night left and day came, Thanksgiving. The world outside the window turned hard and cold. I put on my warmest clothes and a pair of Hobbs's boots, put the turkey in the oven, and hightailed it outside. I would smother if I stayed in that house one more minute. The snow fell, turning the air icy. The water rushed over the rocks not far away. I twirled, a dancer, a child.

That's where Jack and Aunt Ida found me when they came to dinner. I was building a snowman. My hands and toes were frozen, but it didn't matter. Jack laughed, thinking it was all in fun. But Aunt Ida frowned. She knew when she saw a woman giving in to the crazy part of her mind.

"Did you cook them vegetables?" Her voice was stern.

I laughed so hard I couldn't get my breath to answer. Of course I took care of the whole dinner. I was the kind of wife who waited at home until her husband got good and ready to come back.

Nine

The next morning I heard a soft knock on the door. Shelly stood on the porch with a bundle in her hand. It wasn't her day to come clean.

"Shelly?" The sun hadn't made it over the tops of the trees yet.

"I figured you could use some help after dinner and . . ." She looked away.

"And what?" I motioned her inside. The cold went straight to my bones.

"I heard about your visit to the Connors." She bumped snow off her flimsy shoes and stepped inside so I could close the door.

"So. And I guess they know I threw a perfectly good pie in the ditch, along with a pretty tea towel?"

"I didn't hear nothing about no pie. Actually, Mrs. Connor was the one talking, and she was nice, considering. She said you was just plain stupid when it came to your husband." She stopped to see if I would get mad.

"You want some coffee?" I took my cup off the shelf.

"Mama don't believe in it. She says money is too hard to come by these days to be wasting it on coffee."

Hobbs probably owned every family on the mountain—except the Connors. Taking folks' coffee and eggs was stealing and pure meanness no matter how I tried to paint the picture. Thinking about how he held the needs of others over their heads made me so mad I could spit. How could I love someone like him? But I wasn't stupid. I knew if he walked in the door, I'd fall right into his arms. He had some kind of magic over me. Hobbs was to me what whiskey was to Daddy. One glass was never enough for him. He had to drink the whole bottle. I was lost in Hobbs and might never get back to being me.

"I got some milk. You want some?" Again I noticed the pouch in Shelly's hand.

"Yes ma'am."

I poured her a big cold glass. "Here." I pointed to the bundle. "What did you bring?"

Shelly smiled. "This here is from Mama. It's brick dust. If you sprinkle it in front of each door, bad spirits can't come in. She says you need it with someone like Hobbs."

"Thank you, Shelly. Tell your mama I'm beholding." Brick dust, how silly was that? "Shelly, tell me about the man we saw in the woods."

"Has he come back?"

"Yes, when Hobbs had the fire." I looked away. "And the other night."

"I done told all I knew. He was before my time. He don't come visiting me. He visits you."

"What do you mean?" A chill went through my body.

"He's showing himself to you for some reason, Miss Nellie. Ask him."

"Are you saying he's a spirit?" Something familiar about the questions settled in my mind as if it was the last piece to a large puzzle.

Shelly kind of laughed. "He's about as dead as one person can be."

I held up my hand. "I don't believe in ghosts. I told you that."

"You're the one who brought him up." She frowned at me.

"What does he have to do with Hobbs?" I drank my coffee.

Shelly took her time sipping the milk. "Don't know."

"Why do you hate Hobbs?"

"Lord be, ma'am, I don't hate no one." Shelly sat the half-full glass of milk on the table. "Mama thinks he killed my daddy, Clyde Parker."

My head roared. Jack had mentioned him the day I stood outside the barn listening.

"Now don't go fretting over what I think. Mama said Daddy was messing in things he knew better than to mess in." Shelly was quiet for a minute. "Shoot, I wasn't but five when it happened. I don't even remember him." She shrugged. "You can't be all sad about somebody you never knew." Her words were almost a whisper.

"That would have made Hobbs around seventeen. Mrs. Connor said he killed his stepmama."

"Mama says some folks are just born bad. He's one of them. Just be careful. You can't figure him."

"So what spirits come to visit you and what do they say?"

"This here needs a good cleaning." Shelly rubbed on the stove. "He ain't going to let me come much longer. Things are going to get bad."

Fingers of dread walked over my scalp. "He don't care if you're here."

She stopped rubbing the white enamel. "I'll be close by if

you need me. You can go to Mrs. Connor too. She's nice enough."

This made me laugh out loud. What I needed was Mama but I was stuck. If I left and Hobbs came home, he'd throw a fit, chase me down, and punish Mama. How had I come to this knowing? No, I had to stay put to save Mama from getting hurt. And that wasn't some ghost tale.

Ten

That winter on Black Mountain turned out to be colder than any in my whole lifetime. My firewood was running low and still no sign of Hobbs. Christmas was almost on me and this very fact made me sick. Hobbs wasn't coming home. The thought sat on the very bottom of my heart, right there in the quiet place that I hid from everyone else.

Jack would have split the wood for me, but I decided I could do it on my own. I had to learn to do things for myself. In the back of my mind, I believed I could please Hobbs. Eventually he would give in and let Mama come to me. I was young and didn't have a lick of sense. I thought I could turn back time with just a desire. Anyway, splitting the wood showed I could be on my own. Mama taught me how to work for a living. Her laundry business for the fine ladies of Asheville gave me a taste of raw cracked knuckles; one year we even plowed a big field outside of town for a corn crop. We sold it to the farmers for feed. Neither one of us could be called lazy. I could chop wood.

The temperature was around twenty degrees in the middle of the day. Little sheets of ice formed over the still parts of the river. The snow was as deep as ever, no longer pretty, but dirty and gray in most places.

The sun showed through the trees, but it didn't give any extra heat the afternoon I set out to cut wood. I rolled one of the logs upright. Thank goodness Hobbs had sense enough to have a tree chopped down and sectioned. The maul was heavier than I thought. I swung it over my shoulder, losing my footing but regaining my balance. In that moment, a anger for Hobbs boiled inside of me, giving me a start. The feeling was so strong I swung that maul hard and bounced it off the wood without making a dent. Hobbs should have been right there with me. The maul was lighter the next time I swung it over my shoulder. The weight was a burden, a promise. The third blow brought a split in the wood. The anger had turned to pure strength as it moved through me.

Would Hobbs ever come back? Husbands didn't just walk away from their wives. But I knew that was a childish thought. A man could do anything he felt like to a woman. Nobody would stop him from telling his wife what to do. Hobbs was my husband. Our marriage was built on his wants and dislikes. He made the money and owned the land. He owned me. If he said I was stupid, then I was. But the more I stayed alone the more I knew that just wasn't so. It was him who was stupid and mean.

The maul hit its mark and half the log fell away. Warmth spread through me like a spring day. I went at my task for a couple of hours and ended up with a decent pile of wood. My arms were numb and my back ached, but a new strength burned in my muscles. For the first time in my life, I thought I could do anything.

The bathwater turned to a boil just as I heard a truck. I ran to see: it was only Jack. How crazy was I when one minute I hated Hobbs, and the next I was hanging in the window, pining away for love, praying he'd come home?

Jack jumped from the cab and looked directly at the new pile of wood and scratched his chin.

I met him at the door. "What brings you this way?" My thoughts were still cemented on Hobbs, so I almost missed the soft look Jack gave me. I couldn't have him feeling sorry for me.

"I wanted to check in on you." He nodded at the wood. "It seems you've done fine alone."

"I can do anything myself," I bragged. "Come on in." I opened the kitchen door.

He took off his hat. "I could have chopped the wood. I will next time. No sense in not taking my help."

"It's not your place, Jack. If I'm going to live up here alone . . ." These words came to life outside my mind and stopped me in the middle of the sentence.

Jack's face turned pink with the heat of the stove. "I'll help. You're family." He warmed his hands. "You and Shelly have done a fine job with the place."

"She's a good worker."

He looked at the bathtub between us on the kitchen floor. "I won't stay."

The thought of another lonely supper made me sick. "Why don't you stay and eat?" I could see he was about to say no, so I rushed on. "You could stack the wood I chopped while I take a bath."

He relaxed. "It'll be a pleasure to stack the wood. You split wood with your mama?"

"Nah, this is my first time, but Mama and me worked hard." A sharp pain worked behind my ribs.

"You're something else, Nellie." He laughed and went outside. I was smiling for the first time in weeks.

My prettiest dress hung over one of the kitchen chairs. I

soaked in the copper tub while the water worked hard at turning ice-cold. Mama would say I was messing with fire having this handsome man for supper, but I wasn't with Mama. There was no harm in having a meal with my brother-in-law and nothing wrong with being pretty. Jack was a gentleman. And for all I knew he had him a girl down in Asheville somewhere. I closed my eyes and imagined him answering all the questions I needed answered.

Eleven

I cooked the pork chops good and crunchy. The black-eyed peas bubbled on the stove, and the whole kitchen smelled of sweet cornbread. Jack ate so much I thought he'd pop open. Him sitting at the table laughing and talking seemed so natural. I poured us another cup of coffee and brought the apple cobbler to the table. I used apples I canned right after I came to the mountain.

"Lord, Nellie, you're a good cook." Jack sat back and patted his stomach.

"Thank you."

"There are some things about Hobbs's business that can't be denied." He sniffed the coffee. "Folks up here can't buy coffee. They can't buy nothing."

My cheeks burned, thinking about Hobbs and his ways.

"I got to get back home." The dusky gray had settled in the yard. It was this time each evening when I took my coffee to the porch and watched the valley get blanketed by mist.

"Oh, come sit on the porch with me. Talk."

He laughed. "It's too cold to sit on the porch, but you do have a fine view. What is it you want to talk about?"

"Do you have a girl down in Asheville?"

His look became playful. "Ten of them. Why is it that every woman on this mountain wants to fix me up with a girl? Do I look that helpless?"

"Maybe it's because you're such good husband material."

He hooted with laughter. "I don't think you're right about that." A wind rattled a tree branch against the kitchen window. "I'm happy just like I am."

"That's probably good, being happy like you are." Warm feelings were settling in my chest, making it easier to ask my next question. "Did Hobbs kill Clyde Parker?"

A shadow crossed his face. "You change subjects fast." He half smiled. "Did Shelly talk about him?"

"I asked her why she didn't like Hobbs."

He nodded. "There's some things I can't talk about, Nellie. Clyde Parker is one of them. That answer will have to come from Hobbs." He sipped his coffee. "But I wouldn't bring it up."

So I had to think Hobbs killed Shelly's daddy. "Tell me about Hobbs's sister."

A lighthearted smile settled on his face. "What do you want to know?"

"Does she look like him?" I moved around my real question with careful steps.

"She looked just like pictures of her mama. She has her mama's name, AzLeigh."

"Why'd she leave?"

He shrugged and looked out the window. "It was time. She had nothing left up here."

"Aunt Ida said her and Hobbs fell out about her liking your mama. She said he had every right to hate his stepmama since she came into the family too fast."

"Aunt Ida's been making excuses for Hobbs since I came to this mountain and probably way before. She's always had a soft spot for him. Seems he does this to a lot of women. Can't figure it."

I looked away.

"My mama loved AzLeigh like her own. What wasn't there to love? She was everything Hobbs had missing." Jack grew quiet. "When my mama died, AzLeigh hurt just like I did. She loved her that much."

"Did Hobbs have anything to do with your mama dying?" This question had been burning inside since my visit to the Connor farm.

He studied me. "Who you been talking to?"

"Mrs. Connor."

He frowned and shook his head. "That must have been a hard visit for you."

I shrugged off his words. "Did he kill her?"

"She died one night while everyone was asleep. AzLeigh found her the next morning. The doctor said it was her heart." He frowned. "I would have killed Hobbs myself if I thought he put a hand on my mama." He said this so quiet a chill went over my scalp. "Folks give him way too much credit. It adds to his legend as the bad man on Black Mountain."

"So you don't think he's killed anybody?" The relief I felt was in my words.

"I didn't say that. I'm sure he's killed someone. Folks say he killed his first man the day before his mama died."

"Who was that?"

"Merlin Hocket."

The name sent cold through my chest.

"Merlin was a government man sent up here to measure the mountain for taxes. But his problem was meeting Hobbs. They bumped heads because Merlin found Hobbs's still and threatened to bring revenue men up here. He came up missing. Nobody would tell on Hobbs because we deal with our own up here. Problem is we're not doing too good of a job because he's running the show." He slapped his knee. "I got to go. My dear stepbrother would raise Cain if he knew I was here talking with you." He looked deep into my eyes. "Never think you know him cause you won't, ever."

And there was the truth staring me in the face.

I looked away. "I seen your mama here."

"Don't surprise me none. She's probably looking out for you. She knew Hobbs well enough. That's one of the reasons he hated her so bad." Jack opened the kitchen door.

"She walked down the front stairs."

He nodded like we were talking about something as simple as spring coming. "Don't talk to Hobbs about her. He'll ship you off to the state hospital."

"If he even comes back." I cursed the sinking feeling in my chest.

"Oh, don't you worry. He'll come rolling in here when you least expect him. You can't get rid of him that easy. Enjoy your time. Ain't no telling what he'll be like when he comes back." He laughed.

I touched his arm without thinking. It was just a natural kind of gesture. His stare locked with mine for only a few seconds, and then he slid his arm away. "More snow tomorrow." He put his hat on and stepped out the door.

"Don't say that, Jack."

He grinned. "Aunt Ida's knee has been aching up a storm, always does when a big snow is coming."

"Sounds like my mama."

"Why don't you go down and see her, your mama?" He was watching me close.

"How? It ain't like Hobbs left me a way. And he don't like her one bit since she refused to come to our wedding."

He laughed. "Well, sounds like she's got sense. Let's see what Christmas brings."

After he was gone, I sat in the rocker and watched the flames until I got to that sleepy place where I was awake but couldn't move. A sound I hadn't heard in a while, a sound I'd been waiting to hear, pacing around and worrying over, rattled up the drive. I had thought I would dance for joy, but I didn't. And this caught me off guard.

The kitchen door opened. "Well, well, look who's up waiting on me."

I didn't crack a smile. A battle took place in my chest on whether I was going to grab my next breath or not. Hobbs was home.

Twelve

Christmas loomed in the background as I walked through the next few days not giving joy to Hobbs being home for the holiday. Everything in me had up and buried itself deep in some hole. But Hobbs was purely happy and walked around whistling. We never seemed to be able to feel the same way at the same time. Church was the only place I found a peaceful moment, and it wasn't even real peace since Jack sat close by, smelling like clean soap, close enough to let me study the line of his jaw. He smiled here and there, tipped his hat, but kept his distance. He was a fine catch for a sensible girl. Up until I met Hobbs I had been just that kind of girl.

I worked on some gifts, trying to catch the proper mood for the Lord's birthday. It was a time of new beginnings, of birth, shedding our old skins and gaining something completely new. One night the snow fell in big fluffy flakes. I stood at the bedroom window and listened to Hobbs snoring. The soft whispery voice—Nellie—seemed to move through the tops of the trees, through the river, through the very earth itself. The mountain was talking to me, accepting me. I couldn't make out all it said, but I knew the day I could, things would change. For good or bad, I wasn't sure.

On Christmas Eve, Hobbs took out early to do whatever he had planned for the holiday, and I decided to walk to church for the afternoon service. The trees were bare and a brisk wind pushed me up the path. The whole sanctuary was lit by candles. My heart sank and jumped at the same time. In that candlelight, I thought I saw some hope, a way out of the mess I'd made of my life, but that would mean failing. When the good pastor sang out his altar call, I stayed in the pew. I never had been much of a kneeling-in-the-front-of-the-church person. But I prayed God would deliver me from my hopelessness. That's the best I could do. A person should be careful what they pray after. Of course what happened, all that took place, couldn't be left at God's feet. Nope, what came later was like the little purple crocuses pushing through snow to bloom; it was going to happen no matter what tried to get in the way.

On the way home from the service, I stopped at the little cabin in back of Pastor Dobbins's house. In my skirt pocket was a small bundle. I tapped on the door as I stood on the wide front porch. Through the window, I saw the front room washed in lamplight. In one corner was a bed with the most colorful quilt, all bright blues, reds, oranges, and yellows. A big fireplace took over the room, but what caught my eye was the fancy organ in the corner.

"What brings you this way, Mrs. Pritchard?" Shelly's mother had opened the door without me noticing.

My cheeks heated having been caught snooping. "I had a little something for Shelly." I pulled the lacy cloth napkin out of my pocket. "I hope that's all right."

Mrs. Parker pushed the door open wider. "Come on in." She turned her head. "Shelly, we got company."

Shelly appeared in the door of a room to the back of the cabin. "Mrs. Pritchard." Her smile was almost shy.

"I have this for you." I held out the napkin folded neatly around the surprise.

Shelly took it and sniffed. "Oh, you made it." She grinned. "Fudge."

Mrs. Parker's smile was stiff. "Isn't that nice. You thank her, Shelly."

"Thank you, Mrs. Pritchard."

"It's nothing much. I wanted to thank you for all your help. You've been such a hard worker."

Mrs. Parker's face relaxed. "I taught her to be on her best."

"Do you play the organ?" I asked Shelly.

She looked at her feet. "Not good."

Mrs. Parker straightened her shoulders. "You play real good. Go play Mrs. Pritchard a Christmas song."

Shelly frowned but walked to the organ. She placed her long fingers on the keys and played "Silent Night" without missing a note.

I clapped.

"Shelly learned from Miss Faith. She's good enough to play for the church if they let coloreds do such a thing."

"She is very good."

Shelly stood. "Can't I have a piece of fudge?"

"Tell Mrs. Pritchard bye and then go eat one piece."

"Bye." Shelly smiled and ran back to the room with the fudge in her hand.

I sure wasn't used to a shy Shelly. When I was alone with Mrs. Parker, I couldn't find one word to say, but that didn't matter. Mrs. Parker stood in the middle of her small neat cabin and found all the words she needed.

"She won't be coming back to your house. It was kind of you to stop by." Mrs. Parker held the door open.

"Oh, she can come back after Christmas."

Mrs. Parker shook her head. "No ma'am. Your husband stopped by the pastor's house and gave him Shelly's pay. He said he had no use for her work. That you were going to take over the chores."

Sweat broke out on my neck even though it was cold. "I'm sorry. I didn't know. I'll miss her."

"You've grown on her, but Shelly don't belong cleaning your house." Her words were firm. "I don't want her close to Hobbs Pritchard no more."

The air was thick with my silence.

"I guess I need to get home." I wanted to fix things between us, but there wasn't no use.

"I thank you for the thought." Mrs. Parker watched me from the door.

"She's a good worker. I'm sorry if I did anything to offend you." I hung my head and walked.

"Shelly's seen a spirit that's here cause of you."

A ripple of dread went over me.

"The spirit warned her that you're in danger. Did she tell you?"

"No."

Mrs. Parker came close to me. "You ought to use that brick dust I sent. Something bad is going to happen." She held her hand up. "Don't ask cause I don't know. I don't think Shelly knows. But it's bad."

I was silent.

"You're young. You ain't going to listen to what grown folks say."

Night was pulling in on me. She was right, I wasn't listening to no one, not even the little voice in my head.

Hobbs came in late that night, sounding like a drunken Santa. He found me in bed and pushed a ring, a gold wedding band, in my hand. "I never gave you one, so here."

The ring was simple and big, too large for my finger, but the thought was there wrapped up in all his misguided ways, as if God had actually heard my prayer. I couldn't help but smile. "Thank you, Hobbs."

He stood straight. "You better thank me. I do a lot for you. Look at what you have here." He opened his arms to welcome the room.

As usual he stuck his foot in the middle of something good and mixed it all up. "Do you love me, Hobbs? Do you?" We'd been married nearly three months and not once had he said those words. Not even when we said I do.

He had a look of complete confusion.

"Do you?"

"I say it every time I provide for you. This ring here says it most of all."

"You ain't never said it."

"Oh shit! Why I got to? I ain't one to spout words. I gave you the ring." He was getting tired of talking.

I took the ring off my finger and pressed it into my palm. "Thank you for the thought. It means a lot."

"Oh shit, do you have to pout?" He slapped his knee. "Christmas is here and I want my present." He pulled me to him, moving on me fast in his same old way. A laugh struggled to get free of my chest, but I stuffed it down, knowing full well what that would bring me. I was learning my lessons each and every day.

When all the huffing and puffing was over, I watched a slip of a moon riding the tree line. What would happen if I went out to the river and lay down? Let the current pull me under, twist me around? What? Would it take me away from this place? Would it be worth the sacrifice? I wasn't ready to die, not for Hobbs, not at that minute anyway.

Thirteen

Snowflakes fluttered down outside the window the next morning, Christmas morning. It was a beautiful gift. Hobbs slept beside me. Would he even remember giving me the ring? If he was sober, would he want to give it to me? I slipped the gold band on my finger and almost laughed out loud at the size. I didn't want to know where he got it, but something deep inside told me I should know. Some poor farmer had to give up his wedding band on Christmas Eve for a debt owed. I slipped out of bed and went to where my gifts were hidden: one for Jack, Aunt Ida, Hobbs, and even one for Mama. Each gift was homemade and wrapped in tissue paper I found lining one of the drawers in the dining-room sideboard. Each was made from a quilt I'd found in a trunk out in the barn: a hand-sewn stocking that would hold a gingerbread cookie—silly kid stuff, but still good thoughts.

I worked the spicy dough with the rolling pin and cut each cookie with the cutter shaped like a man. We had no tree, no wreath, not even a stocking hanging on the mantel. Hobbs thought it a bunch of trouble, but I had hoped he'd come around. I was coming to see he was hateful and didn't have room for happy thoughts. Maybe he enjoyed being miserable. There were people like that, mean and spiteful, full of poison. I'd seen that side of Daddy before, even though Mama tried to cover his meanness.

The icing, blue, red, and yellow, came out perfect. I added eyes and hair to the cookies. The sugar sprinkles were a childish touch but it was Christmas. There I was, trying my best to bring my memories of Mama at Christmas to life. It wasn't fair I couldn't see her. What was I doing on Black Mountain?

Hobbs stood on the stairs as I wrapped the last cookie. His hair was in a scrabble of curls like a young boy in a hurry to see what Santa brought. I wanted to throw myself in his arms and forget all our starts and stops. The big old ring hung off my married finger.

"What you doing, Nellie girl?"

"It's a secret. Now, go on."

He smiled, looking even more like a boy, erasing those mean thoughts I had. "What you got?"

"Go on and don't spoil my surprise." I smiled.

Outside the window fell thick fluffy flakes.

"Look at that snow falling. It's all too damn sweet, ain't it?"

I ignored him.

Aunt Ida's house smelled like Mama's on Christmas Day. Jack had a big fire burning in the fireplace. He smiled and looked right at me when we came in. "Don't you look like a picture?" Delight lit up his face.

Hobbs noticed my clothes for the first time. "Where'd you get that dress?"

Had I been smart, I would have lied and told him my dress

was old. He sure didn't keep up with what I wore. Instead, I twirled around. "I made it."

Hobbs's eyes narrowed. "Where'd you get the cloth?"

"I found a old dress out in the barn. It was way too big to be one of your mama's."

"It's one of my mama's old dresses." Jack smiled. "And I know she'd be thrilled you used it in such a pretty way. You know she loved to sew?"

I could have kissed him, but I held out my hand. "Did you see my Christmas present from Hobbs?"

Hobbs puffed up. "Put that up, Nellie."

Aunt Ida took my hand and jerked it toward her. "It's a bit big."

"Yes ma'am, but it don't matter. Hobbs gave me a wedding band. That means more than anything."

"Shut up, Nellie!"

Silence filled up all the space in the room. I could have scratched Hobbs's eyes out, but I didn't let one tear fall, not one.

"Don't you have some silly gifts to hand out?"

I didn't even care anymore. I was dying from the inside out.

"Presents?" It was Jack's sweet voice. "I love presents."

I turned around, avoiding Hobbs's stare.

"What you got for me?" Hobbs pointed the words at my back.

I reached in my old feed sack and handed him the gift wrapped in tissue paper. He tore into it like a greedy child. His name was stitched into the cuff of the stocking with some gold thread I found in a drawer. The gingerbread man, with blond hair and blue eyes like his, peeked from the top.

"Ain't that so cute." His words were twisted like the bitterroot plant that grew out in Mama's yard. It had the prettiest white flowers, but it was the thick roots that was used to doctor. He tossed his gift in one of the chairs and walked toward the kitchen. "You got some dressing ready, Aunt Ida?"

"Don't go digging in my food." Aunt Ida followed him but not before she glared at me.

I stood there with that big heavy ring hanging from my finger, holding the other two gifts, lost, lost as a child in some dark woods.

"Is one of them for me?" Jack asked. He had to be the best person ever, but he was as hard to read as Hobbs—different, mind you, but hard to think on just the same.

I passed him his present.

"The gingerbread man has my hat. I don't think I could ever eat it." He smiled.

"You got to cause it'll ruin."

"It's too nice. The stocking is perfect. Where'd you find my old quilt?"

My stomach twisted. "I'm sorry. I found it down in the barn too. It was with the dress."

He shook his head. "It's fine. That stuff was packed up when Mama died. Henry James couldn't stand to look at it. I'm proud to have it as a stocking, Nellie. You found part of Mama for me."

My heart flipped over.

Hobbs came walking into the room. "Did you make him one?"

I twisted the band around my finger and didn't look at him. "I made one for Aunt Ida too."

"Come on, Aunt Ida. You got you a cookie too. Nellie is too sweet."

I studied on him, trying to figure out what was so special about this man. What had I seen down in Asheville?

*   *   *

That night Hobbs stayed home and went to bed at the same time as me. This should have told me something. He caught me studying that huge wedding ring.

"Are you still sulking around?" He was propped up on pillows.

I didn't answer him.

"Oh come on, Nellie. Ain't nothing to be mad about. I'm waiting on you. Give me my real Christmas present."

"I'm tired, Hobbs."

The change in his eyes flashed between us as he jumped from the bed and grabbed my arm. "Get your ass over here and don't talk back to me again. Do you think I didn't see you looking at Jack today?"

The twist on my arm hurt but I refused to give in and cry. "I don't know what you're talking about."

"You like him!"

"No, Hobbs."

His look was mean. "You're a damn liar!" He pushed me. "I don't like being cheated on, Nellie."

"Are you crazy? I'm married." My anger came spilling out. "You know that I wouldn't cheat on you. How can you question me? You're the one who is never home! I left my mama and came here for you. You won't even let me see her. I gave up everything and now you ask me a question like that!" I braced myself.

He laughed as he yanked on my gown. "I guess you're right, little girl. You have to love me if you left your mama. And you're right about another thing. You sure as hell ain't going to see that woman. No you ain't. You're mine. I own you, every part of you." He squeezed my breast until tears came into my eyes. "You're mine." He shoved me on the bed.

There wasn't one thing good about loving that night. I stayed awake for a long time watching him breathe and listening to the cold wind howling. Was this what love was supposed to be? Hell, I didn't know nothing. I'd never been in love before, only puppy love after one of my teachers in high school. I never even kissed a boy on the mouth before Hobbs came along. If what I had with Hobbs was real love, I didn't want any part of it. I thought hard on how I could change things between us. There wasn't nothing, nothing I could do. I fell asleep with that thought.

The next morning his side of the bed was empty. Hobbs's truck was gone. I waited but he didn't come back that night. I knelt on the floor and thanked God for keeping him away. When New Year's Eve rolled around, Hobbs still hadn't come home. Something told me he'd be gone a long time. I prayed he would. I'm ashamed to say I wasn't feeling much like a good wife. I set into a routine and pretended he didn't exist, that I'd never met him. The house welcomed me. The mountain knew me. I wasn't at peace, but I could live with my life. I had settled. What more could I ask for?

Fourteen

I'd like to say I woke up on New Year's Day, looked in the mirror, and understood what being married to Hobbs was doing to me, but that would be a fairy tale of the worst kind. Instead each time Hobbs hurt me, I saw him a little clearer. The problem was, what would he have to do to make me understand the whole truth?

New Year's Day was cold but sunny. I walked over to Shelly's little house.

Mrs. Parker opened the door with a frown on her face. "What you need, Mrs. Pritchard?"

"I need Shelly's help. It'd only be for today." I knew Shelly was there. I could feel her listening.

"Your husband made it clear . . ."

"My husband isn't here and no telling when he'll come back, if he does this time." I looked her dead in the eye. "I want to work in the attic and I don't want to go alone." This was true. "I'll pay her, not Hobbs. He'll never know."

Mrs. Parker studied me for a minute. "You need to go home."

"It's not that easy. He don't like my mama."

Mrs. Parker looked me from head to toe. "You got yourself in a fix. You at least know him now. You know what he can do."

I wanted to tell her about the night before he left, the way he shoved me. "I'll make sure Shelly's all right. I need her in the attic." I looked at the ground. "I'm afraid."

Mrs. Parker sighed. "Well, with the to-do of Christmas behind us, I don't think Shelly will have much work at Pastor's house. I'll let her come for a couple of hours this afternoon. For some crazy reason I'm trusting you, but I don't want her around Hobbs."

"He ain't coming home."

She laughed. "He'll be back before you know it. Bad folks always come back looking for more trouble."

Her words gave me a shiver.

Shelly knocked on my door right as I was fixing my noonday meal.

"Come on in!" I yelled. My heart gave a little lurch of joy.

The door opened with a puff of wind. Cold air was the only visitor.

"What you doing, Shelly?" My laugh sounded hollow.

Shelly didn't answer. It wasn't like her to play tricks. I put down my knife and went to look outside. No one was on the porch. Was I crazy? Someone opened that door. I searched around. When I went back in the kitchen, it was ice-cold, a deep-in-my-bones cold.

In the corner of the kitchen, near the door to the hall, a shadow was forming.

"He's going to tell you what he be wanting soon."

I jumped. The shadow disappeared. "You scared me! Did you knock on my door?"

Shelly only smiled. "You know what they say? If you welcome a ghost into your house . . ."

The room was growing warmer. "What?"

"It won't leave until it gets what it wants."

"Are you telling me a ghost knocked on my door?" I laughed.

She shrugged. "Laugh if you want. You told him to come in, right?"

"I thought it was you!" I was getting mad.

Shelly shook her head and clicked her tongue. "Your mama didn't teach you a thing about spirits."

"She doesn't believe in ghosts, haints, or spirits."

"You just being silly, ma'am. You believe. You have to."

I took in a big breath.

"I seen that ghost with my own eyes standing in that corner. Ain't no telling how long he's been trying to get in Hobbs Pritchard's house." She nodded to the place where the shadow had been. "You seen him too."

"Who is he?"

"It's the man we seen in the woods. The one you seen so much of."

Fingers of cold walked up my neck. "We're going to work in the attic today." I couldn't look at her.

She laughed. "Yes ma'am." She followed me up to the attic.

"I figured we'd start here and work our way back." The room was so big I couldn't see the other end.

Shelly was quiet.

"The newest stuff should be here in the front."

"Yes ma'am." Shelly walked over to a big wooden barrel full of all kinds of books. "Did you hear that?"

"What?"

"Nothing."

The books were a real disappointment. They was all about

horses. Then I spied a small wooden box stuck in the bottom of the barrel. When I bent to touch it, Shelly drew in a breath.

"I wouldn't."

"Why?"

Her lips were a thin line. "Cause it's personal."

"How do you know?"

She took three steps back. "Never mess with private things."

I picked the box up and opened it. A sigh let go in the room. I looked at Shelly, who looked like she was going to run. Inside was a velvet pouch with a necklace covered in red stones.

"Rubies," Shelly said. "Lordy be."

"Maybe." I twisted the necklace in front of me.

"That be her stuff." Shelly took another step back.

"Whose?"

She nodded. "You know. You seen her with your own eyes. She came to visit you."

"It's beautiful." Could this belong to Jack's mama?

"Yep."

"What are you afraid of?" I put the necklace back in the pouch.

"This spirit is hard to figure. I don't know if she be here to help you or him. But I know she can't stop the bad from coming. It's here. It walked in your door today."

A stillness settled in the room. In the box was a lock of steel-gray hair. I ran my finger along its silky softness.

Shelly nearly screamed. "Oh Lord, it be her hair!"

"Stop talking like that. You're scaring me."

She looked past me and her eyes got big. "I can't, ma'am." She looked back at the hair. "Lordy."

"You're being silly." I touched the piece of string tied around the lock.

"He cut it." She looked around me and then at me. "He cut it for fun." She shook her head. "I gotta go and I ain't coming back here no matter how much I like you." And she was gone. I heard the kitchen door slam.

I stood there holding the hair, wondering what in the world Shelly saw that scared her so bad.

Fifteen

January closed in around me like a pack of hungry wolves cornering a lost traveler. No matter how much wood I threw on the fire, I couldn't stay warm. I took to sleeping on the red velvet sofa by the fireplace in the front room. I'd gotten good at chopping wood. Jack tried to help me, but I wouldn't let him. I was driven to take care of me. He came by but never stayed. Sometimes I caught him watching me with his intense green eyes. It was those times that I thought I might ask him to take me to Mama, but something held me back, a hand clenched around some happily-ever-after notion that all things come out smelling fresh and clean. Each day I breathed in the air and fed myself. I went through the motions, but my heart was empty. The days turned into nights and then back into days. Even the spooks didn't show their faces. I was alone. My mind was old and turning inside out with the crazies. Widow Marks lived next door to me and Mama ever since I could remember and as far as I knew she never left her yard. Many times I saw her sitting on her front porch talking to empty air. I was starting to understand why.

One morning I woke up thinking about a garden me and Mama planted the spring after Daddy died. It was full of every kind of flower, and somehow watching them grow gave me reason to hope. That's what a garden could do. I itched to feel the loose dirt in my fingers. I sat up on the sofa, looked outside, and thought I might throw myself off the roof if I had to see snow for another day. The sun was shining, trying to fool me into believing it was warm. I decided to get back to what me and Shelly had been doing before she threw a fit and ran out on me. I went to the attic.

The door creaked like a ghost story. Cobwebs hung in fluffy velvet clusters. It was warmer than I thought it would be up there, probably because of the sun beating on the tin roof. Piles of stuff filled the space, but I figured I'd start at the back this time and give that necklace and hair all the room they needed. I made my way to a tiny window in the corner. The trunk was older than me. I brushed off layers of dust and found the initials "AP." The latch wasn't made for keeping people out. Inside were books with flowers pressed between brittle pages, filled with old photographs of a woman who looked like Hobbs's mama when she was young. In one she wore a fancy dress with a big floppy hat. My favorite was the one where she held a small boy. I enjoyed seeing Hobbs's expression lit up in a smile. I opened one of the small books with lined paper—there were several—and found a willowy handwriting.

May 3, 1913

I gave birth to my first child today. We will name him Hobbs. Henry James thinks I've lost my mind, but he's supposed to be Hobbs. I dreamed the name two weeks ago. Who am I to argue with a dream of this nature? I've counted all his fingers and toes. He's perfect in every way.

I flipped through the book, reading about never getting sleep. Hobbs was of a colicky nature. I opened another of her diaries.

December 25, 1923

I don't understand a thing about my husband. He refuses to allow Mother to send Christmas gifts for the children. I know he has every right not to care for her, but she is my mother. I love her. I hate his pride. I hate this mountain. I wish I had the courage to take Hobbs and AzLeigh home, but what kind of life would they lead in Asheville? They could never be the social birds Mother would insist upon. They are my life.

So my mother-in-law was kept from her mother. I turned to the last page of the next book.

August 14, 1930

Today I go to Mother's for a tea. Finally I am allowed to leave this mountain. So it's terrible that I will be attending this hateful affair. Mother's teas remind me of what could have been. But I'm visiting Mother, and AzLeigh is coming. Yesterday I had a frightful encounter. I was out walking when I ran into a man along the path in the woods. He was one of the government men here to collect tax information. He told me that he found a moonshine still on our property and would have to let the proper authorities know. I explained to him that we didn't make moonshine, but it didn't seem to matter. He was so intent on serving justice. His name was Merlin Hocket. The insistent fool wore his three-piece suit and driving hat while trekking around the woods. I didn't bother telling Henry James. He would only become angry. The whole mountain is in an uproar over the tax people. I do worry Hobbs has something to do with the still. He's getting way too big for his britches.

So there was the story written in my mother-in-law's own hand.

"You can't run far enough to outrun Hobbs." The man's voice was as clear as it could be. I looked around but no one was there. Now I had a name. Merlin Hocket was the man I saw in the woods and who knocked on my door. A ghost. I held the book up to the light. A newspaper clipping fluttered down into my lap.

AzLeigh Renee Pritchard Dead from Fall. The paper was dated August 15, 1930. My gosh, she had died the next day after her writing.

"When the time is right, you'll know what to do." This time the voice sat right next to my ear and I jumped.

"Why are you bothering me?"

The silence was thick. I looked at the clipping.

"What are you doing up here?"

I nearly jumped out of my skin. "You done stopped my heart, Jack Allen. I thought you was some spirit come to get me." My laugh sounded tight.

"Sorry."

"This weather is making me crazy, so I came up here to look around." I put the book back in the trunk.

"Find anything?"

For a minute I thought of telling him about the diaries, about the necklace and the hair, but it seemed wrong. "Naw, just a bunch of old clothes and a few old photos. I can't believe how they dressed."

He watched me a minute too long. "Come on down before it gets dark. I thought I heard you talking to someone."

"You did. Myself. Who else do I have to talk to?"

The sun was sinking into the trees. My bones ached with cold. Still I thought about Merlin Hocket. What did he want from me?

"Have you eaten today?"

"Not yet." All of a sudden I was starving. "But I'm hungry now. I'm going to cook me some eggs and biscuits."

"Sounds pretty good."

"You can stay if you want."

"I might just do that."

"How did Hobbs's mama die?"

Jack turned to lead the way out. "How come we're always talking about Hobbs and his family?" But I could tell from the sound of his voice he was smiling.

"Nothing else to talk about. So, why don't we talk about you. What made you stay on the mountain after your mama died?"

"Nowhere to go, and Mrs. Pritchard died from a fall that gave her a nasty blow to the head."

"All this time I've been thinking she got sick."

"There's a lot you don't know, Nellie."

We were quiet as we walked down to the kitchen.

He sat at the table while I cooked the eggs. Somewhere close by we heard the cry of a hawk. Mama always said hawks were good luck. They represented strength, and the good Lord knew I had to have some to get through this winter alone.

"I'm going to have me a big garden out in the front. You know, where the view of the valley is so good."

"You like to garden?" He smiled.

"I don't think I've ever thought about liking it, but the wet dirt after a good spring rain is the best smell ever. The little seedlings popping up overnight always make me feel like a little girl again. I like the flowers more than the work." We were quiet for a few minutes.

He watched me put a platter of eggs on the table. "It sounds like you had a good life in Asheville."

"Yes."

We ate eggs, biscuits, and ham together, laughing over old stories he told about living on the mountain.

"Me and AzLeigh got in the worst trouble for hiding that skunk in the barn." There were tears in our eyes. "The poor thing was hurt. AzLeigh convinced me he wouldn't spray the ones who helped him. Well, she was wrong about that."

I nearly choked on my eggs. "Stop. You have to stop." I held up a hand, giving in to the giggles that sprayed crumbs everywhere.

"Hobbs threatened to beat me up because his horse stunk to high heaven too. But he couldn't stand the smell of me, so I lived another day." Jack wiped his eyes with his handkerchief. "Me and AzLeigh had to work out in the fields with Henry James for a week. Now, that wasn't no big deal for me because I worked with him all the time. But AzLeigh whined until her daddy sent her home to Ma." He shook his head.

"That doesn't sound fair."

Jack shrugged. "Truth was, I liked working out there in the sun with Henry James. His stories were worth listening to. He always said I'd end up with the farm." A shadow passed over his face. "But I shouldn't have listened to him. I would never be as important as his own flesh and blood. Hobbs got the farm."

A headache worked at the back of my eyes. "I'm sorry."

"I got to be going, Mrs. Pritchard." He winked and gave me a nod.

It wasn't hard for me to see how hurt he must have been. Hobbs had taken the one thing that mattered and never really wanted it. He hated farming. I gave Jack a quick hug at the door and tried not to notice how he stiffened, or how I breathed in deep to catch his smell. All of this was foolishness on my part. Jack wouldn't see me as anything but his sister-in-law. He was good to a fault and only a good woman would catch him one day. That was too bad for me. I had to settle on making him my friend.

After he was gone, I went up to the attic. I got me two of them empty diaries that belonged to my mother-in-law. Then I grabbed the wooden box with the necklace and hair. I settled on the sofa in the front room.

January 23, 1939

I'm going to write my thoughts like Hobbs's mama. Not that they matter nearly as much as hers, but it might help me sort this confused feeling. Hobbs has been gone since right after Christmas and I ain't missing him. I don't expect him back for a while. Actually I pray he don't come back at all. Maybe someone will kill him. That's a horrible thought for a girl who claims to be a Christian. But I got my own bunch of questions for God. Like, why in the world would He let me marry someone like Hobbs Pritchard? If He were real like Mama always said, why would He let Hobbs hurt the people he hurt? Does Hobbs get another set of rules? And what about ghosts? Where do they come from and why aren't their souls in heaven? Mama says there's no such thing, but she's wrong. Sometimes I can feel someone watching me, waiting. And I heard the voice today. Maybe I'm just going crazy. What would I do if I were a man? Cause men can do anything they want. I'd walk right off this mountain and never look back. That's all. That simple. If Hobbs tried to stop me, I'd put him in his place. Where is his place? One of these days I'm going to get the nerve to leave. Until then, I'm going to do more than make do. I'm going to live.

The next morning I put the book and the box in a drawer in the sideboard of the dining room, under some table linens. Hobbs would never look there. A thrill that only a secret can give rushed through me. Jack's mama wouldn't mind me keeping her necklace safe and hidden for a while.

Sixteen

February 5, 1939

We got a good thaw. Thank you Lord. I intend to walk to church. Maybe this week I can start turning the ground over for my garden. I've done some thinking on my questions to God. First, I can't blame Him for all my mistakes. Mama says He gave us free will. But I ain't letting Him off the hook on the free will thing. It ain't right to create humans and then just let them go like a couple of fighting cocks in a chicken pen. We're bound to scratch our way out one way or another. Hobbs is a fighting cock if ever I seen one. He'll spur you in a minute. I may be a girl but it don't mean I can't fight. I'm going to make me a place right here on this mountain. Folks around here have to like me. I'm just as plain as them. I'm going to see my mama too. Maybe I can find the courage to ask Jack to take me. But who am I kidding? That's just a fairy story. If Hobbs finds out, he'll hurt Mama. I can't let that happen.

I chose one of my better dresses, a yellow one with light-pink trim, and then tamed my thick curls into a long braid. I set out walking to church. It was so warm I thought spring had come to stay. No one at church acted surprised to see me, even though I hadn't been since Christmas Eve. At home going to church was like a law that wasn't written down in the Good Book. I took me a seat in the back. Jack was sitting in his regular pew a few rows up. I let him be. The music was perfect for all that was ailing my soul. There ain't nothing like being alone day after day to get a girl to inspecting her life from the inside out. For one thing, I was a terrible judge of character. For another, I believed anything some sweet-talking fellow told me.

The good pastor stood in the pulpit with wild eyes. He was rumpled and looked like he hadn't shaved in a few days. He yelled and screamed so I couldn't understand what direction he was headed, but the congregation seemed to move with his flow, rocking back and forth in their seats.

When church was over, I scooted out the doors, hoping to leave without too much notice. The pastor grabbed my hand. "It's so nice to have you here with us, Mrs. Pritchard. I haven't been able to catch you on your previous visits."

"Thank you."

"You must see my wife, Lydia. She has a ladies' group, and I know she's wanted you to join for some time now." He looked me up and down. "All our fine ladies belong." He pulled his wife to his side, interrupting her talk with one of the women. "Lydia, this is Mrs. Pritchard. We're so happy to have her here. I told her she needed to visit your ladies' group. Its main purpose is to bring women closer to God. As we know from the Bible, this has always been a weakness for females. They wander away so easily."

I stared at him. Did he say that to me?

Lydia plastered a smile on her face and stepped in front of the pastor. "Why, Mrs. Pritchard, we would love to have you in our little group. Ignore the pastor and his thoughts on women. They are from the last century."

The pastor had moved on to talk with others in his flock.

"We meet this coming Wednesday at my house. The topic will be 'How to Make My Home More Prayerful.' We have a wonderful fellowship together." She took my hand in her icy fingers.

When I looked into her eyes, I saw her mocking me. "I'm very busy." How stupid was that? They all knew I was alone with not one thing to do.

"Oh, I know you are, but us proper ladies must show the others the way." She cocked her eyebrow at me. "Maybe your wonderful, handsome brother-in-law would be so kind to bring you." She smiled at Jack, who had come to stand at my left.

"Nellie knows I'll take her anywhere she needs to go."

"Good then, I plan to see you." She looked at me.

Jack took my elbow. "Come, Sister-in-law. I'll give you a ride home."

Lydia Dobbins frowned. "I do hope to see you, Mrs. Pritchard. It will go a long way in the eyes of the mountain. You know, clearing your name from your husband's actions."

Jack pulled me away. Lydia watched me. She was one of those society women who thought they were better than others. She must have been going crazy on Black Mountain. She was a rose in the middle of a bunch of wildflowers. Too bad I loved wildflowers.

February 8, 1939

Okay God, I'm going to this ladies' meeting. I'm going to prove once and for all I'm not like the husband I married. But when I look in these people's faces, I see I'm guilty. I won't never be nothing but bad to them. A good girl would never have married Hobbs Pritchard, and if she did make that terrible mistake, she

*would have owned up to it and gone home. But it ain't that simple.
I've got myself in a mess here and don't know what way to turn. If
I leave, then I'm letting You down. Wives don't leave their
husbands even if they are mean. If I stay, all of Hobbs's wrongs
will be mine till death parts us.*

The weather still held on Wednesday. I took out walking through the woods to the pastor's house. Everyone, even someone new like me, could find the Dobbins place. It was by far one of the biggest and fanciest houses I'd seen. It even had a little tower like a castle. I was praying the weather would hold so I could start on my garden in the afternoon. I would need the exercise to get this stupid meeting off my mind.

Merlin Hocket stood in the curve of the path. Up close he looked downright pitiful. "What do you want from me?" I managed to ask.

The knees of his fancy britches were dirty and one side of his spectacles was cracked like he'd been fighting. He held his cap in his hand and stared straight at me. He looked as real as any person I would see that day. Ghosts were supposed to look scary.

"This mountain plays tricks on people, turns them around, sends them in all the wrong directions. Be careful. You may think it's on your side but it will betray you. Follow your heart. Don't be afraid." His voice sounded hoarse.

The hairs on the back of my neck stood up. "You don't look like no ghost. Did Hobbs hurt you? Is that why you stay on his land?"

A mean look passed over his face and he walked off into the woods.

"Did Hobbs kill you like they say?" I called after him into the emptiness.

I was still sorting things out when I reached the pastor's house. Shelly answered the door. She looked at me like she might jump out of her skin. "Are you here for the ladies' meeting?"

"Yes."

She shook her head and motioned for me to follow her. She wore a starched white apron over a black dress. Was this Shelly's life?

The women were gathered in a fancy room. The windows were covered in lace and the sofa and chairs were made of blue velvet. Lydia motioned Shelly to come pour tea from a silver teapot into tiny china cups. The other women, dressed in worn skirts and blouses, looked as uncomfortable and out of place as I felt. I had made a mistake.

Lydia smiled at me. "Oh, look here. Mrs. Pritchard has joined us." Her smile was real, and I understood me and her were the ones who didn't fit in.

I fiddled with a loose thread on my brown A-line skirt. The button was about to fall off. The room remained quiet. I smiled at the women. Mrs. Connor wasn't among the group, thank goodness. Maybe she had become a backslider like me. The women watched. Their faces told me what a fool I was for marrying Hobbs.

"How's your husband, Mrs. Pritchard?" This came from a pretty, young woman; meanness laced her words.

"He's fine." I spoke as if I had seen him that morning.

One of the women huffed.

"I just bet he is, sweetie. He's always managed for himself. I know." The pretty woman gave me a knowing look that turned my stomach.

An older woman patted my arm. "Hobbs has always been Hobbs. It's his nature. Don't pay her no mind. You can't help who he is."

I could have hugged her.

All the women stared as if I was supposed to speak to this.

A sick pressure worked in my ribs. Hobbs was bad, but I didn't want to talk about him with those women. "Hobbs works a lot."

"Well of course he does. He took on this mountain like a hunter goes after his supper, like falling a squirrel or gutting a deer." This came from the pretty woman.

"Hush now, Darlene." The older woman spoke.

"He took anything worth a darn and left the rest for the vultures to pick over, Mama Park," Darlene sneered.

"Yes he did," spoke a few women at once.

Women when slapped together in the same room could be the meanest of all God's creatures, especially to their own kind. "Does anyone know anything about Merlin Hocket? I saw him on the way here." I allowed these words to settle in their minds. "He talked some kind of nonsense. He looked real to me. I'm not sure he is a ghost."

Shelly rattled the delicate cup as she poured tea.

Mama Park grabbed her chest and took a step back. "Lord have mercy on you, child. You best be careful. Everyone here knows what really happened to Merlin, and he's a bad omen, nothing but bad. He was found in a creek dead two months after he came up missing. See, it's because we kept quiet about the truth that he walks this mountain. He punishes us for not speaking up." Mama Park frowned.

All the women in the room muttered their agreement and this spurred Mama Park on.

"One thing I do know is folks that see him always come to some kind of doom." That word echoed through me. All the women had given me plenty of space. Shelly handed me a cup of tea that sloshed onto the saucer. Lydia came over from seeing to the little sandwiches. She was frowning at me. My being there wasn't helping the meeting like she thought. That was plain in how she tapped her toe.

"Most ghosts look like me and you. You can bet he's a spirit." Mama Park shook off a chill.

"Ghosts do not exist. We know that, ladies." Lydia gave me a "shut up" look. "Can we please change the subject to more ladylike things?" This time she openly glared at me.

The women began to talk about a quilt they were working on. Darlene recited her recipe for pound cake. I slid out the front door. Shelly met me in the yard just out of sight of the house.

"You got to leave this mountain, Nellie. That's what the woman ghost says. She's right upset and nearly driving me crazy. Get on out of here before it's too late. I won't have no part of the bad that is surrounding you. You can fix it but you got to leave right now." Shelly touched my arm and then walked away. I was left there with my mouth hanging open.

Seventeen

I took myself straight to Aunt Ida's. Maybe Mama was right all along. Maybe there was death—mine. Jack was unloading wood from the back of his truck. He stopped and took off his hat.

"Howdy, Miss Nellie."

I tried to smile. "I need to ask a favor."

His face grew serious and little lines appeared near his eyes. "What can I do for you?"

"I want to go see my mama." Women couldn't just leave their husbands, so I had to sort of lie.

He nodded. "You want to go tomorrow?"

My chest felt lighter. "Yes, if you don't mind, first thing in the morning."

Jack took off his hat and ran his fingers through his hair. "I don't want to be out of line, but be careful. Hobbs ain't going to take to you leaving the mountain, and everyone up here is watching."

"They don't like him. They won't tell."

"Not unless they're pushed to pay money they don't have."

He looked over the valley. "Folks might do anything if they're desperate."

"I'm going to see Mama. It's been too long."

"I'll be there first thing." He tried to smile.

"It's just for a visit. I ain't going to give Hobbs no reason to know."

"I know." But I could tell he thought otherwise. It seemed he knew more about me than I knew.

I scrubbed the toe of my shoe in the dirt.

"Your visit to the ladies' meeting didn't go so well?"

"Nothing was said that I hadn't figured on." I shrugged.

"Okay." He slapped his hand on his thigh.

"Thanks."

He jumped off the back of the truck. "I'll take you home."

I climbed into the seat. This time tomorrow I'd be with Mama. Who cared what happened. Mama was wrong; I was coming home. I would dodge the death she predicted. And silly old Shelly could eat her words.

When Jack passed the drive to Hobbs's house, I looked over at him.

"There's one place you need to see before you go back to Asheville." The truck climbed and climbed its way up that mountain until I thought we'd fall backwards. Then Jack pulled over and switched off the engine. "We got to walk the rest of the way. It's kind of tough." He looked at my skirt.

"I can do it."

We took a rough trail, littered with big tree roots, clinging on for dear life. The beautiful straight evergreens were so tall it made me dizzy to look up at them.

We rounded a curve and there we were, looking off a sheer drop, water rushing over rocks and then disappearing. We were at the top of a waterfall. A large gray boulder perched on the edge of the world in the middle of the river.

"This is heaven," I shouted above the rushing water.

Jack grinned. The view was like nothing I'd ever seen. It was one of those rare clear days, and I could look off that mountain into the valley. On top of the waterfall, the world was mine, Nellie Pritchard's. A hawk glided overhead, its wings in a wide span. The air was clean, stinging my chest as I took big breaths. Mama said that a hawk could fly higher than all the birds except eagles and avoided fights by leaving enemies behind. I watched this hawk, and the world turned under my feet. When had Hobbs become my enemy?

When Jack dropped me off, it was with the promise he would be at the house early. I made Mama her favorite chocolate cake as a treat, as a welcome home for me. Then I stretched out on the sofa. I was way too excited to drop off to sleep. Thoughts rolled through my head one after another. Should I take all my clothes? Would Jack try to come back to get me that evening? I hadn't thought of that. Well, I would tell him I was spending the night. Mama would keep me safe. I closed my eyes and saw the hawk floating on the air.

The next morning I wrapped the cake in a towel. I wore my wedding dress. I'd replaced all those silly pearl buttons with practical ones. Jack came early just like he promised and waited by the truck. I opened the door, took one step out, and heard a familiar rattle working its way up the drive. I sat the cake back on the table and took a step back outside as if I were in a dream. Jack's expression turned dark as the noise grew louder, like a funnel cloud barreling in from the west.

Hobbs's truck came rolling into the yard. He was all smiles like he'd only been gone for a few days. My mind went blank. There I stood, nothing but his scared wife, no more than a object like the house or the barn. He jumped from the cab of the truck and crossed the space between us, catching me up in his arms, planting a big kiss on my lips. I couldn't say a word, not a single word. I looked over at Jack, wishing he'd help me. Couldn't he see I needed him? I needed to go see my mama. I needed to be off of Black Mountain. His expression spoke to me like words coming out of his mouth. I wasn't going nowhere. I was Hobbs's wife and he owned me.

"Good to see you made it home safe." Jack's words held none of the anger and disappointment I felt.

Hobbs let me go. "Thank you and Aunt Ida for looking after my girl."

Jack opened the door to his truck and gave one long look at Hobbs. For a second I was sure he would say all the things that should've been said. "That's what we do best, Hobbs, look after what you leave undone. Some things never change."

"You're right about that. Some things never change." Hobbs laughed clear and free of anger.

I was something left behind, something undone. I never thought my happily ever after would be so sad.

Jack went down the drive at a fast clip.

"Don't you dare cry. I'm home now."

My breath left my chest. We went into the kitchen.

He took the towel off the cake. "Chocolate, my favorite." He dug one finger down the middle of the frosting, scarring the perfect smoothness.

Eighteen

Hobbs has been Hobbs since he came home. He skipped right over Valentine's Day and I didn't bother to remind him. Why? My heart's not in this mess. You see, God, I can't figure why You didn't help me get to Mama's. You know Hobbs is bad. He's drinking every single night. The morning he came home he stunk of roses. I couldn't help but think of that girl in the door of the church. Why did he marry me?

At least the weather is still warm and I'm starting my garden. This will help my soul. I thought of walking off the mountain, but that chance was right in front of me and I stayed put. If I stood up to Hobbs, he'd only chase me down and hurt Mama too. Just look where I've come in this marriage of mine.

I put my diary beside the ruby necklace. Each day I opened the pouch and let the stones catch the sun, sparkling. The lock of gray hair gave me the creeps but somehow it seemed right to keep it with the necklace. The drawer squeaked as I pushed it shut. The shadow formed black and oily, the perfect outline of a man.

"He'll do to you what he did to me and to her." The voice took up the empty space in the dining room.

"What did Hobbs do?"

A bitter laugh echoed in the room. "You know what he did. You're a smart girl."

The shadow looked darker.

"You know what to do, Nellie." And then Merlin was gone.

I laughed like a crazy woman.

My garden plot was rocky and hard to turn with a hoe. I worked the dirt, warmed by the sun, with my whole body and mind. The movement kept the images of home from creeping into my thoughts like some sweet dream that I'd have to wake up from. Each time my hoe hit a clod of dirt, I became part of the land, the air, and the mountain itself. I was lost to the heart that drove me to marry. The woods were silent and alive. That's what I loved about gardening, seedlings sprouting through the dirt, a promise that all things can grow. Hobbs wasn't capable of loving me. With this thought, I turned into a woman. The price of two simple words—"I will"—was too high. The dark rich earth yielded to the hoe. The sun sank into the tops of the trees, and a chill spread through me. I scooped up a fistful of dirt. Love was not simple. Love wasn't something I could count on to save me. Love was a story in a book that would never be written by me. I stood there until I could barely see my hand in front of my face.

I must have dozed off in the rocker in front of the fireplace. The whole room turned icy cold, even though I could hear the wood popping. When I opened my eyes, there stood Jack's mama in front of me. She looked tired. Her hair was the same steel gray.

"I see why Jack's taken a liking to you. That ain't going to do him no good or you. He never has been good at seeing things for what they are. You're in a mess and it's partly your own fault. You know how bad Hobbs is. You got to leave. I got that little girl to tell you, but you acted like I wasn't real. You got to leave now! You understand?"

"Did he hurt you?"

"What's that matter to you? He's going to do to you what he did to me. You got to go or face what comes. Either way you will suffer." She reached out and touched my arm. Her touch was like a cool breeze in the spring. "He's going to be here soon. Go and don't let him find you." She dissolved.

My head burned and my joints ached like I had a fever. I was filled with this urge to run out into the dark and never come back. Fog had moved in around the house. The grayish white was thicker than I'd ever seen it. The nighttime would swallow me. I sat back in the rocker. I would leave as soon as it turned light outside.

Nineteen

Hobbs came home that night, pawing me, waking me from a dream of the ocean, where I was going under. He tore my nightgown open. I couldn't get my breath.

"Stop!" I pushed my fists into his chest.

The back of his hand crashed across my mouth. "You're my wife. I own you, girl. I can do what I want when I want." He wrapped my long braid around his fist and pulled me to my feet. "You don't mouth me!"

The smell of whiskey gagged me. "Hobbs, please." And in that moment, before my life took a turn I could never straighten out, I saw the true Hobbs reflected in his blue eyes, the man all his women eventually saw.

He punched my head with his other fist. "Shut the hell up!" Then he shoved me onto the floor on his mama's little braided rug. He didn't even bother to take his pants off. I prayed God would kill him, but God wasn't listening, cause Hobbs kept on pumping me with his meanness. My heart turned black and dead. I guess one could say I was dying, but I clung to the world like beggar lice on cloth.

When he finished his deed, he rolled over, grew still, and began to snore. Finally I had the strength to ease away and make my way out of the house, into the cool mist, where I lost everything in my stomach on the ground.

Daylight seemed like it would never come as I sat in the kitchen waiting. I would tell Hobbs it was over, that he had to take me to Mama's and leave me alone. I would tell Aunt Ida what he had done. Even Hobbs didn't want to be known as a wife beater.

"Silly notion, you know. You can't reason with him. He's not like you or me. Running won't do. You got to take a stand." Merlin Hocket looked fuzzy, like I was looking through a piece of cheesecloth.

"How?" I whispered. The sun was streaming in the kitchen window. The fog had burned away.

"You'll know. It'll come to you." And he was gone. He spoke more sense than anything I had thought up.

Now a smart girl would have walked down that road and found some help, but Hobbs would chase me until he caught me. He would always win. Anyway, I wasn't the leaving type. I walked out to the garden plot. Jack could sow some seeds for me on Good Friday. Mama always said to plant on that day for a plentiful crop.

"What're you doing out there?" Hobbs stood in the door with no shirt, his pants unbuttoned.

I bent down and picked up a clod of soil, crushing it in my fingers, sprinkling it on the ground.

"Talk to me! You tore up the yard! Nobody told you you could do that!" His look was wild. "You ain't got no business doing nothing I don't want you to. You ain't nothing but dirt. Hell, the dirt is worth more. You're supposed to make me a son!"

If I had wings, I'd fly right out into the valley below. "No."

"What'd you say?"

"I'm not going to do anything for you." All the hate must have shown in my face.

He covered the distance between us in a trot, grabbing my shoulders, shoving me to the ground. I tried fighting him, but he was crazier than me. The soil tasted bitter and unyielding. My mind closed and the world went black as he beat me.

When I woke, I was there in the dirt, my dress hiked up over my hips, blood and freshly turned soil mixed in my mouth. The sky was blue. The air was still. God had left me. I struggled to my feet. I thought of going to Mrs. Connor, but I was afraid his fury would be turned on her, so I went to find Jack.

Aunt Ida was washing clothes on her washboard by the river. I saw my face in her look. "Lord God, what happened to you, child?" She dropped one of Jack's shirts on the muddy riverbank.

"Hobbs," I whispered.

She stood. "What did you do?"

"Where's Jack?" I looked her straight in her eyes.

"No need to get him killed, girl. Is that what you want?"

My thoughts were tangled.

"This is just part of life. Husbands do what they want. You think you can just leave? Didn't your mama teach you anything?" Her hand trembled.

"He can't do this. He don't own me." My words were a whisper floating on the slight breeze.

"You're Hobbs's wife. You'll only cause trouble if you go to your mama. She'll pay for your wrongs. You'd better take yourself home and please him. Keep him happy, Nellie. That's my best answer. Learn how to be the wife he needs. That's what women do."

I turned to leave. A dull thought knocked in my head. "I'll never learn."

"What did you say?" Aunt Ida made a couple of steps behind me. "Let me take care of those cuts and bruises."

I kept walking. "No."

"Don't cause no more trouble. You'll end up worse. He's probably left for a while. Fix him a nice supper, make yourself pretty. Surprise him."

I laughed at the blue sky and kept walking, a dip and stumble to each step as if I was going to fall on my face. Aunt Ida kept talking, but the roar in my head drowned her out.

The woods weren't thick yet. It would be weeks before the leaves budded. The path was marked, worn, used. Merlin Hocket stood up the trail. I had halfway hoped I'd come on him. I wanted to turn into him.

"Sometimes you think you know the right way, but you do not. No one can blame you. It takes courage to follow the path that will truly free you, Nellie. You know what to do. You've known all along." He stepped close, and his breath tickled my cheek. Then he was gone.

All that chopping wood gave me muscles that were tight and hard. Hobbs wasn't figuring on that. I'd left some marks on him, but he was stronger. I chopped some extra wood. The ax split the logs. My aim was perfect. I toted the wood inside and stacked it next to the fireplace. I leaned the ax right beside it. Then I heated water and soaked in my lavender oil. My wounds opened. When I was through, I put on my wedding dress. My hair hung down my back. For a flicker, I saw the soft look Jack gave me now and then, but it only brought hate into my heart. Men were men whether they were soft or mean. Their needs came first.

The flames in the fireplace leapt up the chimney, warming the room too much. I waited in the rocker. Hobbs hadn't gone far. The smell of fresh blood would bring him back. A hawk cried out. I drifted off into the sleep of the dead.

Hobbs bent over the rocker, a hand on each wooden arm,

trapping me like a rabbit in a box. "Look at you. I guess a good beating now and then is just the thing. Makes you realize how lucky you are to have me. It makes you see what you got, don't it, girl? I am the boss. You want to know why I married you, Nellie? Because you favor Mama and AzLeigh so much. They always knew how to take care of me. You fit in just fine with this house. But girl, we ain't nothing alike."

I became a ghost, and everybody knows ghosts don't have anything to lose.

"What you smiling at?" His breath could have made me drunk; maybe it did.

"I'll show you if you let me have some room."

He grinned and straightened. "Now don't you try something funny, or I'll beat you again. I may have to beat you once a week for good measure."

I dropped the dress off my shoulders and let it slide to the floor. The bruises—purple, dark—and cuts didn't faze him. He grabbed me with hard, rough hands.

"Slow down. I want to show you what I can do, Hobbs. Nice and slow like." I guided him to the floor on the rug his mama had hooked. I knelt beside him and left my regrets in the shadows. The person who mounted Hobbs turned the wind into the hot breath of the devil. I embraced the heat and hammered him into submission. When he tried to speak, I placed my finger to his lips.

After he fell into a deep drunken sleep, I untangled my body from his. In that moment, I could have walked away. The ax weighed heavy in my hands. I slung it over my head. The room spun and thunder rumbled in the distance, shaking the floor of the house. The fog would come rolling in soon. I splintered my prison, spilling my sin all over his mama's little rug, and I deeply regretted that.

The fog moved in at dawn, rolling into the open windows,

giving me the feeling that I was living in a dream. I worked with efficient strength as the sun burned through. I fed the flames, leaping in the fireplace, until I finished. The flames of hell burned for hours, and then they died down to embers and became hot ashes, littered with a bright hot glow here and there. When they were cool enough, I sprinkled them over my garden plot, turning dirt as the moon rode the horizon. I would plant the seeds in neat rows. I would tend the garden, and then I would be free to leave.

His head was all that remained. Even fear, hate, and revenge couldn't bring me to destroy his face. I pushed the head through a hole in the hollow tree on the edge of the woods. The moon slid into the tree line as I climbed the stairs to the bedroom. I slept as if I were a child in Mama's bed.

Later that morning, I cleaned the cabin until the tips of my fingers peeled and cracked open, but still the rancid smell remained. I couldn't scrub my sin away no matter how hard I tried. So I chose a big rug from the bedroom upstairs, dragging it in front of the fireplace. No matter how right my actions were, I was wrong. In my deed, I destroyed my life on that mountain, but at the same time, I became part of its soul. The mountain owned me and always would. It used me to take away the evil that haunted its people. Nellie died with Hobbs. Who was worse, me or him?

February 17, 1939

How long can I live with this deed? Where can I go from here? God, I know You don't want to hear from me, but Hobbs beat me. You let him. He would have killed me. Freedom isn't freedom after all. God, I'm not sorry. And that's my sin. You don't want to listen to me. I don't blame You. I will live and walk this earth knowing that anyone can do bad things. I keep studying that old hollow tree. I loved him. Once upon a time Nellie loved Hobbs Pritchard.

Twenty

A person can tell how they're loved by how much they're missed when they leave this world. Three weeks after Hobbs's life ended no one had asked a question; not one soul had come to visit. No one sensed his spirit had left the earth. Like a fool, I was still living in that house like I was stuck, like the mountain kept me prisoner. Time moved in and out as if all was good. My food was almost gone, but that didn't much matter. I wasn't hungry. I floated from one room to another trying to paint my deed as a good upstanding choice. The truth stared me in the face, cracking the mirror in our bedroom, a long deep slit from one corner to the other. But still I had no regrets. My feelings were sliced away. Hobbs stood in every shadow. His scent marked our bed. I burned the fine linens and closed the upstairs room. His laughter filled my waking hours. On more than one night, I searched for him by the hollow tree, but he wouldn't show himself. Somehow he knew he had won with the fall of the ax.

I slept like a dead person. A weariness owned every bone of my body, and I took to feeling sick each morning. I walked through my days losing count. One morning Jack came knocking at the door. I thought of sitting still. Maybe he would go away, but I knew he'd let himself into the house and find me sitting on the sofa. I went to greet him.

His forehead wrinkled. "You don't look good, Nellie. I should have been up here before now."

I swallowed the rank taste of hate in my mouth. He had no business caring. "I'm fine." Past him was the ever-changing valley and of course the turned dirt of the garden.

"You don't look yourself." He held me with his stare.

I almost laughed in his face for being a fool, a stupid fool who couldn't see the devil standing in front of him. "I need me some seeds." Before someone came and hauled me off to jail, I had one thing to do, one mark to leave.

"You do have a nice big garden plot." He looked at the garden. "You said you and your mama did a lot of gardening."

His remembering didn't soften me one bit. "I turned that garden, but Hobbs"—his name hung in the air like ice crystals frozen on a glass windowpane—"doesn't like that I tore up the yard. He got right mad." My words were flat.

"I guess he left again?" Jack looked everywhere but at me. "Aunt Ida said you came down to visit a few weeks ago, but Hobbs didn't come with you. She's been worrying over him like always." He cocked his head to the side. "It ain't like him to leave without a visit with her."

"He breezed in here long enough to spoil my trip to Mama's and left. I can't say why he didn't come see Aunt Ida." The bitterness of my words could have poisoned a person.

"You still want to go to your mama's?"

I looked into his green eyes and wanted to slap his face. "No, the time for that has come and gone." I just wanted him to leave.

"You want to make me a list of seeds?"

He stood beside the kitchen table as I wrote the list on the back of a brown paper bag.

"What is that smell, Nellie?"

My pencil stopped for only a second as I wrote the name "asters." "I burned a ham real bad last week. I guess you could say I turned it black to the bone. It's a wonder I didn't burn the house down. The smell won't go away. Hobbs was right about my cooking."

Jack watched me. "Ain't nothing like burned meat. You must have burned it something terrible." He tested me with one of his grins.

"I did." I scribbled the rest of the list and handed it off to him.

After studying the paper, he looked up and laughed. "Flowers, you want nothing but flowers?"

"I need something pretty in my life. They're for Hobbs too." This was true.

Jack's face darkened. "You sure he ain't done something to you?"

For a second, I thought of confessing, but the moment passed without a word. "He was Hobbs, nothing but plain old Hobbs."

He folded the piece of brown paper and put it in his front shirt pocket. "I'll bring these back soon."

"Good."

Funny how I didn't even like him anymore.

Instead of getting in his truck, he walked around it and headed out to the hollow tree.

I got a little light-headed.

"You got a dead smell out here by the tree," he yelled.

I shrugged my shoulders. "I can't think of what died."

He nodded and walked back to his truck. "I'll be back soon with the seeds."

When his truck disappeared down the drive, the stone sitting on my chest got lighter.

It took me two mornings before I decided I had to do something. I sat down at the kitchen table and wrote me a letter.

> *Dear Mama:*
> *You saw my future and you was right. It pains me to say that. I was wrong. I did learn something. I learned how to chop wood and be alone. I'm going to grow me a right nice garden with all kinds of flowers. I think of you often. I think most about the trip we took with Daddy that time. You remember? Do you remember what I told you? I wasn't but nine and I already knew more than I should've. But if you don't remember, I'll understand. It was so beautiful there. Wasn't it? I'll always love you.*
>
> *Your daughter,*
> *Nellie*

I sealed the letter and walked it down to Jack. Aunt Ida was hanging clothes in the side yard. She turned a frown on me. "Have you seen Hobbs lately?"

"He hasn't been back since he beat the stuffing out of me." I tried to contain the bubbling rage in my head.

"He always tells me when he's leaving no matter what."

"He didn't this time. Maybe you mean as much to him as I do." I let these words sink in. "You can never tell about old Hobbs, can you." I handed her the envelope. "Could you make sure Jack takes this to the post office the next time he goes?"

She took the letter but never looked me in the face. This

gave me a power over her, but it was too late to care about such things.

"Jack's got you some seeds and some lime. He said you've got something dead up there in the yard." She picked that time to look me straight in the eyes. "What died?"

Without missing a beat, I laughed. "I had a coon hanging around some time back, nearly drove me crazy at night shuffling here and there, but I haven't seen him in a while. I think he crawled in that hollow tree and died. Good thing. I believe I would have killed him myself soon."

Her eyes grew big. "That stuff is on the table in the kitchen. Jack will mail your letter. He's got a right soft spot for you. You don't need to be causing trouble between him and Hobbs."

I threw back my head and laughed. "Oh, I don't think I could do that if I tried."

"You be careful, now. That coon could have been rabid, and it's as dangerous dead as alive."

"I could almost guarantee he was rabid, but I can't see how he can hurt me no more."

The ground turned with ease as I planted the seeds, marking each row with the names of flowers: black-eyed Susans, zinnias, pansies, sunflowers, and snapdragons were just a few. While I was tossing the dirt, my hoe hit something hard. My heart did a little flip. I half expected to grab something like an elbow or finger bone. The jar was partway out of the ground. Inside was a big roll of bills—more money than I could have ever imagined. I didn't even count it. Finding the jar explained why Hobbs didn't want me digging a garden. I removed five one-hundred-dollar bills, and then an extra four. The rest—still a big wad—I put back in the jar and buried it with the seeds and him. I set out for the church. The thoughts that crowded my every hour parted like the Red Sea.

The spring shot out of the pipe. The cup was in the same place Maynard left it. I looked over my shoulder just to make sure no one was around. The water splashed into the tin cup and I placed it to my lips, sipping in a baptism. I dropped the cup and unfastened my skirt, dropping it to the ground. Next I took off my blouse. I slid off my slippers. The water numbed my feet as I squatted beneath the flow of water. I stayed there until my hair was soaked, until the bills tucked into my bra were soft.

God, please heal the evil side of my heart.

The sun sank low in the sky as I walked into the Connors' yard. This time I was prepared, no longer that pitiful little fool. I knocked on the door.

One of the younger boys opened it, staring at me.

"Is your mama here?"

"Yes ma'am." He ran away, leaving the door standing open. The room was neat and homey with quilts and a big bowl of apples on the table. How did they get fresh apples this time of year?

"What you want?" Mrs. Connor looked tired.

"Maynard can come home and here . . ." I shoved five of the one-hundred-dollar bills into her hand.

She unfolded the wad. "I'll not take any money." She pushed the money back at me. "Did you take a bath with it?"

"It ain't my money. I found it where Hobbs must've buried it. You split it up with all the people he owes. You tell Maynard to come home like I said. It's safe." I turned to leave, tired to the bone. "I'd appreciate you don't tell anyone where you got that." I nodded at the money.

"You done killed him, ain't you? Lordy mercy, you killed him." She smiled, making her look years younger.

I couldn't speak.

"You won't hear me breathe a word. If you killed him, good. He had it coming to him, Nellie. You did us all a service. Don't you ever feel bad. You walk off this mountain with your head held high. You remember, you'll always belong here. You're one of us now."

If only someone could have said that earlier. "Would you do one more thing for me?"

"What you need?"

I pushed two one-hundred-dollar bills at her. "Would you make sure that Shelly gets this? Tell her she was right, and I love her for trying to save me."

"Folks will always remember you, Nellie Pritchard." Mrs. Connor smiled, taking the money. "She'll get this. You can count on me."

I left her on the porch, watching me.

"Nellie, you ever need anything, you let me know."

I nodded and walked home as dark pushed in around me. My time was running out. Soon Aunt Ida would start to snoop around and find Hobbs's truck up near the waterfall. It was time for me to leave.

Twenty-one

And just as I predicted, Aunt Ida had worked herself into a dither. She had sent Jack down the mountain with my letter and orders to find Hobbs. When Jack came back with nothing that evening, she insisted on paying me a visit. They were waiting on me when I got back from Mrs. Connor's.

Aunt Ida stepped out of that truck with a determined look. "Jack went down and talked to Rose this morning. That's Hobbs's girlfriend in Asheville."

Jack wasn't looking at me.

A deep rage cracked open in my heart.

"She ain't seen him in over a month. That's when he came home last."

"Oh, you mean the day he beat me?" I spit the words at her. I hated her for the unfailing love she had for Hobbs.

She skipped over my words. "She's known him longer than you. He wouldn't keep from seeing her. Something is wrong."

I bit the inside of my mouth until the salty taste of blood seeped onto my tongue.

"What kind of clothes was he wearing the last time he was here?" She was yelling at me with all the hate I felt.

"I couldn't quite make them out. I was trying to stay alive and my black swollen eyes got in the way."

Jack stared at me.

He helped kill Hobbs, just like Aunt Ida. They knew what he was and never had the guts to stop him. Only me. I did.

"I guess Aunt Ida didn't bother telling you about my beating and how much she helped." My hate bubbled over. "He had on his overalls and blue shirt."

"I want to see in that house." Aunt Ida stamped her foot. "I want to see what she did to my boy."

"That's Nellie's house too, Aunt Ida. You can't just go in." Jack touched her arm.

"I don't care!" she cried.

"Go on in. It's no place of mine." I stared at Aunt Ida.

"He's my boy." She was pitiful.

"You go on in there. All that is mine is a few old dresses."

Jack reached out to me, but I stepped back. "Go on with her. Get your fill." They were mean words.

Jack and Aunt Ida went inside. I sat down on the edge of my garden. The ground was warm and moist. Through the front window I saw the ghost of Jack's mama following him around the room. I wished with all my heart I could tell him what all I knew. When they came out, Aunt Ida went straight to the truck, but Jack walked over to see me. His mama followed right along. She smiled at me, but it was a pained smile, as if to say nothing ends, nothing gets settled.

"I want you to go with me tomorrow so we can look over the land, see if we can find some trace of him. He has lots of enemies. You could be in danger."

I laughed. "You come in the morning. I'll go then."

Jack nodded. "You should have told me he beat you."

Jack's mama shook her head and walked back into the house.

"Why?" I spoke around the lump in my throat.

"Because."

"So you could help me like you did the morning he came home and spoiled my trip?" I stared at him. "You come on back in the morning." The hatred I felt drained out of my feet. The healing had begun.

He nodded.

Twenty-two

That night a storm came like I knew it would. It was the kind of storm that showed up on the heels of warm air too early in the spring. Its power built in the sky and crashed through the heavens, shaking the foundation of the house. The mountain was telling me good-bye.

I found Hobbs's old blue shirt and overalls. I stood in front of his shaving mirror, cutting my hair until it was right close to my head and stuck out like a boy's. His cap pulled down on my head perfect. In the mirror was someone who looked Hobbs Pritchard in the eye and lived.

Merlin Hocket stood in the front room.

"He's gone."

"Yes, but just like you, I will never rest. Hobbs Pritchard will always be a haunting. I'll never move past what him and this mountain did to me." He turned and walked through the closed front door.

Right before dawn a fog rolled in, and I took out walking through the woods. I wasn't a bit scared. I knew enough not to walk off a cliff. It wouldn't much matter if I did. I had my feed sack with two dresses tucked inside the bib of the baggy overalls. I left the others behind. The dresses I brought would be used for the baby clothes that I would need. I had two hundred dollars down the front of my shirt. That would do me for a while.

The fog was hard to see through, so I was on the road before I saw Jack's truck making its way up to the house. I tucked my chin in my collar and looked straight ahead. I released a prayer to heaven. God was listening cause the truck never slowed down. When Jack got to the house, he'd find a nice fire burning in the fireplace, breakfast on the table, and a note saying I'd gone for an early morning walk to clear my thoughts. I wrote how much I loved Hobbs, and how I couldn't live without him. Nellie was gone forever.

The last time I saw Black Mountain was in the side mirror of the Connors' truck as Mrs. Connor and Shelly drove me down the mountain. The hawk I'd seen at the waterfall was circling in and out of the fog, a flash of wing, a sharp cry.

Part Two

Josie Clay

Twenty-three

If you want to know how Nellie Pritchard got herself into the mess she did, you got to know parts of my story. See, Nellie belonged to me, my only child. Sometimes I could have sworn we were one and the same, but at other times, we was on the opposite ends of the earth from each other. The good Lord knew I did my best to send her in the right direction just like my mama did me and her mama did her. It's a weakness trying to keep our daughters from making the same mistakes. But I didn't make one bit of difference. I didn't stop one thing.

The day that nice young man Jack Allen came down from Black Mountain with Nellie's letter in his hand brought the hardest day I ever looked into with my eyes open. The paper felt hot to touch. That was my warning. I tried not to show my fear, not to jump to conclusions. I thanked him and sent him on his way. I hadn't heard a word, not one word, from Nellie since she called herself marrying Hobbs Pritchard.

Those few short sentences told me her future. We had come to this, me and her. I would have went to cry on Marge's shoulder, but she had passed on two months earlier. I told myself, *Josie, if you can pull off this one, you can do anything.* God never gave me more than I could handle, but I had to take issue with Nellie committing one of the worst sins in the Good Book. She might as well have held a gun to her own head. But doom was exactly what I saw in those tea leaves. She made her choice, and the part of me that is pure woman understood all the way to the bone. So, I packed up my clothes, got in my old Plymouth truck, and took out to meet her. I cursed myself the whole way for not marching up that mountain and putting Hobbs Pritchard in his place. I failed as her mama. Me and her daddy made our share of mistakes and brought a lot of history to our little family. I guess it could be said we passed on our habits, some good and some bad. We didn't know no better. Just like everyone else, we were writing our lives as we went.

One of the worst things I ever done in my whole life was hurt my mama by going against her wishes. She always wanted something better for me than she had for herself. Ain't that the way of a mama? She gave me her own dream of getting a decent education. Me? I thought that was pie in the sky. Girls didn't go to college. Most of the time they didn't even finish high school before they up and married a man picked out for them. Shoot, women weren't even allowed to vote. How could any of us be something big like a doctor or a judge? Mama told me from the start that if I married, I wasn't going to see anything but struggles. Did I listen? Shoot no. The day I saw Owen Clay standing in front of the church congregation, smiling his toothy grin, I fell in love with him. As if I knew what love was. In front of me stood what I wanted more than anything, and I figured if he had any wrongs, I could iron them right out like a wrinkled dress shirt. Lord, that's the worst thing a woman can do, love a man so much she can't see reason. It's a disease we women have carried in our blood since Eve. Cause wasn't it Eve that got blamed for that mess in the garden? Mind you, she was dumb. I'm not arguing one minute about that. But what did she have to go on? She didn't have no mama or daddy to blame for being bad examples. She got roped into sin by a smooth-talking serpent. Sometimes I wonder if Satan didn't reveal himself in the flesh. And don't you know he had the most beautiful eyes to stare into. It's them eyes that get us women each and every time. Anyway, I figured Adam put Eve up to that apple-eating incident. Don't you know she went home after talking to the snake and told Adam what was said? I can hear him now: "Eve, I bet that snake knows what he's talking about. Why don't you go on over there and pick us a couple of apples? I got a backache."

Nobody held a gun to Adam's head and made him eat the dern thing. But you wouldn't know it from the way the preachers tell the story. Lord no. I bet if a woman could stand in the pulpit for one hour, she'd set the congregation straight. But women didn't have no voice in the church when I was coming up.

I married Owen in 1918 on a sunny April day. He was a good husband, but I'm not going to lie, he had his ways. He had no tolerance for my talking. I learned to keep my chattering down. He also didn't see one reason for me to have any money of my own. I found that out the hard way.

"Look here, Owen, what Daddy gave us for marrying. I bet we could buy a house." I fanned the bills out in my hand. A dark look flew over Owen's face. Then I saw white. He hit me three times before I let him have the money. Now, don't get the wrong idea. Owen wasn't a wife beater. He only hit me one other time, when Nellie was eight, and he was drunker than a coot. That one don't count.

A week after he took my money I stood in the kitchen

stirring navy beans and baking cornbread. I thought we could crumble the cornbread into sweet milk. Lordy, that was a treat to me. Owen worked at the stone quarry and made a decent living. We had us a little rented house near the church.

His old Buick had a ticking in the engine that nearly drove him crazy but he couldn't ever make it stop. When he turned down the road coming home from work, I'd hear *tick, tick, tick*. I'd run my hand through my hair and practice my smile.

Owen was early on that afternoon. When he came in the door with a big smile, I caught my breath. He was pretty to look at when his face was lit up.

"Come here, girl." He wrapped his big hands around my waist and lifted me into the air. "I got you a surprise." He sat me down on the floor again.

I giggled, caught up in his happiness.

He held a big key in front of me. "I bought you something today."

My stomach churned and sweat broke out on the back of my neck.

"Aren't you even going to act happy?"

"What's that key for?" I turned on my big fake smile.

"Come on and I'll show you." He pulled me by the hand.

I still had my apron on, but I didn't raise one word to him.

We drove and drove through the streets of Asheville. Almost like he didn't know where he was. A couple of times I held my breath because he went down streets with big fancy houses, but then he turned onto Settle Road. All the houses were four-room boxes, sitting next to the tracks. He stopped in front of one with peeling yellow paint. Surely I could give it a new paint job and plant some flowers out front.

Owen slid the skeleton key into the key hole, wiggled it, and then turned. "This is our new home, sweetie. We're going to have our babies here."

I managed not to scream. "This looks real nice, Owen." A mouse scurried across the kitchen floor.

"See, we got us a big window in the living room." He beamed.

I wasn't sure what we were supposed to be looking at through that fancy window. More little run-down box houses or a train coming through, I guessed. "Mama's chair will be perfect there." I pointed to a corner. Mama had given me a green upholstered high-back chair. "The room will be real pretty." This was the thing. Daddy gave us enough money to buy a big fancy house. But I couldn't ask no questions. Women didn't get involved with the buying and selling. Owen probably spent it on drinking anyway.

We made a handsome couple, Owen and me. He was tall, dark, and had deep brown eyes that convinced me he was always right. Next to him, I was small and quiet in a pretty but simple kind of way.

"I wish my mama had lived to see this house. It's not as fancy as our house in Darien, but it's ours." He grinned.

I got a tiny glimpse of the man I married, the man I had to find peace and make a life with.

Twenty-four

We'd only been married two years when I found out I was going to have Nellie. It was the summer of 1920 and women were busy winning the right to vote, meaning my baby girl would come into a world that gave women a better life.

Owen just made a face when I pointed it out. "Women already got the world by the tail. Men work and they stay home looking pretty. How hard is that?"

I wanted to throw a shoe at him. He's lucky I didn't. My being with child made me hate him at the time.

The day my pains started, I sent word to Owen at the quarry to meet me at the hospital. We had argued for two months about having the baby at home. Owen felt hospitals were a waste of money. Me, I didn't see any reason to live in the past. The truth was I didn't like having a baby one bit.

My neighbor, Marge Marks, took me to the emergency room in her Model T, talking to me the whole way. I don't know what time Owen showed up but I do know thirty-six hours later Nellie came into the world and I promised myself I'd never have to go through that again.

"It's a girl, Mrs. Clay." The nurse spoke softly.

A girl. I wanted a girl. Nellie was the prettiest baby I ever laid eyes on. She didn't even cry. I fell in love.

Owen hovered in the door with a put-out look on his face. He was fretting on how he had missed a day of work. "So, it's a girl?" His voice was flat and disappointed.

"She's the prettiest baby I've ever seen." I flashed him a big smile that invited him to join me.

"Hm." He walked to the bed and peeked into my bundle.

"I think we'll call her Nellie." I waited.

Owen's lips drew up into a sour look. "Nellie. Where'd you get that name?"

The truth was I dreamed it one night early on, but I didn't dare tell him. He didn't hold with dreams or any superstitions. "I just thought it was a right pretty name."

"I was thinking we'd call her my mama's name, Pauline."

Owen never would speak about his mother, and now he wanted to name my child in honor of her. Something wasn't right. "Oh, that's a pretty name, but why don't we call her Nellie Pauline?"

"Why not Pauline first?" He was watching our baby close.

"Don't you think we need to keep your mama's name just for her?"

He thought a minute. "Yeah." With one of his knuckles, he softly rubbed Nellie's cheek. She turned, searching with her mouth. "One day I'm taking you to see where your daddy is from, little girl." His forehead was smooth. Owen had his good sides and they always made me happy when they showed up.

So that's how Nellie came into the world. She dodged a bad name and charmed her daddy. Owen wasn't all over me every night and that was the best gift I could have gotten. Frankly all that business was boring, dull as tarnished brass. I took care of our little house and Nellie. Owen never came home to an empty table, and I never did without anything I wanted. I guess you could say Owen and me had come to some kind of agreement in our marriage.

Mama came across town every Wednesday to see her new grandbaby. Lord, she loved Nellie better than anything. She loved her so much she never brought up my mistake of marrying Owen, even though she must have seen evidence every time she walked in my door. One Monday morning, Mama came strolling up the walk wearing her prettiest hat and dress. That wasn't like her.

"Mama, you're dressed up today. You got a doctor's appointment?" I was glad to see her because Nellie had been fussy for days.

Mama's smile was weak and she looked a little pale.

"Are you okay, Mama?"

She went straight to her chair at the kitchen table. The sun poured in the yellow curtains she had made for the windows. "I'm better than I was early this morning, Miss Josie."

That was the name she called me when I was little and she had to give me some bad news.

"Don't you want to see Nellie?" Normally she would have grabbed the baby first thing.

She folded her hands in her lap and tilted her head just enough to catch the sun in her blond hair, not one bit of gray. I got to thinking on how old she was. She sure wasn't old enough to be a grandma. "I think I might have something catching, but I wanted to peek at Miss Priss this morning." She stood and looked into the cradle.

A little shudder ran across her shoulders that seemed suddenly frail. "It's really kind of selfish. Lordy, this baby is going to see some hard times, Miss Josie, hard times." She had tears in her eyes.

I never got mad at my mama, but I was angry in that instant. "What's wrong with you today, Mama?" My words were a bit sharp, but she was whispering to Nellie and didn't pay me no mind.

Mama stood up straight and pulled on her dress. "I got to go now. I just wanted to see you and tell Nellie a thing or two."

I reached out to touch her, but she pulled away. "What's wrong, Mama? How'd you get here? I don't see the car."

For a minute she looked confused, but then her face cleared. "You take care now, Miss Josie. I love you so much." She moved to the door and Nellie began to wail.

"Wait and I'll walk with you." I turned to get Nellie.

"No need."

The door clicked as I pulled Nellie from her cradle. "Let's go see where your grandma is going. Something just ain't right."

Mama wasn't anywhere to be seen. A horrible feeling crawled under my skin.

Marge was sitting on her front porch. "Josie, who you looking for?"

"Did you see my mama?"

Marge looked at me a little strange. "Ain't been a soul on this street for the past hour."

I didn't argue. I thought of using Marge's phone to call Daddy, but I knew he'd be in the fields. The strange feeling stayed with me into the afternoon.

I was making my midday meal when I heard Daddy's truck crunch the gravel in the drive. He had never come to my house. I threw open the door, trying not to show the panic in my chest.

His face was a gray color. "I need you to come with me, Josie."

"What's wrong, Daddy?"

"Now, girl!" Daddy wasn't one to yell at me, mostly because I stayed on his good side.

"I got to let Owen know and get the baby."

"Hurry. I'll stop at the quarry."

I wrapped Nellie in a blanket and rushed out to the truck.

Daddy didn't speak. He drove like he was somewhere else other than behind the wheel.

"Did Mama make it back home?" I wasn't looking at his face because Nellie was cooing. She'd been in a right good mood since Mama left. When Daddy stopped the truck in the middle of the road, I looked up. "What's wrong?"

"Are you pulling my leg, Josie?" His tone told me he was angry.

"No sir. She came by this morning. She was dressed up pretty in her church clothes. She told me she was feeling poorly. I thought she seemed confused." I didn't tell him what Marge said.

A car behind us started honking its horn. Daddy didn't make a move. "You're too old for lies, Josie."

Tears stung my eyes. "I ain't lying." What was wrong with him?

He pressed the gas, and we headed for the quarry. "I ain't never believed in haints."

"Neither have I." I said this in a sharp voice.

A shadow fell across his face. "If you're telling the truth, and you ain't never been a liar, then you saw a ghost today."

I looked at the side of his face, studying on him.

"Your mama died this morning."

Cold air filled my lungs.

"She was still in the bed when I left out. It wasn't like her, but I let her rest." He let his words sit between us a minute. "I told her to get up and call you to come take her to the doctor. I left her there."

I couldn't open my mouth.

"Are you listening, girl?" He looked over at me. "We got to get in touch with your sister." Emily was older than me by six years. She'd been in Oklahoma for four years with her husband, Pete. She wasn't going to come home. I knew this in the bottom of my heart. She was living high on the hog with her big farm and all. Nope, Asheville was dust under her feet.

"When I came home for dinner, your mama was still in bed." His voice broke. "I got mad cause I was hungry. I even yelled. When she didn't answer, I went to look. She had this horrible look on her face like she died hurting. God help me for my selfish acts."

I'd seen Mama after she left her body behind. What had she whispered to Nellie?

We stopped in front of the quarry. My heart was beating in my ears.

"Go get Owen. We got a funeral to plan."

I'd watched Mama prepare my granny's body. I knew what to do. The women in the family cared for the dead. It was my job since Emily wouldn't be home. There would be lots of ladies from church coming over. They were gossipy old busybodies. Our whole church was against just about anything fun. Their view of Jesus involved a man who frowned on anything that might make a person happy. It was hard for me to swallow, but out of respect for Mama and Daddy I always did what was expected of me and went to church.

Mama was on her back, a sheet pulled up to her neck. "Lordy, Mama."

Daddy had covered the mirror and stopped the clock on the fireplace mantel. The covering of the mirror ensured that her spirit wouldn't be trapped in the world, and stopping the clock marked the time of death. But not in Mama's case. Who knew when she died?

Mama's body would be placed on the dining room table. I removed the lace tablecloth.

"You need something?" These were Owen's first words since we picked him up from the quarry.

"You can get some water."

He nodded and left.

Nellie had fallen asleep and was on a pallet next to the table.

Owen was back with a big bowl. "Do you want me to move your mama in here?"

I nodded, pouring some of Mama's perfume into the warm water.

He returned with her body, which didn't give in to him like it would if she were still breathing, but in his arms, Mama looked like a child. A sob caught in my throat, but I swallowed it down.

Owen placed her body tenderly on the table where she had served a dinner each Sunday after church. At that moment, I thought I could love him until we were both old. "You need me to stay here with you?"

I wanted to ask him if he did this for his mama, washed her, got her ready for burying. "I'll be fine. Just keep everyone, especially the nosy church ladies, out until I'm through."

He nodded. "No worry." He lingered in the door. "I'm sorry for your loss. She was a good woman and I know she loved you a lot." He kept his eyes on Nellie sleeping in her innocent little world. "Come get me if she starts crying. I think your sister wants your dad to come stay with her."

A knot grew tight in my thoughts. "I'll think about that later." Daddy always loved Emily best. She made something of herself by leaving this town. "I'll call you if I need you." We never said what we intended to say to each other, me and Owen. Maybe it was this death that softened us.

"Owen."

He was watching me, listening in a clear-eyed kind of way.

"Most of what is between us is good." There.

He stood still and then the door was empty.

"I need you," I whispered, but to who I wasn't sure.

The soft washcloth—one of Mama's best—smelled like the fresh clean spring air. I dropped it in the bowl of water and perfume; a light lavender smell floated around the room. Mama's silver brush weighed heavy in my hand. Her clothes had to come off, but I couldn't do that just out of the blue. She was my mama. I had to work up to the task. The silky purple scarf wrapped around her head hid little blond curls. I ran my fingers through her thick hair, working her scalp like I'd seen her do each morning. The brush moved through her hair as if her body still owned her soul.

"Mama, you got the prettiest hair," I whispered in her ear. The tulip trees were in bloom and some of the yellow, green, and orange flowers fluttered in the breeze to the ground. I don't know how long I brushed. Then I worked her old flannel gown over her head. The sight of her body was comforting. I pulled off one of her socks and then the other. Her toenails were painted a beautiful bright pink. Oh, the ladies of the church would have just died. Using makeup or nail polish was considered vain and a sin. But there were those fragile toes, shining for all to see, a secret, a joy. The sight stirred something inside of me that broke me open. My tears fell for the first time since I understood she was gone. I couldn't help but think of Mary kneeling to wash Jesus' feet in the expensive perfume and drying them with her hair.

Gently I worked the soft cloth over her feet. The perfumed water made a puddle on the shiny table finish. This memory would be preserved in the watermarks. I reached on top of my head and released the knot of hair. I rubbed Mama's feet until the water and perfume soaked into the strands. Mama was gone.

She was buried two days later on a warm spring day. I watched the pine box being lowered into the big empty hole. I held Nellie in my arms. Owen stood beside me. Already I could feel him moving away from that soft place we had found. Mama loved me enough to come see me before she left the world. She wasn't no ghost, just a spirit on its way to heaven. Amen.

Twenty-five

Like I said, the summer after Mama died women won the vote, and boy did that set Asheville ladies to singing. I was too sick at heart to care. So it took me until the 1924 presidential election before I wanted to use my right and cast my vote. Owen finally agreed but I could tell he didn't like the thought one bit. Three-year-old Nellie was our common thread, our reason to smile at each other sometimes.

"Why do we want to take a child with us to vote? Miz Marks said she'd watch her. Voting ain't no place for a little girl." Owen spoke around his chewing tobacco that he'd taken to using.

This was one time I intended to have my way. "She's going to watch her mama vote for the first time. I want it to stick in her head; otherwise she's liable to forget how many women fought for this right. We worked hard."

Owen spit out the back door. "You didn't work at nothing."

Owen was wrong. I had attended me one meeting of the North Carolina Equal Suffrage League. Those women were serious about getting the vote and a lot more. Mama took me. It was a side of Mama I didn't know. She believed in women standing up for themselves.

"It's important to me Nellie goes." I looked him dead in the eye.

"Oh, what the hell. I ain't standing here and arguing with you. You take her with you. Voting ain't some woman's parlor game."

I wanted to point out it was his first time ever bothering to vote. Ain't that the way it went. Some folks wanted a right so bad while others had the privilege and never used it.

The courthouse had a line running down the stairs. It seemed I wasn't the only woman who took my voting serious. There were more women waiting than men. My vote was going for President Coolidge. He'd done a fine job since he took over for the late President Harding. As we worked our way to the voting booth, Owen took me by the elbow. Sweet little Nellie held my hand and flashed a smile at me. "What we doing, Mama?"

I squeezed her hand. "We're doing something mighty fine, Miss Nellie. We're exercising our voice."

Owen huffed and whispered in my ear. "Now, when we get there, Josie, you make your vote for John W. Davis."

For a minute I stopped following the line and looked at him. "What?"

"Keep walking." As I obeyed him, he spoke louder. "I ain't having no wife of mine shaming me by voting for a Republican."

A couple of women ahead of me looked back with sympathy. God help us women. We lived in a free country but couldn't do what we wanted. Nobody was telling Owen how to vote. But none of this came out of my mouth. I should have shouted my thoughts from the highest tree, but instead I said one word: "Why?"

He cut a look down at Nellie and then at me. "Because John W. Davis is from West Virginia, Josie. Do I have to spell it out for you? You ain't got enough sense not to vote Republican."

I stared at him like he had three eyes.

"Mr. Davis is from the South. Everyone knows it's time to have someone from the South become president. You understand that?"

I pulled Nellie in front of me and kept moving up them steps right into the courthouse. I had every intention of voting for who I wanted. He wasn't stealing my wish.

Mrs. Vera Jones nodded for me to take my ballot to the open booth.

"Remember what I said," Owen said, loud enough for all to hear.

When Vera placed the paper ballot in my hand, she smiled. "Make your choice, Josie."

And that's exactly what I marched off to do. Then I noticed Lyle Hamby taking the ballots when folks were finished. Lyle and Owen worked together. They did some drinking together too. Nellie and me went into our booth. I inserted the ballot and stared at the machine. I almost wished I'd stayed home. What kind of fool was I? A law wasn't going to change one dern thing for us. I lived in North Carolina. President Coolidge's name came first on the ballot.

"Mama?" Nellie tugged on my skirt.

"Wait, sweetie. I got to think." The thin black curtain was nothing, no protection at all. My courage drained right out of my feet. Owen would know before I got home if I didn't vote the way he told me.

"Mama, are you going to do what Daddy told you?" Nellie had a worried look on her face. Lord in heaven, I'd taught her how to bow down to men.

I squatted in front of her and whispered, "Nellie bird, when you grow up, you don't have to do what any man tells you to do. Okay?"

She looked at me with her big brown eyes.

"Promise?"

"Okay, Mama." She smiled.

"Good."

I stood and made my vote for President Coolidge. "And Nellie, I did exactly what I wanted to do, not what Daddy wanted me to do."

Owen stood by Lyle. I held Nellie's hand tight and marched over to the table. Lyle stopped talking when I pushed my ballot at him. Owen didn't say a word. He was so sure of himself, so positive I'd never go against him and follow my own mind. It was a shame I couldn't tell him.

"I can't take that, Josie." Lyle smirked.

My head spun.

Owen puffed. "You got to fold it yourself and put it through the slot." He looked at Lyle. "And they gave them the vote."

And Owen never knew I went against him. But I always had it planted away in my thoughts. I went against him and followed my heart.

Twenty-six

Owen Clay was a man to be reckoned with. The year Nellie turned eight he decided we was taking a trip to his hometown. I don't know how that bee got in his bonnet but it did and there wasn't no talking him out of it.

"Owen, that's a long way to drive."

"I'm driving and you're going, nothing to worry on." He never looked up from his newspaper at the kitchen table.

Nellie had her hands in dough, doing her best to make her own biscuits. She was doing pretty good for her first try. "We could take a train." Nellie smiled.

"Sorry, sweetie, the train only goes as far as Savannah. Darien is another sixty-something miles down the coast. We got to drive. You'll like it."

Nellie nodded.

"What are you doing over there, anyway?" Owen's voice always went soft when he spoke to our girl. This made our marriage worth all the ins and outs.

"I'm learning to make biscuits like Mama's."

He laughed. "Well, I'll have one of those when you're finished."

Nellie laughed. Both Owen and me smiled at the same time.

"Why you so afraid of this trip, Josie? We're going to spend the night in Atlanta, stay in a fancy hotel. You'll get to see the city."

"I'm not afraid." I said this sharply and knew that's exactly what was wrong. I was scared to death.

"We'll have us a good time." He opened his newspaper and began to read again.

I never had left the state of North Carolina. Shoot, I'd never been past Asheville's city limits.

We set out in the old Buick for what seemed like another country. Who in the world had heard of Darien, Georgia?

"Tell me about the ocean, Daddy." Nellie wore a wide-brim straw hat with a yellow ribbon. Her dress was the prettiest butter-colored check with a full skirt.

Owen smiled as he watched the road. "It's the biggest body of water you'll ever see." He seemed to move away from us into his own world. "Once you hear the ocean, the sound will stay in your head. It will visit you when you're low and need some help. The ocean is living and breathing."

"I can't wait, Daddy. Drive fast."

"But you got to remember Darien is inland. It's on the Altamaha. All around you will be marsh, and the smell of salt is the best smell in the whole world." He gave a little shiver.

"What's the Altamaha, Daddy?" Nellie wiggled in her seat with excitement.

"That's a mighty river, girl. It takes the fishermen out to the sea each morning and brings them home each night. It's like this here highway, except for boats. Darien is a fishing town and has been forever. The sea is in everyone's blood."

"Were you a fisherman?" Nellie was finding out more than I knew about her father.

"Should have been, Nellie bird. My daddy was a fisherman, but when he died at sea, Mama never got over it. She even let the bank have his boat for next to nothing. She told me if I ever went to sea, she'd make me leave home. I did and she did what she threatened. That's how I ended up in Asheville."

Nellie was quiet.

"So, you just stopped fishing?" How could he have kept this from me?

"Everybody thought I was jinxed. It was pure stupidity." He glared at the road and his knuckles turned white because he was gripping the steering wheel so hard.

"Why was it stupid?" Nellie sang out.

Owen's face softened. "Fishermen believe in signs and such. Shoot, they believe in ghosts." He cut a look at me. "We know there ain't no such things, but they are ignorant and believe."

"Oh."

"Anyway, after all was said and done, I came to Asheville." He had relaxed.

"I can smell the salt." Nellie cheered.

Owen laughed. "You keep on smelling that salt. It will take you places. Darien is the best place I know."

The first time I saw the tall buildings I couldn't believe they were real. They stood off in the distance like some pencil drawing on what seemed to be the edge of the world. We'd been riding so long my legs were numb.

"That's Atlanta." Owen said this in a quiet way.

Nellie sat up straighter. "Look at how big the buildings are, Mama."

"We're going to stay there?" I nodded at the city.

Owen never looked at me. "Yes ma'am. We're going to stay at the Georgian Terrace. That's one of the fanciest hotels in Atlanta."

"A hotel?" Nellie said in wonder.

"A fine hotel," Owen laughed.

My fears were lost in his laughter.

I'd never in my whole life stayed somewhere as fancy. Our room had the softest and best-smelling cotton sheets. When Owen went into the bathroom to clean up, Nellie and me rolled around on the bed just to feel how it bounced.

We had dinner in the restaurant downstairs. The tables were covered with white linen and the napkin rings were real silver.

"Daddy, can we live here?" Nellie had a plate of fried chicken and mashed potatoes. Her face glowed in the soft candlelight. Lord, it was almost like the honeymoon me and Owen never thought of having. And of course Nellie was along.

"Wait till we get to Darien, honeybee. That's where you'll want to live, both of you." He smiled. "It's in your blood, Nellie. You'll know as soon as we drive into town." Owen took a big bite of his steak.

"How far is Darien from here?" My chicken pot pie melted in my mouth.

"It's about six or seven hours." Owen winked at Nellie.

I tried not to let the air out of my lungs in a huff. "How in the world did you ever find your way up to Asheville?"

"Looking for dry land, Josie."

Nellie looked like a princess at the fancy table. She was meant to have fine things. A cold chill walked up my arms, but I didn't pay it a bit of attention. We were having a fine time.

Twenty-seven

We drove into Darien before the sun went down the next day. Owen took us over the big river and straight to the dock, where the shrimp boats were lined up for the night. The air smelled like salt, tangy and sharp. Nellie jumped from the car as soon as it stopped and ran to the edge of the dock.

"Careful now, there are gators in these waters." Owen put some chewing tobacco in his lip.

"Where are we staying?" I heard a little splash and looked in time to see a small alligator slide off a log into the brownish river.

"I told you there were gators," he said to Nellie.

She clapped her hands and bounced up and down on her toes. "Look, Mama."

Owen nodded to a worn house in the bend of the river not far from where we stood. "That's the old homeplace where I grew up. My daddy was born there." He pulled a key out of his pocket and showed it to me.

"You've had this place all the time we've been married?"

He frowned. "Yep. Don't start making this a problem, Josie."

"Why are we here?" All of a sudden I understood this trip was much bigger than showing me and Nellie where he grew up.

"I'm here to sell the house, and I want to show you the cemetery. You'll have to bring me here for burying." He watched Nellie, who gazed down in the water. She looked up and smiled. I wanted to grab her and go home. The air was thick with a omen that Owen would never profess to believing.

"Can we live here forever?" Nellie yelled.

Owen's face melted into a smile. The bad moment was gone.

"What about all your friends?" I spoke ahead of him.

Nellie's face grew serious, and she looked so much like Owen I had to look away. "I can make new friends, Mama."

Owen gave a little chuckle. "I just bet you could too. But we're here to sell that house over there. A friend is going to buy it."

"Who?" How could this be news to me?

"A man I used to sit on that very dock and fish with. He's buying it for his sister who never bothered to get married."

"Owen, how could all this happen without me knowing?"

His cheeks turned red. "I don't owe you my past, Josie. It's no place for you."

The words stung my heart.

"This will be your money when I die."

A chill walked into my heart and closed the door. I'd never thought of a life without Owen. A woman had to have a husband. They couldn't live on their own. That was just a fact of life. "Are you dying?"

He smiled and walked to Nellie. "Nope. I'm getting rid of an empty house. A house with bad stories. It's just that and nothing more."

We were so different, me and him. We were together because that is what men and women did. They got married.

The salt was so strong I could taste it, but I couldn't make myself come in from the front porch that faced the river. Imagine a river nearly in a person's front yard. Like Nellie, I began to wish I could live in the little town. Somehow I had it in my head a life in Darien would be simpler. The magic Owen must have felt as a boy was catching like a sore throat. The air was full of fancy little fairies hidden out of sight. I was turning into a little girl.

Nellie's voice carried out of the upstairs bedroom. Her and Owen had been talking a long time. I rocked back and forth. A blue-gray bird flew through the moss-covered trees, unfolding long legs, landing in the marsh. Several other white and gray birds dipped in and out of the river. What a world this was compared to Asheville, with its mountains and rushing creeks. This river moved so slow I couldn't see a current. The wind rippled along the water, a lazy movement at most. Time stood still as clouds built high and moved across the hazy sky. Just a hint of cooler night air ruffled my blouse. Nellie talked and talked.

"I love yellow. Mama tries to always give me something yellow to wear. She made this dress."

Now why in the world would she be telling her daddy about a dress he already knew about? Then I saw Owen's familiar figure walking down the path to the house. I stood. Who was Nellie talking to?

"I love the mountains and so does Mama. It's a real nice place to live. I think you're wrong. I don't think I'll ever come here to live even when I grow up."

Owen ran his fingers through his head full of dark hair.

"You want to walk to the cemetery so I can show you the family plot?"

I shook off Nellie's talking and pointed to the blue-gray bird. "What kind of bird is that?"

"That's a blue heron. Mama always said that if you're seeing a blue heron for the first time, it's because you're standing on shifting sand and you need balance." He looked at the marsh.

"What about me, Owen?"

He cocked his head at me. "What about you?"

I took a deep breath and watched the heron. "Where am I going to be buried if you're down here? Husband and wife are normally buried together."

"I figured you could be buried right beside me if that's what you want. I always got the feeling you didn't much want that, Josie. We ain't been much of a couple." He walked in the direction of the street. "Come on and we'll look at our resting place."

The whole thing didn't make a bit of sense to me. "Let me get Nellie."

All was quiet in the house. "Nellie, let's go walk with your daddy."

Nellie came through the door wearing her pink sleeveless jumper. "What kind of walk? Are we going to look for some gators, Daddy?"

Owen winked at her. "I bet you could catch one."

"Who were you talking to, Nellie?" I ignored Owen.

"A lady who used to live in this house."

Owen snorted and walked up the path to the street.

"Don't make up stories, Nellie. You'll make your daddy mad." But I knew my girl wouldn't fib.

Her hurt showed in the way she wrinkled her nose. "I ain't lying, Mama. She said her name was Pauline like my middle name. She lived here for a long time."

Lord Jesus in heaven, my baby was talking to ghosts. "What was she doing in this house?"

"She's stuck." Nellie looked at me with a serious stare. "I think someone killed her. She's a ghost."

"Nellie, I don't believe in ghosts." I nudged her to move down the path.

"What about Grandma? You said she came to see us after she died."

"She was a soul on her way to heaven. She wasn't no ghost stuck here on this earth."

"Pauline said she can't remember what happened. She asked me all kinds of questions about Daddy."

A chill spread through my whole body this time.

In the cemetery Owen showed us where his daddy was buried. "I'll be right here and you will be there." He pointed to the space that wasn't marked by stones.

Nellie was running all around. "This man here was in the Revolutionary War, Daddy."

"Plenty of them. There's a fort not far from here."

"Where's your mama buried?" I held my breath.

Owen frowned up.

"I'm your wife. I don't know anything about your life here."

He took a deep breath. "There's some things that don't need to be pulled out of someone."

Dread welled up in my stomach.

"Mama wasn't buried here because it wasn't right. The church refused her." He watched Nellie moving away from us.

"Why?"

He waited so long I figured he wasn't going to answer me. "She hung herself. The church can't abide someone killing themselves. Neither can the fishermen. I was considered tainted." The air was still, not like at home where the heat bugs started singing before the sun got behind the trees. She killed herself. This explained mostly everything about him.

"I know you don't believe in such, but Nellie was talking to someone this afternoon that she called Pauline."

He looked like the saddest person in the world. "Folks say they see her walking down on the dock at night. I'd hate to think she's still here. She hated this town and wanted nothing more than to go back to Atlanta. Then Daddy died and I became a fisherman. It was way too much."

"That must've hurt real bad, Owen."

His face fell into a pitiful look, and he turned from me and walked to the next family plot. There's always something more to a person's story, things held deep inside too painful to tell.

Nellie stood near the Episcopal church in deep thought. It was time to take my girl out of that haunted town. Owen's mama was so lost she hung herself. She was stuck in the place she hated the most. Spirits were real, and I could only pray that they left my baby alone. But I knew that was pie in the sky.

Twenty-eight

On November 20, 1930—some dates just stick in a person's head—Owen was sitting in the kitchen before work, reading the newspaper. I was frying his bacon and eggs while Nellie ate her oatmeal before she took out for school. She was in the fourth grade and smarter than a whip. It was nearly Thanksgiving. Nellie had been studying on gifts she wanted Santa to bring. Santa was going to have a tough time visiting a lot of the kids. The bottom had dropped out of the whole country, and it all started with a bunch of stocks in New York City. People everywhere were losing their jobs because whole companies were going under. Folks in Asheville had been living high on the hog for so long they couldn't see the bad coming. The city had built the fancy new library out of Georgia marble brought up here on trucks. Owen had been put out about that, seeing how he worked for the quarry and they had fine rock. Then the city went and built a brand-new courthouse, shipping in Tennessee limestone. What a waste when the old courthouse was fine and dandy. Mostly everyone was living way beyond their means. Shoot, if a person wanted a new house they just went to the bank, got themselves what was called a loan. The bank gave them the money right then. Owen didn't believe in monthly payments.

"Did you hear that the county is in money trouble?" I tried not to let my worry show. The county was a big customer of the quarry.

I had started me a laundry business in the year since we'd come back from Darien, and Owen wasn't a bit bothered. There were so many women in the big fancy houses who didn't want to do their own clothes. I filled the need by giving extra detail to their fine things. Washing, mending, and pressing was my gift. "Eagerly, that's Mrs. Hamilton's maid, told me she heard Mrs. Hamilton talking about how the whole county government might shut down." I was worrying on my business. See, I was making some good money off those bundles of clothes delivered by colored maids in chauffeured cars on assigned days. Mrs. Hamilton had Mondays, a prime day, because she paid the best. Mrs. Tiller sent hers on Tuesdays and so on. I was pretty good at sorting things out. I kept Fridays open for those ladies who had emergency needs.

"We don't have a thing to worry about, Josie. Our money is right in that old jar under the bed. You know that. My job at the quarry don't depend on the county. Other folks need rock. I've been there long enough to make it through a slowdown. And your colored-maid friend is still in good enough shape to gossip. It's the foolish who is hurting right now. Hard workers like us will be fine."

But something told me that was a bunch of hogwash, that things was about to break loose and hurt everyone.

As Nellie and Owen headed out the door, I didn't even get a tingle of something bad coming. I waved and then set to work on my own laundry before Eagerly showed up with Mrs. Hamilton's bundle.

By lunch word had spread all over town, even on Settle

Road, that Central Bank and Trust Company had shut their doors for good.

A soft little peck on my back door made me jump. Marge Marks stood there on my step, wringing her hands. She'd grown so old since Mr. Marks had passed. I worried on her a lot. She was just like family.

"All my money's there, Josie. What am I going to do? The city is going to have to close down."

"Don't you worry none, Marge. I ain't going to let nothing happen to you." I put my arm around her bony shoulders and led her back to her house. "Me and you are family. Things will be okay." I only hoped I could keep that promise.

She looked at me with watery green eyes. "Aren't you glad Owen wouldn't put his money in the bank?"

"You'll be okay. What's mine is yours." A secret satisfaction welled up in me. For once I was proud of Owen thinking backward. "Lord, here comes Nellie early from school. They must have shut the school down. You go on in your house, Marge. I'll be right here."

Nellie had a scared look on her face. "Mama, teacher says all the money is gone. She was crying, all the teachers were, even the principal."

"We're fine for now. Daddy doesn't keep our money in the bank."

Her shoulders relaxed.

A bad feeling took up a place just under my ribs. "Still, I think you need to run over to the quarry and let Daddy know what has happened. We might need to make a plan."

Mrs. Hamilton's car moved slowly down the street.

"Go on and tell him about the bank. Ask him if I need to do anything. Tell him that Widow Marks's money is gone. She's crying and carrying on." A desperate feeling spread through my chest.

"Okay, Mama." Nellie ran up the road.

"Where's she off to?" Eagerly wore her starched white uniform and black shiny shoes. The bundle of clothes was in her arms.

"I sent her to tell Owen about the bank."

"You got all your money there?" She looked concerned.

"Naw. Owen doesn't abide by banks."

"Good thing." Eagerly looked over at Carl, Mrs. Hamilton's chauffeur and Eagerly's husband. "Miz Hamilton don't seem too worried for herself—I figured she's got her money in some other bank—but Miz Tiller has been beside herself ever since word came early this morning. She be waiting for Mr. Tiller to come home. He's a bigwig in the mayor's office, you know."

I nodded.

Eagerly had been with Mrs. Hamilton since she turned twenty. She was kissing fifty. "We never put our money in the bank. Carl said if they won't let us coloreds eat at the lunch counter, why would we give them our money? We'll make do as long as Mrs. Hamilton needs us." There wasn't a trace of worry in her face.

"Looks like that other shoe has finally fell," I said. "I've been reading my tea leaves and it don't look good. I see nothing but hard times. When I cipher them, I can't tell who for. That's real foggy. This bad feeling is bigger than just my family and smaller than me and you. Maybe it means Owen's going to lose his job. Or maybe it's Nellie. I just don't know." I gave her that look women give each other when they know the burdens each other carry. "Come on in and have a cup of tea." I took the bundle of clothes, knowing full well Eagerly wouldn't come in. I liked this woman better than any woman I'd ever met and I didn't care what color she was, but us sitting down and having a nice cup of tea wasn't done. She could lose her job or worse.

"Naw, can't today. You keep reading those leaves. You got

the gift. If not for you Carl would have been bit by that moccasin. It was your warning that made me go look after what he was doing. He wouldn't have seen that snake."

I couldn't take no credit. I told her that. But she insisted my warning saved his life.

"Let me know what you hear after Mrs. Tiller."

"I will." Eagerly turned to leave.

A ripple of dread spread across my chest through somewhere deep in my body. Why had I let Nellie go to the quarry alone on a day the town was let loose with grief? I couldn't concentrate on Mrs. Hamilton's clothes. I stood in the kitchen window, watching the street.

When the strange truck turned into the road, I was still there. The truck had ASHEVILLE STONE printed on the side. My heart turned over as it slowed to a stop in front of the house. Still I stood in my place. A man with a round belly got out of the truck. He was Owen's boss. Then I seen my Nellie. The air left my lungs as I ran out the door. Little sounds of grief pushed from my chest.

Nellie's eyes were rimmed in red. "Mama," she sobbed, burying her face in my stomach.

Owen's boss—I couldn't place his name in my mind—took off his cap. "Mrs. Clay, there's been an accident."

Those words echoed in my ears and down my spine. Part of me went weak with relief because my baby was safe. The other part of me became tight and rigid.

"Owen was killed, ma'am." There it was, the picture the tea leaves kept trying to form. "The chain broke and a big stone fell. He never understood what happened."

But I knew Owen had been understanding this for over a year. He'd been waiting. "Did my girl see her daddy die?" The words began to spin.

The man nodded. "Yes ma'am." The words were quietly

tearing my mind apart. I had no deep love for Owen, but all the same I felt part of my soul was missing.

"There's something we need to talk about."

Nellie sobbed. I had no one but her. No one.

"Can we talk later? I got to think."

Owen's boss took a step closer. "We got to do something with the body, Mrs. Clay," he whispered.

Yes, the body. Oh God, his body. Something had to be done.

"You want me to send him to the funeral home? It's a right nice place."

What did a huge rock do to a man's body when dropped from that high? "Yes." I whispered into Nellie's hair, "Why don't you go wash your face. I'll be right there."

She never looked at me, only nodded and walked in the house with her head hanging down.

"Owen took out a big life-insurance policy a year ago. That should help some. I'll get you the paperwork."

Oh Owen, you knew. All the times I hated him for his coldness seemed a sin. "Thank you."

And Owen's boss was gone, leaving me standing in the yard.

Mrs. Hamilton's big fancy car turned down the street. My shoulders went slack. Eagerly got out and came to me. "I'm here." I cried into her neck. I cried for Owen and what we never had. Somehow I had to convince Nellie to marry a man she loved and who loved her. But better yet a man with the same mind as hers. I cried because I didn't know what I was going to do. A part of me wilted away that day.

Eagerly gave me a squeeze. This is what friends did for each other.

"He had a death policy and I didn't know."

She nodded.

* * *

By the time the funeral home put Owen in his shining oak casket, I was set on my purpose, my direction. Nellie turned quiet on me and never once did we talk about what she saw that day. She wouldn't have any of my coaxing. I took a big part of the life-insurance policy to bury Owen in Darien. Me and Nellie rode in the front of the hearse. Nobody came to stand by his grave as he was lowered into the ground. Who could I call? He wouldn't have wanted anyone else there anyway.

"There's the woman I talked to from Daddy's old house, Mama." Nellie pointed to a clump of trees at the edge of the cemetery.

My blood froze in my veins. A beautiful woman dressed in the prettiest pink suit watched us. When I blinked, she was gone.

"Did you see her, Mama? She just disappeared."

"I didn't see a thing, Nellie." My words were cold.

Nellie looked at me like I was crazy. My whole world was upside down and some old ghost wanted to make it worse. "I mean it. No more talking about that woman. You didn't see nothing, understand?"

"Okay." She looked away from me.

I had hurt her feelings. The last thing Nellie needed was to have her crazy grandmother's spirit chasing her through life.

"Mama." Nellie looked at me.

"Yes."

"One day I'm going to marry someone just like Daddy."

I wanted to correct her but shame filled my heart. Owen was her father. I couldn't talk bad about him. "Nellie, I'm going to tell you what my mama told me. Don't go looking for some fairy-tale marriage. They're not real. And never fall head over heels for no man, save some love for yourself."

She was quiet and studied me like she was a adult. "Mama?"

"Yes."

"Someday I'm going to live here in Darien."

"No you won't, Nellie. No reason to. We're from Asheville, me and you."

"Yes I am. You'll see." Her stubborn look reminded me of Owen. Maybe she needed to think this to be closer to her daddy.

"And Mama . . ." She took my hand. "You're going to live here with me."

Of course by the time eight years rolled around and Hobbs Pritchard showed up, I had forgotten that Nellie ever said such a thing.

When I read her letter that nice man brought down Black Mountain, I saw her plain as day standing in that graveyard. The air was cold when we put Owen in the ground. Nellie stood there watching. I caught a glimpse of the woman she would become and how she would change on me, how she would hunger after a man to replace her daddy. No one story is completely free of pain, and Nellie's was dotted with more grief than she deserved. But I had no doubt she saw something that day besides the ghost of Pauline Clay. She saw her future. She knew that something trying was on the horizon.

Part Three

Shelly Parker

Twenty-nine

Nada was right proud of my gift. If she could have bragged on me, she would have shouted from the top of Black Mountain. But we didn't have no one to talk to, only each other. We was the only Negroes on the mountain and that made for a mighty lonely life. All I had was Faith Dobbins, who made me her baby doll until I got old enough to be her maid. But she did teach me how to read and write real good. Nada said I had to be careful and act dumb because smart coloreds were punished. It was just a fact of the times.

Nellie Pritchard was the first white person to treat me like a regular girl. Of course I never let on because Nada would have frowned on the whole business. She was my mama and one of the best conjures to come out of New Orleans, who happened to work for a pastor and his family. In those hard times, work was work. Folks from all over the mountain came to her for everything from a corn on a toe to catching a husband. That's why Nada thought my gift was something special, except we had to hide it from Pastor. He was strictly Christian in his thoughts.

The day Hobbs brought Nellie up the mountain Nada kept sniffing the air. "Something is marching our way, Shelly. I can't tell if it's good or bad. I think a little of both."

That was the evening a woman spirit came in my room. See, that was my gift, seeing haints stuck on earth for one reason or another. This woman was one of the friendliest spirits I'd come across. Those were the kind of spooks who might do anything. She stood in the corner of my room, a tall figure.

"Why you here?" I couldn't be nice cause she might use it against me.

The woman studied me so long I was sure she was one of those silent ghosts. Then she moved close to my bed. "I've come because of Hobbs Pritchard."

Now this didn't put her on my good side. "You in the wrong place, ma'am. I don't go around the likes of him or anyone attached to him."

The woman smiled. "You're a smart girl. That's why I'm here. You'll be a good helper. I always stood up to Hobbs."

"That ain't something to be bragging about, seeing how you're dead and all."

She didn't pay me no mind. "I want to save that new little wife of his."

"I can't help you."

"Hobbs will ask you to come work."

"You be crazy, woman."

She looked me over. "Hobbs will hire you to clean. You will help me by telling that little girl to go home. That's the house I died in, you know."

"That ain't one bit comforting, and no ma'am, you got it all wrong. My mama would never let me work for the likes of Hobbs Pritchard."

The woman laughed and walked right through the wall. She was one mixed-up ghost, thinking I would be working for Hobbs Pritchard, not in a month of Sundays.

Ten minutes later Nada waltzed into my little room off the kitchen. "Shelly." The name was full of concern.

I was in some kind of trouble. "Yes ma'am."

She sat on the side of my bed. That's when I knew something was wrong. "Shelly, Mrs. Dobbins has done something without asking me."

That woman never asked. She was all about ordering.

"She does what she wants. This time she's crossed over the line." She waited. This was bad all the way to the bone.

"Mrs. Dobbins has promised Mrs. Ida Pritchard that you will go help out at the old Pritchard place."

I sucked in air. "Nada," I managed.

She looked away from me. "Shelly, it's finished, done. My hands are tied."

"Throw a spell."

Her shoulders sagged. "You're going. Mrs. Dobbins said you're old enough to work on your own."

But I knew the last thing Nada wanted was me to go under the same roof with a murderer.

Thirty

So the first time I laid eyes on Nellie Pritchard she was standing in that nasty kitchen looking as lost as a mountain girl in a big city. She was pretty to look at with them light-colored curls scooped up in a tail like a horse. Nada said that Hobbs Pritchard had a way with girls that just dumbfounded her. This new wife had to be stupid when it came to men. You could smell his meanness for miles away.

The first day she worked right alongside me, getting her pretty hands all dirty. That house was in sad shape. We worked quietly. After we'd been working in the front room for a while, I looked up and saw the man spirit looking in a window. If not for the glass, he could have touched Nellie as she polished a table. At first I thought the man was real. Most of the time when spirits appeared, they looked odd in some way. But he seemed normal except for the wild look in his eyes. He wanted in that house something bad. The hairs on my arms stood straight up.

I refused to stay there one more minute. "Mrs. Pritchard, I reckon I'd better head home."

She glanced out the window, but the man was gone. "Hobbs will be here soon. Thank you for all your help." She held out her hand. "I'll see you in two days."

That girl wasn't nothing but trouble. What did she think, I was going to shake the hand of a white woman I was working for? "Yes ma'am." I laced my fingers behind my back.

The old woman spirit hovered on the stairs. "Tell her to leave this house now."

I looked the other way. "I got to go, Mrs. Pritchard." And I was gone out that back door. Of course I couldn't get the man spirit out of my mind. He was a strange haint.

Right before I fell asleep that night, a thought came to me clear out of the blue. The man spirit was Merlin Hocket. I sat straight up in bed. Everyone knew about Merlin and the doom he brought.

Hobbs Pritchard was a walking, talking mess of meanness. I wasn't never going to tell Nellie nothing those spirits wanted, no way, nohow. I was staying out of it.

That turned out to be a lie. I was with Nellie when she saw Merlin Hocket in the woods, even if she refused to say he was a ghost. But it felt real good to know someone had the same gift as me, even if they was dumber than a doornail.

Thirty-one

The young girl wore a plaid dress with a deep-blue shawl draped around her shoulders. I watched her standing by the church for the longest before I knew she was a spirit. I was down behind our cabin that butted up to the old Daniels Cemetery, washing the Dobbinses' clothes. Mrs. Dobbins didn't like me to hang the laundry close to the house. I guess she wanted folks to believe she never cleaned her underthings. This girl I seen was older than me but not grown. Her hair was long and red. That pretty kind of deep red. Her thin frame looked like she might break in half. I watched her as I scrubbed Mrs. Dobbins's cotton underpants.

The girl stared right at me.

"Here we go again," I said into the wind.

She picked her way through the headstones, careful not to step on any graves. Her feet were tiny, and she didn't have on no shoes. That's how I knew she was wearing her burying clothes.

I scrubbed those underpants like it was my favorite thing to do. This little old haint caused the hairs to stand up on my neck. Just as I straightened the pair of cotton underpants on the clothesline, there she was, moving toward me not two feet away.

"You go on now," I fussed.

"Hobbs is bad." She had her hands folded in front of her.

"I'm about sick of hearing about Hobbs," I said.

Her eyes were a cool gray. "They searched for me, you know?"

"Who you talking about?"

"Near the whole mountain. And I was right under their noses. It took them two weeks to find me and by then, they couldn't tell what happened. That's how he planned it."

"What's your name?" I couldn't remember no search.

"Patricia, but I was called Patty."

"What be your last name?"

She cocked her head to the side. "Harkin."

The Harkin girl that came up missing when I was eight. Lord be, not many people mentioned that death. They was scared of bad luck. Nada always said there was something fishy about her dying. "Why you around now? That was a long time ago."

"It's that dern girl."

"What girl?" But I knew.

"The one he brought up the mountain. She needs to leave soon. If she don't, bad will touch her family from here on out." And the Harkin girl turned and walked away, disappearing into the cool breeze.

This here was more than some ghost tale.

Thirty-two

I worked at Hobbs Pritchard's house every Monday and Thursday. I had better sense than to try and talk to Nellie about them spirits again. She wasn't going to listen to me none. You could see it carved in her face. She was one of those who had to find things out on her own. Anyway, one of Hobbs's buddies got himself killed when Maynard Connor blew up Hobbs's still. Nellie acted like she didn't know nothing. I had a hard time believing she was that stupid. But Nada said sometimes we play dumb to keep the truth away.

The night before Thanksgiving, Mrs. Connor came to get Nada to throw a protection spell for Maynard. I sat over in the corner so I could hear any good gossip she might bring.

"That wife of Hobbs Pritchard brought herself to my door today." Mrs. Connor looked older than Mrs. Dobbins, but Nada said that wasn't the case. She was younger by five years. That's what life on this mountain did to a pretty woman. It worked her over good.

Nada was putting together a bag of herbs for Mrs. Connor.

"If you want to call that little slip of a thing a Mrs. She ain't nothing but a girl." Mrs. Connor cleared her throat. "I was pure-out mean to her. Couldn't help it after all the bad blood between Hobbs and me."

Nada looked up from her work. "Well, I reckon that could be expected."

"She's as stupid as they come. She thought I'd be her friend. She acted like she didn't know a thing." Mrs. Connor got quiet for a minute. "She ain't nothing but a girl, someone's daughter. I bet her mama is sick over her."

"I bet you're right, Mrs. Connor."

"Hobbs Pritchard has done things we can't even guess at." Mrs. Connor sighed.

"He's one of those people who have no feelings."

Mrs. Connor nodded. "What about that Harkin girl a while back? He was sweet on her and her daddy ran him off."

I was putting the story together. Lordy be, Hobbs had been involved in that Harkin girl's death.

"And there's his stepmama. We all know about that." Mrs. Connor clicked her tongue.

And in those words, I felt purely tired. Poor old Nellie. Her life was as empty as a rain barrel in August. She needed one person on her side. I guess it was going to have to be me.

The day after Thanksgiving, I took myself over to Nellie's house uninvited. I figured she needed some helping. You'd think I'd learn not to get in folks' business, especially a white woman's. The snow was a foot deep in places and there I was wading through it when I saw Patty Harkin standing by the big iron gates of Daniels Cemetery. See, the Daniels started the church about a billion years earlier. All that was left of them was the graveyard and a stone plaque saying Negroes could never be buried there.

"Hey you, colored girl," Patty yelled.

I ignored her.

"You going to see his wife, aren't you?"

I studied the road in front of me.

"Tell her if she knows what's good for her she'll get out of that house. He's going to do to her what he did to me. You'd better tell her cause she ain't got long. He's going to stop you from going there soon."

"You go on and tell her yourself. She can see spirits," I yelled. But Patty Harkin was gone. There wasn't nothing about the future I could change, but in my pocket I had me some brick dust. It was perfect for scaring away bad spirits. Mama's dust was so strong it would probably bar Hobbs from his own house.

Nellie looked faded around the edges, maybe just a little crazy. She wore a big smile, too pretty and alive. Mrs. Dobbins did that a lot, and she was on the edge of entering the state hospital on most days. When I gave Nellie the dust, I could see she was holding back a laugh. I wanted to pinch her. She kept bringing up Merlin Hocket, but on that subject I wouldn't budge. She was bent on believing in Hobbs and that was something I just couldn't understand for the life of me. We worked together and then I left. Not one spirit showed itself, and for this I was thankful.

By the time I was headed home, dark wasn't far off. Some folks thought just because I saw spirits all the time, like some people seen birds in the trees, that I wasn't scared. Most of the time I got over that fear quick enough, but Hobbs's ghosts put me in a jumpy place. I couldn't tell what direction they were going in or where they would stop. It sure enough put the fear of God into me. If my counting was right, Hobbs Pritchard killed himself four people and got away with it. Merlin Hocket, his stepmama, Patty Harkin, and my daddy.

Daddy came to see me one time when I was about six. I

was picking flowers out back, and he walked out from behind a tree.

"Shelly, you be picking some nice flowers." He had the kindest eyes, but I could tell he was sad.

"Nada said you are dead, Daddy." I backed away.

He squatted down and pulled up some clover. "Your mama is right."

"Why can I see you?"

"You got a powerful gift, Shelly. It's going to be a thorn in your side, but you can help people too."

"How?"

"You'll know when the time comes. Just follow your heart."

"How'd you die?"

"Little girl, you listen to your daddy, never get mixed up in bad. You understand?"

I nodded.

"I got mixed up with a mean man. Naw, 'mean' is too nice a word. He was what some call evil. He could kill a person without showing no feelings. He killed me cause I crossed him. I told him I wasn't going to sell moonshine no more. That's what did it. He never even acted like he was mad, just killed me with a big old knife."

I held a hand full of black-eyed Susans.

"He stabbed me, little bit, and then acted like it was a accident."

"Who?"

"Hobbs Pritchard. Now, you stay away from him. He's going to get close to you one day. Stay clear of him dead or alive."

"Shelly, who you talking to?" Nada walked over to me. Daddy looked at her and I thought he might hug her, but instead, he walked away.

"Daddy."

Nada stared at me. "What he want?"

"He said Hobbs Pritchard killed him and made it look like a accident. He said I should stay clear of him."

Her hand trembled. "You do as you were told. Hobbs Pritchard would just as soon kill as not. One day he's going to get his own. His kind always do." She was talking more to herself. Her attention snapped back to me. "Throw them flowers down and get in here. We got some clothes to wash for Mrs. Dobbins."

"Yes ma'am." I let the flowers fall to the ground, marking the place where I seen my daddy.

And that's what I was thinking on while hoofing it home in the dusky light. So I didn't even notice Patty Harkin standing behind me in the cemetery.

"If she dies, it'll be because of you."

I jumped ten feet. "I ain't wanting to talk to you."

"You know you want to know how he killed me."

"My daddy said to stay clear of anything to do with Hobbs Pritchard."

"Yeah, and now you're working for his little wife."

I took two steps away. "I don't want to know nothing about Hobbs. I ain't telling Nellie nothing."

Patty Harkin studied on me a minute. "Did you ever think I'm here for a good reason?"

"I told you I don't care."

"He stuffed his handkerchief down my throat and hit me in the head with a log so many times I lost my face. He told me I deserved to die because I didn't love him."

"Shut up!" I was sick of haints. "Nellie won't listen to nothing. She thinks she loves him and she don't believe in ghosts."

"But she can see Merlin and Hobbs's stepmama. He's going to kill her. It'll be on your head." She was gone. Shoot, could a ghost do anything besides drive me near crazy?

Thirty-three

Christmas brought Hobbs to Mrs. Dobbins's door with a dark look on his face. "Here's that colored girl's money. I don't want her at my house no more."

"Did Shelly do something wrong?" Mrs. Dobbins never got too flustered with folks on the mountain, but Hobbs had her in a dither.

"She's colored, ain't she?"

Pure anger washed over me and ran out my shoes. Nada said we was supposed to ignore white folks' ways and remember they're the ignorant ones. But sometimes I thought I might pop wide open. Nada came up behind me where I was standing in the kitchen and placed a hand on my shoulder, reading me like one of her spells.

"My wife is lazy. I don't know why I ever married her. She ain't nothing like my mama. She's going to clean my house like a good wife should." He shoved the money at Mrs. Dobbins.

"I'll make sure Shelly doesn't go to your house again."

"You best believe there'll be trouble if she does." He stomped out of the room and slammed the front door.

Nada pulled me back from the door just as Mrs. Dobbins stormed through. "Shelly, do not go to that Pritchard house again."

I was polishing the already polished silver. "Yes ma'am."

"Did you say anything to offend Mrs. Pritchard?"

"No, we got on real good."

"That Hobbs Pritchard is as mean as they all say. Our church is better off without the lot of them." She made a show of putting my money in a jar inside the cupboard. "For a rainy day."

Yeah, whose rainy day?

When Mrs. Dobbins left, Nada turned from the kitchen sink and went to the cupboard. She pulled out half of the rolled-up bills and pushed them at me. "You can't be thinking on that anymore."

"We'll get in trouble." I took the money anyway.

"How? It's yours."

"Nellie's in trouble." This slipped out.

"You seeing haints around her?" Nada went back to the sink.

"Yes ma'am. Something is going to happen."

"It don't take no spirits to tell me that. You can't go around her no more."

"Yes ma'am."

You could've knocked me over with a straw when Nada came to me on New Year's Day saying I could go help Nellie one more time.

"You said I couldn't go. Hobbs don't want me there."

"He's gone for now. That girl's got to have some help.

You go over there and tell her what you know. Get it over with. Then come home. That's all you can do. The rest is up to her."

"Yes ma'am."

By the time I got to Nellie's house, the worst had happened. Merlin had weaseled his way in and was standing in the corner of the kitchen all cocky. Nellie seen him. I know she did, but she only laughed at me for being a fool. That put my feelings on my shoulders. I followed her up to that creepy attic where she found the wooden box. It was a burying box that folks put keepsakes in to bury with their loved ones. The bad had started and couldn't be stopped. I know that now in hindsight. When Nellie pulled that necklace out, my stomach went sour. Then she touched that lock of gray hair, and chills moved through the air. All of a sudden I saw what Hobbs had done to his stepmama. I watched it play out. He held a pillow over her face. She struggled something terrible before she ran down and her spirit left her body. He pulled her out of the bed and onto the floor so it looked like she tried to get up but fell dead. Her name was Bess, and her heart was good. She was the old woman spirit.

Bess appeared behind Nellie in the attic and nodded at me. "You got to see what she'll do if she don't leave."

Nellie didn't hear her, only me.

I saw it all in clear pictures. Nellie holding the ax over her head. Blood, Lord Jesus, the blood. Them horrible vacant eyes where Nellie had gone out of her mind.

The room grew too little, and I got myself out of there. I don't even know what I said to Nellie. She was a curse on me and I never warned her about a thing. Later, when I calmed down, not telling her what I seen weighed heavy on me.

A week later, I slid off from the Dobbins' house with the thought I would stand on Nellie's doorstep and tell her everything I saw. But I never got down her drive. Merlin Hocket stood in my way. He was a mighty little man. Not much taller than me and little boned like a boy. But his face told me I shouldn't mess with him.

"Go home, little girl. Don't shadow Nellie's door."

"I got to tell her some stuff and then I'm through."

"Leave things as they are. She's a softhearted girl. I'll not have you convincing her to leave. I need her. You understand? Nellie will come out alive."

I opened my mouth but never got to say a word.

"If you tell her about Hobbs's murdering ways, she'll go for the sheriff. She'll get it in her head that more can be done. The right thing. That will be her death. If you tell, I'll bring down the worst kind of curse on your family. I'm too close to let you destroy my work." He stared at me with pure hatred.

In my heart I knew I was lost to helping Nellie. What would happen would happen. Nellie's future was sealed when she married Hobbs Pritchard. I had to trust Merlin. I left him standing in the road. And to this day, I've never stepped on Pritchard property again.

The night Nellie chopped Hobbs's head off I woke up out of a deep sleep with a scream echoing in my head. A cold sweat covered my body and for a minute I was sure Nellie had died. I wasn't a baby, but I wanted to go sleep with Mama in her bed. What if Hobbs showed himself to me?

Time went by, and I didn't hear a thing about Nellie or Hobbs. Then one afternoon I seen Nellie walk out behind the church to God's spring. That water had healed the worst snakebite on my arm and saved me.

I understood why Nellie stripped down and washed. She was baptizing herself. God's finger was touching her soul.

*   *   *

The next ghost to come visit me was Merlin. I was hanging wash on the line and there he was, standing behind one of the Pastor's nice white shirts.

"If you want to see Nellie, be on the road in morning, early. There'll be a truck, wave it down."

"I thought you'd be finished with the mountain since Nellie did what she did."

He threw his head back and laughed. "I'll never be finished with the Pritchards." And he was gone. He was a spiteful spirit.

But I listened to him and got myself out on the road early the next morning. And sure enough the Connors' truck came rolling up the road. It was so foggy it was there before I could think about it. I waved like a crazy person. The truck stopped.

Mrs. Connor opened the door. "Lordy Shelly, you nearly gave me a heart attack in this fog."

"I come to ride with you. I want to see Nellie one more time."

Mrs. Connor opened her mouth, shut it, and opened it again. "I don't want to know." She reached over and pressed some paper in my hand. "That be from Nellie." Two one-hundred-dollar bills is what I had.

Mrs. Connor shrugged. "Don't ask."

I saw Nellie before Mrs. Connor did. She looked like some little old boy coming down that mountain road. When she got in, I scooted in the middle. She looked at me, thought for a minute, and then said one word: "Shelly." That was all that needed to be said. I rode all the way to the train station in Asheville. We left her standing on the platform, waiting on a train to God knows where. Before we left I gave her a hug and whispered, "I seen you in the spring. You'll do just fine. Don't worry. That's healing water."

*   *   *

So it was over and done. The whole mountain soon tired of
buzzing over Hobbs missing. They was happy, if the truth
be known. As for me, months at a time would go by before I
thought of the people he murdered.

Hobbs waited three years before he appeared to me,
standing on my front porch like he'd come calling. "Rose is
coming up this mountain. This mess ain't over by far. It ain't
never going to end." And then he was gone, leaving me to think
on who in the world Rose could be and what wasn't over.

Part Four

Rose Gardner

Thirty-four

My first memory was of Mama making a deal with one of our neighbors to sell me for a thousand dollars. The poor woman had lost her husband in the Great War with Germany, and she was lonely in an awful sad way. I was three years old but smart for my age. The widow taught me to cook, read, and cuddled me on her lap. When the time came for Mama to turn me over and take the money, she backed out. So, somewhere inside her mixed-up mind, she truly loved her only child, me. But all the same, I worried that the widow had been my only decent chance in life and one day Mama would abandon me for good. I never complained about fending for myself and made good use of the time. At five I had read the Bible through twice and found a wonderful book called *Tom Sawyer* that I swiped from a bookstore next to the shop where Mama worked. Often people looked at me with pity in their eyes: *Poor Rose, she has the worst kind of mama.* But I loved her all the same with my whole heart, the kind of love that saw no wrongs. I taught Mama to read better, did her nails, and cooked her supper, hoping these things would keep me in her favor.

Mama was a beautician who ran the numbers and conjured hoodoo spells on the side. By the time I was fourteen, she had taught me everything I needed to know about men. Useful stuff like how to get jewelry, trips, and good meals. How to make them smile when they wanted to beat me instead. I was born in Louisiana, right in the heart of hoodoo and voodoo country, New Orleans. But Mama pulled up our roots, and I couldn't remember a thing about the city. We moved around the South, living in every state below the Mason-Dixon Line. Mama couldn't abide Daddy and pretended he never existed. Sometimes she made out that my birth was no different from Mother Mary's divine conception. That was my mama just full of herself. So I never had a steady male figure in my childhood. Mama looked just like Mary Pickford, and this got her a lot of attention, but the kind of men Mama picked was here today and gone tomorrow. She wore her welcome out with every relative we had and some who weren't even kin.

When I was seventeen, we landed on our feet in Atlanta, but not before I had attended ten different high schools and gave up altogether. Mama said I was smarter than any of the kids I was going to school with. She was right, but still I wanted to go. She had found work in a decent beauty shop right close to Oakland Cemetery. The year was 1938 and times were hard. The Depression wouldn't go away even with President Roosevelt's New Deal. Women—even the well-to-do ones—weren't having their hair done as often. Too many times I had seen the line for the mission's soup kitchen snake around two blocks or more. Men, women, and even kids would wait and hope they would make it through the door before the cutoff. People were living in tents and lean-tos made out of cardboard near the railroad tracks. On many nights I fell asleep to the sound of the railroad men rounding up the hobos, scattering their pitiful belongings. They always attacked at night to catch these poor souls off guard. I wished I knew a spell that would make times get better, but hoodoo didn't work on that big of a mess, or so Mama said. She and I shared one room over the beauty shop. For me that room was enough. Being with Mama was always enough. She made sure our stomachs were full and we had a roof over our heads. Sometimes it took me smiling pretty and sitting next to her latest boyfriend to get him to cough up the rent, but this was a small price to pay to keep our tiny family intact.

One day Mama sent me to buy her special perfume—Chanel No. 5—from Rich's department store. She said a woman had to keep herself up because you never knew who might come walking in the shop to whisk her away. That one small bottle of perfume cost five dollars, a fortune, a week's worth of food, Mama's paycheck. After I had the perfume safe in a brown sack, I took my time and watched the trolleys come and go. The air was heavy, hazy, and thick that morning as if a bad storm was going to roll in from the west. My hair had turned into a million tiny curls. I came upon a crowd of men, pushing and shoving their way into a small business. The sign above the office read TYLER'S EMPLOYMENT AGENCY. A young man with a neat haircut, dressed in a crisp white shirt and a sharp blue tie, walked out from behind a tall counter where he had been helping several men at once. Men who all looked the same, rumpled dress coats and dusty dark pants. Their shoes had seen better days, with heels run down to nothing. Some didn't even have shoelaces. The look of irritation on the young man's face turned to surprise and then fear when he saw how many men were outside on the sidewalk.

I was only a few feet away and could smell the men's sweat. Lines cut across their faces with worry and something like rage. The young man pushed the door closed and turned the lock in one motion, leaving the crowd outside to roar their disapproval.

Two men just on the other side of the door yelled words a girl shouldn't hear. One of the men had a cap pushed down on his head, hiding his eyes. His fingers formed a fist. The man hit the glass with one swift motion. The glass turned into a spiderweb and took flight. A rather large piece struck the young man in the forehead. A red stream of blood splattered over the blue tie.

"The paper said you have jobs!" yelled the man who shattered the glass.

A touch on my arm made me jump, and I dropped the brown bag on the sidewalk. A sickening crack let me know what I had done as the brown paper turned wet and the air smelled of flowers. Mama would kill me.

"Young lady, you need to go home. Things are about to get ugly. No place for a girl." The man speaking had once been handsome. His dress jacket told me he had known what it was like to have money in his wallet before the world turned upside down. I bent down to pick up the pieces of the bottle; a fist caught the man's jaw. I was knocked to my knees. Sirens and whistles told me the police were near.

"Go on now." The man's eyes were the bluest blue. "Go!" He gave me a push.

I left the bag of broken glass and ran until I could see the beauty shop. Mama would be livid. There wouldn't be any explaining how I broke her perfume. When I swung the door open, the bell tinkling, relief flooded my chest. Mama smiled her sweetest smile. "Well now, here is my beautiful daughter, Rose."

Our luck had changed, and it came in the form of Mr. Homer J. Carson, a fancy business owner from North Carolina, who happened to drop in the shop for lemon shampoo. Lemon shampoo for a man; I just couldn't imagine. Mr. Carson owned the only rock quarry in Asheville and his business was doing just dandy thanks to the WPA and all its projects in the South.

He took one long look at my mama as if he were drinking a glass of ice tea on a hot day. Mama packed up her hoodoo, quit the numbers, and put on her entertaining hat. The change was that easy. Homer J. Carson married her before she slipped away from him and moved us to Asheville, the city of romance. Mama sure made me want to throw up with that one. Her move into a new high-society life and pretending that our old life never existed might have fooled some, but I, Rose Gardner, her daughter in every way, knew better. When she looked at me, she couldn't help but remember exactly where she came from, the beautician who ran numbers, conjured spells, and almost sold her only child for a thousand dollars. She couldn't hide behind her pretty smile, behind her clipped and proper words, and that's what made her decide I needed to change too. But her lessons in determination led me up Black Mountain almost four years after Hobbs Pritchard came up missing.

I was the daughter Mr. Carson always wanted but never had. His late wife, Jessica, who was everywhere in Mama's new home—on the walls, in the closets, and even in the kitchen, where her apron still hung on a hook by the stove—wasn't crazy about children. Mama didn't marry Mr. Carson to make him forget his wife. She didn't marry him for love or romance. No, as long as he gave her lace dresses, new hats, and a hefty allowance, Mama was in heaven.

She warned me to stop using the hoodoo she taught me, told me to put those backward ideas behind me. And I listened, and even gave it a try, until Hobbs Pritchard came into my life. I'm the reason Hobbs came up missing, a misguided spell.

Because of Mama I met Hobbs. If she hadn't been having one of her fancy parties, where ladies whispered behind her back, where she could never measure up to dear Jessica, my life would have turned out completely different. She had ordered a hundred of those dainty finger cakes that a girl could pop in her mouth and let the icing dissolve on her tongue, even though Mama told her it only added weight to her hips.

Hobbs showed up with the bakery's deliveryman, who was his poker buddy. He tried to sell Mama homemade liquor to serve at her party. Mama could see straight into his soul and see herself. I'm sure that's why she detested him on sight.

"I don't want moonshine. I've moved on to better things." She laughed and turned her back, motioning the deliveryman to follow her in the house with the boxes. "You do understand my husband owns the stone quarry?" She flung this over her shoulder like a dart at a dartboard, smack dead into the bull's-eye.

I watched the whole scene play out while sitting on the back porch swing. Hobbs probably wouldn't have noticed me if I hadn't laughed. Any girl on this earth could see how handsome he was, but his looks weren't what made me tingle. Excitement vibrated off him with a fiery energy.

"What are you sitting out here for in those fancy clothes? Shouldn't you be helping your mama with her high-and-mighty party?" He sneered.

I stood and met his stare. "I don't give a damn about my mama or her so-called friends. I'm bored to death. This city is dead."

He threw his head back and laughed at the sky. And it wasn't a nice laugh. "Come on with me into your mama's garden. It seems right pretty. Maybe we can find something alive in there." Again he laughed.

Mama prided herself on Jessica's flower garden, famous for its hedges that formed a maze guests loved walking through. I held out my hand and he helped me off the side of the porch.

Hobbs lit a cigarette, and we kept a lazy pace, not touching, even though I wouldn't have minded. As soon as we were in the middle of the maze, he pulled me to him and kissed me.

My body melted into him. I had to be a lady and not let things go too far. "Excuse me, but maybe I didn't want to kiss you." I'd been kissed plenty of times. Shoot, I even let some boys go to second base before I halted their fun. That was my intention with Hobbs.

He kissed me again, long and sweet.

In the kiss I tasted danger. "Your friend should be ready to leave." Even I could hear the lack of conviction in my voice.

"Let him go. I'm a big boy." He kissed me again and pushed me against a tree, tugging at my dress and underwear. I tingled all over.

"This is enough." I was more determined.

"No teasing, little girl. I know there's not one thing ladylike about you."

His hard part freely bobbed around. God, I couldn't help but be amazed since I'd never seen one before.

I pushed his chest with all my strength. "I'm going back to the house."

"Nope. Don't fight me. You know you want this." He held me without much effort.

I wiggled but it didn't make any difference. The first push hurt but things moved so fast I couldn't even cry. He finished before I could summon the air to yell. I never imagined my first time would be pushed up against a tree in the middle of a hedge maze. I always thought I'd be in love, but Mama always said love doesn't have a thing to do with anything.

He zipped his pants and looked at me. "What's your name?"

Mama said not to give my gifts away. No good man wanted to buy the cow if he could get milk free. I looked at the ground. This wasn't going like I wanted.

"Hobbs Pritchard is my name." He touched my hand and

turned to walk away but came close again. "I'm coming back to see you. Meet me here at midnight."

"Rose, Rose Gardner." His scent of whiskey and sweat was on me.

"I'll meet you right here, Rose Gardner."

"I know hoodoo." Was this a threat or an offering?

He kissed me one more time. "I just bet you do."

A rush of energy ran through me. Did I hate him or love him? There was no in-between place.

"I like you, Rose. I like you a lot. Do you like me?"

"I don't know."

"Good. You can find out." He was gone before I could say another word.

I was left straightening my dress and hungering after a man who most would say was the worst kind of creature. But he liked me. I needed someone to like me.

When I met him that night under the moon, he held a rose—a rose, mind you—in his fingers. Now, that took some thought. His hair was combed back straight. "This is for you."

I took the blood-red rose. "Thank you."

He shrugged. "I've been thinking on you all afternoon." He didn't sound happy.

I waited.

"It was your fault that I did what I did. You wanted me to do it. I'm never wrong. I thought you'd been around some."

"I haven't." I was wearing my prettiest blue dress.

"You got me confused, Rose." He lit another cigarette. "You might be different from the girls I come across. How old are you?"

"Twenty," I lied.

"That's young, but not too bad. I don't want no trouble from that mama of yours."

A breath caught under my ribs. "My mama doesn't care if I ever come back." The truth after so long sounded sad when released into the air.

"I don't know. I ain't scared easy and you scare me. I ain't got it in me to do a proper courting or be a proper beau. I might be gone for good tomorrow." He was quiet. "I've done bad things, and the truth is I will probably do them to you. See, I'm telling you stuff that is best kept to myself. I can't always control how I do things. My mama was disappointed in me when she died. Let's just say the women in my life have been real let down for good reason." His face was calm.

I was hooked. He was telling his heart to me. "I'm not looking for a proper boy; that would be boring." I swirled the rose in my fingers.

"I ain't no boy, Rose. I'm twenty-five going on twenty-six."

"Well, if you leave me at least I had some excitement."

He smiled and pulled me to him.

"I don't care what you did, Hobbs."

"Don't say that, Rose. You would care." He said this into my hair. "You might be different, Rose Gardner." Kisses led to more kisses, and we took our time with the moon looking down on us. Something deep inside me said Hobbs Pritchard had never taken his time for anyone else. And that would be the only thing I was right about when it came to him.

When we rolled over on our backs, looking at the sky, I knew I would be Hobbs Pritchard's girl forever, until he died and then some.

"I like you, Rose." He lit another cigarette. We stayed there until the stars faded and the moon fell away.

Thirty-five

Things between Hobbs and me went fast, knocking the breath out of me. We moved at full speed for five months. I would meet him on the street, and he would take me to one of his poker games, where I sat at his side as a good-luck charm.

One night we stood on the street outside my house. "Hobbs?"

"Yeah." He scrunched up his forehead.

I kissed his cheek. "Are you my boyfriend?"

He laughed so hard my cheeks heated. "I guess I am, Rose Gardner. I guess I am."

"Haven't you ever had a girlfriend before?"

"A long, long time ago. Things didn't go so well. I haven't had no use for it since then."

I nodded. "You won't be sorry being my boyfriend."

"You're changing all the wrongs, aren't you?" He touched my cheek and laughed.

"Maybe."

I was sure we'd get married. We saw each other four or five

times a week. But then one week in late September he didn't come. At first I didn't think a whole lot about it. He was Hobbs after all and probably got sidetracked playing poker, and he was winning. Another week came and went. I waited and thought about the pretty girls that made eyes at him. But we loved each other. I decided to check around and see if someone killed him or the law caught up to him.

He was sniffing out a little girl serving at the soup kitchen, one of those do-gooders. Miss Nellie Clay was her name, and she was as sweet to look at as a honeysuckle vine loaded with blooms, or so Hobbs's friend at the bakery said. I let another week go by.

On my next visit to the bakery, Hobbs's friend reported the news. "He's marrying her today down at the little Baptist church close to the soup kitchen. Hobbs Pritchard getting married. I pity that girl."

Without giving my actions any thought, I slapped him cross the face.

"What the hell is that for? I didn't do anything."

I walked away, moving in the direction of Hobbs. He couldn't marry Miss Nellie Clay. He loved me. That much I knew. When I reached the church, I ran right to the doors with every intention of stopping a wedding. Hobbs held his new wife in a passionate kiss. She was tiny and fragile where I was tall and strong. Something powerful ran between Miss Nellie and me as our stares met. Her long blond curls hung away from her face. She was prettier than me. If I had to compare myself to this girl, I was an elephant dressed up in ribbons and satin to disguise my tough hide.

I left without a word. My life was over. Hobbs was married. All the way home I shook with a rage I was sure would kill me. I hated him, hated her. I wasn't thinking straight when I finally ran into my room, shut the door, and dug deep in the back of the old cupboard. Hoodoo isn't something to be taken lightly, especially when a person believed with all her heart in its power. I threw a spell with a twist. This conjure would make Hobbs Pritchard hunger after me until he left that pretty, perfect wife. It was so powerful I wasn't sure how fast it would work. I lit a candle, placed it in my window, and waited.

Six weeks later, two days before Thanksgiving—my third candle was burned to the nub—still no Hobbs. The sun was shining bright, and the redbirds were singing. I could smell winter in the air, my favorite time of year. I wandered out into the maze, barren and dead. Deep in the hedges a twig broke behind me. I turned and the sun nearly blinded me. A person stepped towards me and blocked out the sun. My heart raced. Hobbs stood there grinning as if he'd only been gone a couple of days. He caught me to him. I breathed in his scent of whiskey and cigarettes. My body was home, in the place it wanted to be.

"You're the only one for me, Rose Gardner. Why'd I ever think different?"

I pushed him away. "Well, you decided a little too late, didn't you, Hobbs? You picked her over me because she's little and pretty."

"I'm sorry." He pulled me back to him. "She's all bones, girl. You got something none of the girls in these parts have."

"Really, Hobbs? Did you tell Miss Nellie Clay that too?" I let her name float between us with its shiny sharpness.

He wrapped his arms around me tighter. "I was dumb. I know I was. I wish I could go back in time and change it all, Rose. Nellie ain't you. You're smart, pretty, and strong. You set me straight. But most of all you know me inside and out. I can't hide anything from you. I'm weak and you know it. But I got to have you. Get your clothes. I've had enough of this seeing you here and there."

"Why would I? You're married." But as the words came out, I knew I'd follow him anywhere.

He laughed. "If that's what marriage is, I don't want no part of it. I want us. Don't you?"

"You'll leave Nellie?" I relaxed in his arms.

"Pretty much."

"I know you love me, Hobbs. We'll get married and have a good life."

He pushed away. "I ain't talking love, girl. I'm talking souls. That's more important than love. Don't you think?" He was looking at me as if he might have mistaken me for some other girl.

"Mama will never let me come back again."

"What is it with girls and their mamas? You're grown. Twenty ain't a kid. What do you want?"

"If you don't leave Nellie for good, we're over." I didn't want him to know I'd lied about my age.

He grinned. "Go get your stuff."

Every girl wanted parents that cared enough to watch over her like a hawk. I slid out of the house without Mama even noticing. My suitcase wasn't too heavy. Mama could go about her new life without reforming me. Living with a man was not tolerated by the Asheville women, especially if said man was married and known for breaking the law.

Our little house sat on the edge of town facing Black Mountain, Hobbs's favorite place in the world. When I looked at its large shadow, I thought of one thing only: Nellie. She sat in our new place as if she belonged. She had to understand that I had him first.

We didn't have a stick of furniture except a bed. That's all we needed. For the first days, we stayed there most of the time. We ate among the rumpled covers. We laughed and talked.

"Tell me about your family." I'd always wanted a brother and a sister.

Hobbs was propped against the pillows. His face turned hard. "I got a sister, who up and ran away, and a stepbrother that gets in the way all the time. Mama and Daddy have been dead for a while. And I got Aunt Ida. I love her. She knows me like you."

"Why did your sister run away?"

"Sour grapes. She wanted more than she got out of life."

"Why don't you like your stepbrother?"

He laughed. "Jack wanted the same girl as me when we were young. Her name was Patty Harkin."

"Who got her?"

The dark look on his face bothered me. "No one."

I put my head on his chest. "I bet it was you."

He sniggered.

"Does she know where you are?"

He rubbed my head. "She who?"

I slapped at him playfully. "Who? You know who."

"Why you got to let Nellie in this room?" The air in the room had changed. Nellie walked right in and soaked into the walls. "I don't want to talk about her. I'm here. That's where I want to be." He looked out the window at the mountain.

"We need to talk about her sometime."

"Why? Why can't we be like this, Rose?" He opened his arms out as if to catch me as I fell. "Why has life got to be all tied up in a nice neat package?"

I'd been wrapping my beautiful package ever since I was little.

"When I look at you, I see what the world can be. All the girls I've met want something from me. Mama wanted me to be like Daddy. AzLeigh wanted me to be strong and hold her up. You don't expect nothing of me, Rose. Can't we just be together like we are now?"

"What does Nellie expect?" I whispered, but he covered my mouth with his lips.

That night we made Lonnie as the full moon shone through the window. Of course I wouldn't know for a while. All I wanted was to have Hobbs there with me. He had a wandering eye, a fondness for other women. Men were like this unless a woman got herself a Mr. Carlson, dull as paint drying. Hobbs was worth my effort.

I snuggled into the crook of his arm. "Why'd you marry her?" I waited to see if he would answer.

He was quiet so long I was sure he wouldn't. "Mama would have liked Nellie. She would have approved."

A lump grew in my throat. "She wouldn't have liked me?"

"That's why I'm with you, Rose. You're right the opposite of any girl my mama would have chose."

Simple.

The last time I saw Hobbs, he was headed back up the mountain to leave Nellie for good. He knew about the baby and his tenderness came out. It was his idea to go end his marriage. He walked out the door promising to be back as soon as possible. As he drove out of sight, I realized he might be lying to me just like he lied to Nellie. What if he never came back? What if he really didn't love either one of us? A familiar feeling of dread ate away at me. Nothing was ever going to work out with Hobbs, nothing.

Thirty-six

Two weeks later I sat straight up out of a dead sleep. *Rose! Rose! Oh God, Rose!*

I heard Hobbs like he was sitting on the side of my bed. Mama always said that each soul calls out when leaving the world. My name sat in the air and left me empty inside.

I stayed in the house living off money Hobbs left me. Just over a month went by and Jack came knocking at the door. I'd been spending all my time alone, never going out in case Hobbs came home.

One look at Jack and I understood all the reasons Hobbs hated his stepbrother. He was tall, quiet, and unruffled. He wasn't much to look at like Hobbs but he was peaceful, a lake of cool clear calmness.

He took off his wide-brimmed hat. "Are you Rose?"

"Yes." I fought the urge to laugh like a crazy person. "Are you Jack?"

He took a step back. "Yes, but . . ."

"I just know." I opened my door wide. "He's dead, but you know that, don't you."

Again he looked at me. "When's the last time you saw him?"

"He was headed back home to break off his marriage. Over a month ago."

"How do you know he's dead, then?"

"Just do."

He looked at the floor. "Do you know who did it?"

"I got my guesses, but you can't blame a person on a hunch."

He nodded in a no-nonsense way. "I'm sorry to have bothered you."

"No bother."

"You need to go home to your family." He looked at the bulge under my shirt.

"Thank you." The edge in my words broke the kindness in his expression. I didn't need his pity. I'd do fine one way or another, just like Mama.

Jack stepped out the door, put his hat on his head, and gave me a nod.

I watched his truck until I couldn't see it anymore.

Thirty-seven

I never intended to go up Black Mountain. Half the time I was angry at Hobbs for dying when I needed him the most. In all fairness, I wasn't so sure had he lived we would have been together.

Women without men were lost to making any kind of decent living. Mama proved this to me. My life took a hard turn after Lonnie was born. It wouldn't have taken much to put me in one of those lean-tos by the tracks. So I turned to what I knew. I threw spells for people. I became the local hoodoo woman. Some of the most important people in Asheville, such as the mayor, came to me. Love and money were the top two wants. One time I conjured a love spell for a girl from the uppity side of town. Her mother knew Mama. She wanted to marry Mr. Perfect so bad she would have done anything. Maybe she was sleeping with him, and that's why he was dragging his feet. Who knew?

"Here's what we do." I took the rose she brought me. With part of the petals I made some rose water. Then I took one of the big soft velvety petals and handed it back to the girl. "You write his name on there." I handed her an ink pen.

She looked at me strangely.

"You have to believe or it will not work."

She nodded and wrote her beloved's name.

I took the petal and soaked it in the rose water. "In the night and in the day, love will find this boy some way." I placed the wet petal in her open hand. "Now, you go throw this at his house. When you do, picture yourself wearing a wedding dress in a church. That should do the job."

She gave me a long look. "Okay." She wrapped those pretty, long fingers around the petal.

"Good, now go."

She tripped out of the little house.

A week later she showed up on my doorstep. "He asked me to marry him. You did it!" She pressed a twenty-dollar bill into my hand. This was the most I had made on a spell. Most of my customers wanted something for nothing.

I wasn't making ends meet for Lonnie and me. Mama refused to have me at her house. So I was reduced to following in her footsteps, showing wealthy men a good time. If not for Lonnie, I would have put an end to my sorry life. Then one day Mr. Carl Ramsey Sr. offered to take me to the seashore. Just the sound of the invitation in his mouth was lovely, special. I begged Mama and she agreed to take Lonnie but vowed to call the state if I left him with her one minute longer than I promised. I guess she had forgotten her old life altogether.

Mr. Carl Ramsey was one of those men who liked to act way younger than he was. This was evident by the strands of hair combed over his big bald spot. As if no one could see the scalp shining beneath. Girls like me helped him feel twenty. He promised we would stay in a nice house on the coast, where I'd be waited on hand and foot, along with swimming and laying around in the sun, not a bad way to earn some money. I needed the rest. The day we were leaving I stood in front of the mirror.

"You see what I've come to, Hobbs? Even you wouldn't want me sleeping with old men for a living. I'm tired and I miss you." I pulled my brown hair back in a ball at my neck. "It doesn't matter because if I could do it all again, I would. I have Lonnie. He's so sweet and cute. If you could see him, you would have straightened out your life."

The house on the beach turned out to be old as the earth but big, and it was on an island off the Georgia coast. Not a maid to be seen. The first day we arrived, Mr. Carl Ramsey wanted to keep me in bed all day. I should have seen that coming, but I was hoping. No man had complained about my performance under the sheets, but this old man couldn't seem to get enough. Between him and the sound of water rushing in and out all hours of the day and night, I couldn't concentrate. I kept seeing Hobbs standing here and there. When Mr. Ramsey wanted to eat supper—that I cooked—in bed, I took a long walk on the beach. I walked into the deafening wind, thinking of the ocean and how easy it would be to drown.

Rose.

I looked around for Hobbs.

Go home.

"Where's home?" I shouted into the wind.

The air stilled for a minute. *The money is there. Go get the money.*

Ah yes, the money. Hobbs never was much of a giving person, but he did look after me. He told me there was plenty of money stashed away all over his farm.

"I'm tired, Hobbs." The tears in my voice made me quiet.

Black Mountain, Rose.

Could I manage it? Could I find the courage to go up that

mountain and take what was Lonnie's? I was at my rock bottom. The wind grew still again.

I turned around and nearly ran back to that old house. I insisted Mr. Carl Ramsey take me home right that minute. And yes, I understood I would not receive any pay. For the first time since Lonnie's birth, I had a plan. Hobbs had spoken to me.

Thirty-eight

M y first close look of Black Mountain was through the window of a car Mama gave me. She thought staking claim to Hobbs's place was my best idea. Finally I was wising up and following her example. Lonnie was asleep on the backseat. Each place was just as Hobbs described. The Connor cabin stood in the middle of where the road forked into two, a narrow island of land. Aunt Ida's house was down the left side of the split, sitting in the bend. If I went a mile farther, I'd come to Hobbs's house on the right overlooking the valley.

I parked in Aunt Ida's yard, opened the car door, and got out, watching the house with hands on my hips. I stood there until Aunt Ida waddled out on the front porch.

"Who are you? Is that you, Nellie?"

At the sound of a strange voice, Lonnie sat up in the backseat. "Mama."

"I'm Rose Gardner, and this is my son, Lonnie. I'm sure you've heard of me." I opened the car door for Lonnie. I wanted to ask about Nellie. What happened to her? Was she still in the house I came to take? Well, she could just move over.

"I've never heard mention of a Rose. I'm watching for Nellie, Hobbs's wife."

I yanked Lonnie close to me, which caused him to wail like a cat in heat. It wasn't his fault the old biddy was telling the biggest lie I'd ever heard. "Hush now," I said sweetly, but that only made him yell louder.

"You hurt that baby." Aunt Ida came off the porch like she would take Lonnie away from me.

"This is Hobbs's son. We live alone in Asheville. I'm Rose, the girl he loved. I know he told you about me. He said so."

"He told a lot of things, girl." Aunt Ida cut me a stare. "He was the meanest boy that ever walked this good earth and it caught up to him. But he was good to his aunt Ida." The old woman had the look of someone who had come to the end of her frayed rope. "He never had no children with Nellie. He came up missing. I'm guessing he might be dead."

"Is Nellie up there living?" I nodded to the road.

She looked at me hard. "Nellie was never found, girl. She's been missing nearly as long as him. She's probably dead too. No kids to be had here."

I fought the urge to yell. "This is Hobbs's son. I promise. Can't you see him in his face?" I turned Lonnie's little head in her direction. "See him."

She came close. Lonnie tried to hide behind my skirt. "I reckon Hobbs never had no son."

"He had this one, Aunt Ida."

She studied me. "He liked women, the younger the better."

"Yes, I suppose you're right." This knowledge never changed the ache in my chest.

"I let Nellie down. I didn't help her when Hobbs near beat her to death."

A cold chill walked up my back. "He never raised his hand to me." The glimpse of Hobbs's life with Nellie turned my stomach inside out.

Aunt Ida put her face in Lonnie's. "How do I know this is his boy?"

"Look at his eyes."

She looked at Lonnie, and he watched her back. "Hobbs; Lordy, Hobbs, you're there. You're alive in this boy." She shook her head and touched Lonnie's light hair. "I loved your daddy more than anyone would ever know."

"I still love him." I spoke in my softest voice.

"Yes, you knew him like me. He didn't show that to many. Mostly he showed the side Nellie knew. He wasn't all bad. And if you knew that sweet part, you couldn't help but love him."

The sob stuck in my chest hurt. "I love him. He sent me here. Came to me on the beach and told me to come."

She nodded. "His old place is empty, just like Nellie left it that day. I wouldn't let Jack mess with any of her stuff. I was hoping she'd come home so I could tell her I was sorry for not helping her. He beat her bad. But it was because she was so sweet and just like his mama and AzLeigh. He ain't never kept that anger down. You can live there if you like, but they say Hobbs's soul is stuck. The young boys have seen his ghost, and what I hear it ain't a pretty sight, seeing how he ain't got no head. That's what they say. It could be hogwash." Tears filled her words and she nodded up the road as if she could see the house.

"Hobbs doesn't scare me. He can stay right there with me." I turned back to the car.

"We found his truck near the waterfall. No sign of him. Didn't find a bit of blood or nothing. It's like he just walked off this earth, but we both know that couldn't be. Lots of people wanted him dead. They didn't know him like you and me."

I opened my mouth to agree, but I couldn't speak.

"I tried to tell that wife of his he would hurt her. But she wouldn't listen. Now, if he had brought you home, I would have known he was in love. But that girl was bound to get hurt. I just hate she had to learn it all the hard way."

"It's the only way most of us learn." I helped Lonnie back into the car.

"I'll help you all you need. You're family, having that boy and all. Good luck, sweetie."

"I make my own luck, always have. I'll take care of myself. That's what Hobbs and I had in common. We know how to make something work."

The house sat in the clearing as if it were left over from another time and life. For the longest, I studied the weathered wood from inside the car. What in the world had I been thinking?

The front door pushed open almost on its own as if someone were waiting on me. I walked to the large fireplace and stood. A cold chill washed over me. Upstairs a door closed, and I could have sworn I heard a sigh. "Hobbs," I whispered. But all was quiet.

"Where we at, Mama?" Lonnie tugged on my skirt.

"This is going to be our new home." I led him to the stairs. "Come on and let's have a look." I opened the only closed door. The bed was a beautiful four-poster affair. I touched the bare mattress. At one time fine linens had dressed the bed, white ones with a delicate lace border; they belonged to Hobbs's mama. I knew this. Pictures came to me sometimes. I saw the bed made, elegant. Romantic.

Lonnie pulled open a big wardrobe with double doors. There hung Hobbs's clothes. I took a shirt off the hanger and held it to my nose. I still caught his scent around the musty smell. Grief oozed in my chest like the disease his death had become. With the shirt to my nose, I prayed Hobbs would appear. Is that why I had come? To find Hobbs? I caught my reflection warped in a large mirror. One long crack ran diagonal from one corner to another. The reflection rippled, turned dark as night, and I saw the headlights of a truck moving down a steep road. The crack was visible again, clearing away the vision but not before I got the heebie-jeebies. I'd glimpsed something about Hobbs, about his death.

"You crying, Mama?" Lonnie looked at me with solemn eyes.

With the salty tears on my lips, I laughed. "No, sweetie. Look at this mirror. It's just ruined." I dropped Hobbs's shirt on the floor. "Let's go downstairs and have a look at the kitchen."

I wouldn't sleep in the room. I wouldn't even enter the doorway again, but this was crazy thinking. How could I live in a house and never go in a room? It wasn't living. I wanted life.

The first thing we needed was food. I had a little money Mama insisted I take. I think she was feeling guilty about the way she'd treated me. I opened the cupboard door. A flash of gray shot across my feet. I screamed, which caused Lonnie to break into sobs, wrapping his arms around my legs so I couldn't move. My breakfast churned in my stomach.

"The house ain't been lived in for a while. Mice take up in empty places." Jack stood in the door. "Ain't no wood or food. Tough place to lay claim." His words were guarded, quiet.

He kept a safe distance from me, hovering in the doorway. His looks were just as homely as I remembered.

"I don't have a choice. This is my chance, my only chance." Why in the world did I choose to be honest with him? "Is there somewhere I can buy food?" Why hadn't I thought of buying groceries in Asheville?

"Folks always willing to help around here, but they won't

take your money. They're funny like that, solid plain folks. We best get you a late garden in for extras this winter." He sighed as if this were his job, a burden on his shoulders. "You do know how to can vegetables, don't you?"

I didn't even stumble. "Yes." At least I was back to my old self. "I should have planned better." I held out my hand. "I'm Rose Gardner, and it looks like I'm going back to Asheville to buy some food."

He looked around. "This is a mess, but you could make it work if you had a mind to." He walked past me. "You know, kids around here see Hobbs out by that hollow tree." The tree stood on the edge of the woods with limbs like some kind of creature's arms. "He ain't never showed himself to me, but I don't guess he would anyway." He looked out the window. "Nellie turned into another person up here."

Damn, he was sweet on Nellie. What made everyone love that girl? "When you marry the wrong person you change." I wanted to stomp my foot and scream. "I'm not Nellie. Hobbs didn't change me a bit. I guess that's why we loved each other so much. We accepted who we were, the good and the bad."

Jack looked me over as if searching for a crack in my honesty. "We ain't talking about the same Hobbs Pritchard."

"He could be decent. He was good to me, but like all of us, he had his faults, and getting caught up with young women was one of them. Nellie's pretty looks outshined mine and he married her. But in the end, he came back to me."

"Where'd you get the idea you weren't something to look at?" He studied me with his green eyes.

Under his stare my cheeks grew warm. I looked away. "I'll be okay. I know how to take care of myself."

"I'm sure you will. You might just make it after all. You remind me of someone I knew."

"Who?"

"AzLeigh Pritchard, Hobbs's sister. She was one smart girl. She didn't take anything off of people." His voice was tender.

"I've heard about her."

"Yep. I'm sure you have."

Lonnie pulled on my skirt. "Mama."

Jack looked at him for the first time since he shadowed the door. "Hello, little guy." He held out his large hand. Lonnie took it instantly. "We got to get you and your mama some food. What you think?"

Lonnie smiled. "I love cookies."

Jack threw his head full of dark curls back and laughed a belly laugh. "You look just like your daddy, the good parts he never seemed to use." He ruffled Lonnie's hair. "Too bad Hobbs never got a chance to know his son. It might actually have changed him."

"I thought the same thing. But he had his easy ways too."

He gave me a doubtful look. "Never saw them myself, but AzLeigh used to claim the same thing. Said that's the reason she kept giving him one chance after another. Me, I learned early on not to go back for more."

"Do you know who might have killed him?" It seemed the wrong question to ask a person who disliked Hobbs so much, but I asked anyway.

A quiet pall fell between us, but finally he spoke. "Who can say? So many people hated him." He patted Lonnie's back. I could tell he had a firm belief in who hated Hobbs enough to kill him. "We'll stock the cupboard."

"I'll pay. I don't want charity. I was working up until I decided to make this change."

He cocked his eyebrow. "What kind of work? It must have been pretty bad to up and quit a job nowadays." His smile was wonderfully clear and free of all the junk hanging on my shoulders. How could I tell him something that would make him think less of me?

"I cleaned houses for a living," I lied. "Lonnie's too big to take with me now. He gets into everything. I had to come up with another life." The story ended true enough, but I couldn't look my son in the eyes.

"You're starting fresh here." He turned to leave. "I'll be back in a little while." And he was gone out the door.

Lonnie ran after him. "Bye, big man."

Jack turned around and studied my boy with his cool green stare. "Bye, little man." He looked at me. "I'll bring plenty of food. You can pay me by cooking some suppers. Poor old Aunt Ida can't remember half her recipes and mixes up the ingredients."

Thirty-nine

Jack was in and out of our lives, helpful but distant all the same. I wasn't looking for a friend. One day while searching halfheartedly for Hobbs's money, I found Nellie's diary and a beautiful red garnet necklace pushed into a sideboard drawer. The necklace wasn't worth too much but Nellie probably thought it was a treasure of rubies. Hobbs could have bought it for her, but his style was to win gifts at poker games. I fastened the clasp around my neck. The stones caught the sun. I liked the fact that I didn't know its story or real worth.

I read the diary in less than thirty minutes. The few pages were revealing. Nellie started out innocent. Her last entry sent a shiver up my back. Hobbs destroyed something deep inside her. The thought crossed my mind to give the diary to Jack, but that would spoil the story that Nellie died because she walked off into the woods with a broken heart. Could Nellie have killed Hobbs? I burned the book in the fireplace.

* * *

Lonnie and I moved into a small bedroom tucked near the attic door at the end of the upstairs hall. This turned out to be Jack's old room.

"You didn't want the big bedroom?" Jack had stopped by to help with the garden.

"No." I busted a dirt clod with the toe of my shoe.

"Why? Have you seen anything?"

"If you mean Hobbs, no."

He nodded to the garnet necklace around my neck. "I was thinking more like my mama. I don't believe in things like that, but Nellie said she saw her. That there is Mama's necklace you got on." He turned his head and the brim of his hat hid his eyes.

"I'm sorry. I found it in a drawer in the dining room. It's not worth anything, so I thought I would wear it."

He pushed his hat back. "I wonder how it got to the dining room. The last I knew, she was buried with it."

The words made my thoughts scramble at once. "Oh, I can show you the drawer where I found it."

He shook his head. "I don't doubt you, Rose. I'm just wondering how the necklace got out of Mama's casket. Maybe Henry James had a change of heart, but I doubt it."

I took the necklace off and pushed it towards him. "The box is in the same drawer."

Again he was still. "Don't worry none. I don't think you had anything to do with it." He half grinned. "I mean, you weren't living here then."

"I'm glad you can joke."

He shrugged. "It's just another mystery on this mountain full of them." But I could tell he was concerned.

I dropped the necklace into his open hand.

"I got a keepsake. There's not many of those." His finger curled around the red stones. His sadness stood between us.

"I chose the small room because the big bedroom is haunted with something besides ghosts. That room has Hobbs in every corner." I watched his face become stern.

"I know you didn't like Hobbs. I know he was mean to most of the people on this mountain, but he wasn't mean to me, Jack. I loved him."

He nodded. "Every person, mean or not, must have someone they try to love." Then he cocked his head. "Did you ever go against him?"

"I told him he had to leave Nellie or else I'd go home." A seed of truth. "He came back here to leave her."

"We'll never know." He took his hat off and ran his fingers through his curls.

"Know what?"

"Whether he was going to leave her or not. Whether he was going to come back to you. Whether he would have been there for little Lonnie." His words weren't mean, but they did hit a mark inside.

Lonnie ran full steam across the yard to Jack, pulling on his arm. "Come and play, please."

"Lonnie, Jack is busy with the garden."

"Come play." He tugged harder. "The man near the tree says you're good at playing."

"What did you say, Lonnie?" I looked around the yard.

Lonnie ignored me. "Come on. The man says you can teach me to throw a baseball."

Jack looked at me. "What are you talking about, little man? What tree?"

"He's right there by the tree with the hole. He's watching us. He's my friend."

"I don't see anything, Lonnie."

My son looked at me like I had three heads. "He's there, Mama." Then he pulled on Jack's hand. "Come on."

Jack gave a little smile. "Does this man have a name?"

Lonnie shrugged. "He won't tell me. He said it would upset Mama. He likes her a lot." Hobbs was talking to my baby.

Jack looked at me. "Well, I think we should go play some ball." The two of them walked off toward the barn. This quiet man was becoming part of my son's life whether I liked it or not.

The shadow leaned against the hollow tree with its arms folded over its chest, a position I'd seen more than one time. "Hobbs." The sweet scent of whiskey and cigarettes surrounded me. "Hobbs Pritchard," I whispered.

Forty

The summer months were hot during the day and wonderfully cool at night. I was content in my new life. The small garden near the kitchen was full of vegetables. The tomatoes were big and red. My favorite supper was a yellow squash sliced with fresh onion and cooked in butter. Next spring I planned on having a larger garden near the front of the house. The mountain had become my home, a safe friend. *"You'll stay here the rest of your life,"* it whispered in my ear.

Slowly Hobbs moved to the back of my mind. I went days without even remembering his face. Jack grew to be a silent friend, even though I knew nothing much about him.

"So, did you ever have a girl, Jack?" I said this in a matter-of-fact way. I didn't want him to get the wrong idea.

He paused ever so slightly with the maul over his head. "Yes I did. The problem is Hobbs had a liking for her too." He lowered the maul. "We both know how easy it was for him to get what he wanted. Patty loved me, but Hobbs wouldn't have no part of it. He followed her everywhere, making her life miserable. Her daddy threatened to call the sheriff up here."

"Why didn't you marry her?"

His face turned trouble. "She came up missing."

A prickle went down my neck. "What happened?"

"They found her two weeks later, dead." He took a deep breath as if the whole scene still lived in him. "I was the last to see her alive. I walked her home from a church social and left her at the top of her drive. I should have walked her to her door, but she shooed me off. Henry James could get upset if I was late coming home." He leaned on the maul. "By the time they found Patty, well, it wasn't pretty. Animals got ahold of her." He looked away.

"How horrible."

"Could have been a bear that killed her. They will do that if they're caught off guard. But I don't think so." Then he looked me dead in the eyes. "Sometimes you just know something but you don't have no proof."

A thickening in my breath made it hard to speak. "You think it was Hobbs?"

He looked at me with a wiry smile. "If I could have proved it, I would have killed him myself."

I looked at my feet. I didn't want to know this about Hobbs.

"Did you ever think, Rose, you didn't really know him at all?" Jack hoisted the maul over his head and split the log in half.

Searching for Hobbs's money became serious. I wanted Hobbs's treasure. Then I could live anywhere and do anything. So, one morning bright and early I decided to go snoop around the hayloft. I dug through the hay like some kind of fool.

"What are you doing?"

I jumped a foot. "Good Lord, Jack!" I fell back into the hay and laughed harder than I had in the months since I came.

"What you digging for, Rose?" He wore a half smile.

For a minute I thought of lying, but my new life deserved better than that. "I'm looking for money."

"Ah, Hobbs's loot. You must have been talking to our good ladies on the mountain. Before you came, I had to run kids off from up here all the time." He laughed.

"It's not funny. I want to find that money so I can do what I want for the rest of my life."

"You don't have to leave here, Rose. I'll help."

His words sat on my shoulders. We were quiet. I was afraid to look him in the eye for fear I'd see pity.

"Now, don't go getting mad cause I offered to help you."

This made me warm in a silly way. "I'm trying to make it on my own. You've done way too much."

"You let me decide that." He held out his hand. "Get out of the hay, Rose. You make too pretty of a picture there." His cheeks were pink.

I took his hand and allowed him to pull me out of the hay.

Forty-one

September, with the last of the summer heat, rolled in with no signs of cooler weather. I woke one morning in our quiet little bedroom. The sun was bright. The river churned, and even though I couldn't see the water the sound seemed to fill the space in my mind. I closed my eyes and melted into its music. What would happen if I followed the river up the mountain? I needed to clear my mind. I'd been spending too much time with Jack beginning most of my thoughts.

"Mama, what you doing?" Lonnie's curls fell over his forehead, making me think of Hobbs in the morning.

"We should get out of this house and go on an adventure."

Lonnie sat up and clapped his little hands together.

"Come on. We'll follow the river up the mountain. I hear there is a waterfall somewhere."

"Yes, yes." He jumped up and down on the bed.

The sweet sound of my own laughter surprised me. I was healing. I was moving past the tethered places inside me. "Breakfast first."

* * *

Lonnie ran ahead of me. The wind was blowing, keeping the heat of the day away. The red bee balm dotted the sides of the road. The bell tower of the church hung in the sky ahead, a simple, quiet plainness. The river was to our right. The banks were covered with smooth moss-coated rocks.

As Lonnie and I followed the path the river grew louder. Lonnie would run to the water and dip his feet in, throwing rocks. I stood still, allowing my many thoughts to disappear. We moved at our own speed. The trail forked. One snaked through a thicket of trees. The other was steep, climbing higher up the mountain. I was pulled to the lower path. Sunlight sprinkled the packed dirt. A cluster of monarch butterflies sat on the edge of a mud puddle. They appeared connected, their wings opening and closing at different times like a silent orchestra.

Lonnie smiled at me. Open and close. He ran right up to them but they continued to work their wings. Then I walked closer, and they burst into a graceful, gliding flight around our heads, like a magnificent dream. My heart opened with the dance they performed in the air. My boy whooped and stomped but still these beautiful creatures fluttered around in no hurry. One landed on my chest, opening and closing its wings, so delicate it looked like paper. Slowly each butterfly moved into the forest until only my guest was left.

"She likes you, Mama." Lonnie watched in awe.

"It seems so."

"Touch her, Mama," Lonnie begged.

I ran my finger close to her feet. She hopped on in one flutter. I held her close to his face, and just as I went to touch her wings, she took to the air. Twice around our heads and then into the woods. The sound of the water moved around us, a melody running through me. Life was right there waiting in the same place it had always been, waiting for me to catch up, to see my new way, new road, a butterfly in flight.

"Mama, look." Lonnie's words were almost lost to me.

The water tumbling over the sheer rock cliff stopped me in my tracks. *If there really was a God, He was right there in the water, the rocks, the butterflies, and the forest, not in a church with a bunch of people.* At the foot of the waterfall, before it took off as a river, was a pool surrounded by rocks. Then I noticed an opening behind the wall of water.

"Come on, Lonnie." I took his hand, and we picked our way over the rocks until we stood under the cool wet overhang. The waterfall fell in front of us. A cool spray hit our faces.

Lonnie smiled, holding out his hand, touching the water, splashing it back on us. "We're the waterfall."

And we were the water. I closed my eyes and allowed my wings to emerge, cracking open my tough skin. I slid off my shoes. The water was so cold I couldn't catch my breath. The wind blew through the tops of the trees and I shivered. Hobbs stood on the bank, watching. Everything went dark. Lights, truck lights, crashed through small trees, settling with a loud hissing sound into a good-size tree trunk. I wrapped my arms around my waist. The vision disappeared.

"What's wrong, Mama?"

"I'm fine, sweetie."

"You look scared."

"No." I stepped out of the water onto soft moss. "We'd better get home."

"I like it here."

"Yes, we'll have to come back," I said, shivering to the bone.

When we reached the road, I took the opposite direction. I saw the back end of a truck pointing down the embankment about fifty feet away. I'd have known that truck anywhere. "Hobbs."

"That's my friend's name. He said you knew him." Lonnie smiled.

I pulled the door open. Nothing; not even his smell. Then I saw a ring, a wide wedding band, on the floorboard. It was hers. She drove the truck up here. She killed him. I clinched the ring in my hand so tight it left a print on my palm. All our actions travel a road that comes home to us at some point. His fate had been in this delicate girl's hands. I didn't know how I knew all this, but I knew it. I put the ring in my dress pocket and cried the first tears since Hobbs died, a baptism in grief.

Forty-two

Jack was backing up his truck when he saw us walking into the yard. "You okay?"

"We went to the waterfall. We got to stand inside of it." Lonnie danced around. "Mama caught a butterfly."

Jack smiled. "Well, it sounds like you had a good walk."

I touched the ring in my pocket. "What do you know about Nellie, Jack?" The sadness still came in waves.

"Hey, Lonnie, go get us some of those cookies your mama made yesterday."

Lonnie smiled. "Okay." He ran off into the house.

"I should have told you about the truck."

"Aunt Ida told me when I first came here." I fought the tears away.

He rushed ahead of me. "We couldn't get the truck out. I tried."

"You probably were the only one." I slid the ring on and off my finger inside my pocket. "I know you hated Hobbs, but he was the father of my son and he was the man I loved. It hurts to see that truck hugging that tree, clean, except . . ."

He nodded. "Except what, Rose?"

I pulled the ring out of my pocket and shoved it at him. "This, this ring was on the floorboard of the truck."

His eyes got big but he wiped the look off his face quick as a flash. He took the ring in his fingers.

"Do you know who it belonged to?" I knew. It was a trinket from one of Hobbs's poker games with me sitting right there beside him. Before Christmas. He had promised to give it back to the man. He promised.

"I think so." At least Jack wasn't a liar.

"It belonged to Nellie. It had to belong to her because I was with Hobbs when he won it in a poker game. He gave it to her probably for Christmas." I spat the words at him as if he was the one who caused all the trouble.

"I'm sorry," he whispered.

"She was the one in the truck! She drove it off the road!" I was screaming the words.

He stepped forward. "You don't know that."

"I do! Why would the ring be in there? She would have kept it."

In my heart, I knew if I turned to the hollow tree, the shadow would be right there, waiting for Jack's response.

He shrugged.

Lonnie burst from the house with a plate of cookies, allowing a few to slide off onto the ground.

"Just forget it, Jack."

"Don't." The one word was a warning. "Let it go, Rose, before it swallows you up."

My anger served no purpose pointed at him. "Maybe."

"I know."

He had given thought to Nellie being the one. He'd been through it over and over in his mind.

Jack took a handful of cookies.

"Lord, you love sweets better than anyone." I tried to laugh.

"I got a big favor to ask of you." Jack spoke around the cookies.

"What?"

"The kids have got it in their heads to have a Halloween carnival. They want to have it at your house with a big bonfire, games, and food. They're afraid you'll say no."

How could I? I wanted to belong to that mountain so bad. "Sounds like fun. Of course we'll have a carnival. But why do they want to have it here?" But I knew even before he opened his mouth.

"They think it is haunted."

I laughed. "Well, they're probably right."

Jack smiled.

"You have to stay for supper. Lonnie will be disappointed if you don't. I'll send a plate home to Aunt Ida." She never left the house now.

"You don't have to twist my arm. I'll stay. We can talk about the games we'll have at the carnival."

When was the last time I played a game? I couldn't remember. "I always wanted to play bobbing for apples."

"Then we have to add that one to the list. How about I be the pumpkin carver? The whole mountain will come. Well, except for the good pastor. He refuses to have anything to do with the devil's night, as he calls it." Jack laughed.

Pastor Dobbins was a real stick-in-the-mud. Watching paint peel on the side of a house was more interesting than listening to his sermons. That's why I didn't bother to go to church; that and I didn't know what I thought of God. Oh, I believed, but He played favorites. This left the rest of us on our own to make the biggest messes out of our lives.

"We'll have a party, a Halloween carnival."

"Yes we will." Jack smiled. He was becoming a trusted friend.

Forty-three

Halloween came and the whole mountain was set for the big party. Right before sundown, I went into the woods to get some pretty leaves—orange was my favorite—to decorate the tables. A little girl stood on the other side of the creek. She wore only a slip, the frilly old kind that touched the ground.

"What are you doing out here in the woods dressed like that?"

"I come here all the time." She was pale, sickly looking.

"You need to come with me. I'll get you home."

She smiled. "I'd be happy if I could." In her hair were tiny rosebuds attached to pale pink ribbons. I thought it odd she'd have fresh roses in October.

"I know your mother would hate it if I left you here alone. What's your name?"

"Katleen Morgan. You're going to have a big party?"

"Yes. I think I met your brother, Tyler."

She giggled. "Couldn't be. You're going to make him mad."

"Your brother?" The child was talking in riddles.

"No." She stepped toward the creek and stopped. "A question will be answered and a riddle will form."

"Come with me so I can take you home." The girl must have been touched in the head.

"Can't."

"The weather is turning cold and it's almost dark. You can't walk around in what you're wearing, especially in the woods."

"I don't like the dark."

"Well, come over here and let's go. Be careful not to wet your slip."

"You'll make him mad."

"You're not making sense."

The little girl giggled again.

"Rose, are you out here?" Jack called from the edge of the woods.

I turned. "I'm here by the creek. I've found a little girl." I looked back but the girl was gone.

Jack made his way through the trees and undergrowth to where I stood. "Did you say you found a little girl?"

"Yes."

He looked around.

"I know. She was right there." I pointed across the creek. "I'm not crazy. She was wearing a slip."

"Folks say the whole mountain is haunted, and that it takes all sorts of forms." He smiled.

"I'm not joking. That child is going to freeze to death or get lost or eaten by a bear."

"I ain't heard of no one being eaten by a bear in a long time. Did she give you a name?"

"Katleen Morgan."

Jack thought a minute like he was going down a list of people living on the mountain. "Never heard of her, and I know pretty much everyone up here."

"Maybe she's visiting."

"Don't get many visitors and no one has company right now."

"I'm not crazy, and what happens up here that everyone doesn't know about?"

He laughed. "You ain't crazy. And not too much happens that doesn't get passed around. There's no little girl visiting right now." He took my arm and led me out of the woods. "We're going to have us some fun tonight, Miss Rose. Are you ready?"

I looked over my shoulder but no one was there.

Forty-four

The party began with a rush of kids trying to do everything at one time. The yard was full. The fire blazed, providing lots of light. We had paper lanterns and the half moon hung in the sky. Lonnie followed the big boys around like a shadow, but they didn't seem to mind. He was a strange little fellow who spent most of his time alone and happy about it. Maybe he wasn't different. Maybe all little boys liked playing by themselves. Jack stayed close and part of me liked this, even though I knew we were just friends.

I looked after the bobbing-for-apples game. The night air was nippy, but our guests didn't seem to care the water was ice-cold. My mind was on my frozen hands, which were so painful I almost didn't notice a ruckus coming from the woods. The noises blended in with the party's commotion, but the second burst of loud voices brought a sharp hush to the crowd, as if everyone noticed at once something wasn't right. My first thought went to Lonnie. I strained to see around the people.

"Look here! Look here!" It was one of the teenage boys. I moved toward him.

Jack touched my arm and nodded. "He's right there in the thick of the excitement. Them boys are stirring up some ghost story or another. It's Halloween."

My whole body turned fluid with relief. "What do they think they're doing? I was scared to death."

"Ah, they're boys. Don't have no brains to speak of." Jack smiled and moved toward the one talking so fast he was hard to understand. "What's all the excitement about, Charles Ray?"

"Jack, look what we found in the hollow tree, right inside that hole. Look. We ain't playing no gags. This is real."

"What's . . ." When Jack stopped speaking I moved to get a better look.

A bony face perched in Charles Ray's hand. What kind of joke was this?

"I want to hold it." Lonnie reached for the horrible treasure.

I crossed the distance between us. "You don't touch it, young man." I grabbed his arm.

A skull with big vacant eyes stared out at me. Hobbs's features formed over the bone. I looked to see if anyone noticed, but they didn't. When I looked back, it was into the empty eyes of the skull, but I knew what I had seen.

"Who you think it belongs to?" Oshie Connor shouted at Jack, as if the noise of the crowd still existed.

It was Hobbs, of course, the father of my son.

"It's my friend." Lonnie spoke as if his answer was normal. "He's always out there by the tree."

I choked on the thought.

Jack came closer but didn't touch the skull.

"So he's been here all along," Oshie almost whispered.

The crowd buzzed. My heart turned empty like a ghost ship on the water.

"We got something to talk about now." Jack spoke so everyone could hear.

Charles Ray placed the skull in Jack's hands.

"I'll call the sheriff tomorrow, but I don't know what to do with this until then." Jack looked at me.

"Put it back." The tree had been Hobbs's grave all this time. "It seems only right."

He nodded. "The sheriff will want to see it like it was before Charles Ray found it."

"Leave him be. Don't even bother the sheriff."

Jack studied me a minute. "We have to call him. It's the right thing to do."

Ah yes, the right thing to do. I'd almost forgotten. "I guess you're right."

"Let's tell ghost stories!" This came from one of the teenage girls.

The group rushed off; Lonnie pulled at me. "Let me go, Mama. I want to go with the big boys." I should have held him close to me so he could never be hurt, never find out who his scary friend really was. He was my heart.

Jack stood beside me as I released my grip on Lonnie and he ran off.

"So, that boy found Hobbs's skull. It doesn't seem real."

Jack gave me a worried sideways look. "Lonnie found the skull, Rose. Charles Ray took it from him."

"Granny's going to tell a ghost story. You got to come listen." Oshie ran up to Jack.

I crossed my arms over my chest. "Lonnie found it?"

"Ah, don't worry. He was exploring like the big boys." Jack made the whole incident sound normal, as if kids found skulls every day.

I went to sit around the fire while Jack went back to the tree. I wasn't so sure I wanted to hear a ghost story, but I didn't want to sit alone.

An old woman, all bent over with a cane, looking like a witch herself in the firelight, spoke to the crowd. "I got a good one. Sit down, little ones." All the kids clambered around the fire. The old woman sat to the left of the fire. Shadows from the flames gave her a spooky look. I moved closer to Lonnie, watching Jack still standing by the hollow tree. I wondered what he was thinking. Had he figured out it had to be Nellie who killed his stepbrother?

The old woman settled in a kitchen chair. "It all started when I was a bit of a thing. Long before Hobbs Pritchard's mama was brought to this mountain." She turned her gaze on me. I imagined she'd been a pretty woman when she was young. "The government had sent a newfangled teacher—Miss Palmer was her name—up here from Raleigh. That's the capital."

"We know," the kids yelled.

"She had it in her mind to save us kids from ourselves. You know, not many come up here and take to Black Mountain's ways. Most of the time she walked around with a headache she swore we caused. But she did learn us about Halloween."

The kids, now quiet, listened like they were in another world.

"She'd tell us the darndest stories about kids in Raleigh dressed up in costumes, going door to door promising good luck for treats and bad luck for empty hands. This sounded like heaven to us kids up here on Black Mountain. In those days, we had no time for foolishness of any sort. I purely loved a party, and I told my best friend, Mary, who thought we ought to have us one of those nights for our own.

"So Mary being who she was, much older than her ten

years, took herself right up to Miss Palmer and asked if we could have a party like that. I always admired Mary for the way she stood up for us to the grown-ups. Miss Palmer wasn't sure it would work here on the mountain since we were so spread out, and then she got an idea.

"She guessed we ought to have a big get-together with games, treats, and ghost stories like this." The old woman turned her smile of perfect teeth on the group.

"Of course, this mountain has always been full of ghosts. We all know it. It breathes like any human here. That's why we don't much get scared when we come across something odd. But, back then, I'm ashamed to say I was right scared of ghosts, but worst of all I was scared of the dark. I was scared of this old mountain."

"Oh, that can't be," a tall boy yelled from the back.

"It is, son. When my granny told ghost stories, I always listened and never was a bit worried until I got into bed and the creeps crawled right in with me. Many a night I slept with the covers over my head even in the one-hundred-degree heat.

"Anyway, it was my luck that Jim—he was my big brother— hated being stuck with me and ran off early to the big party. I was left with the supper dishes. Mama was down in her back, and Daddy, well, he had done drank himself into a dither, passing out on the floor. My granny wasn't much on walking, especially in the dark with her bad eyes, so I was left on my own.

"The wind had picked up some, and I tried not to put too much thought into the sweater I left hanging on the rocker at home. Mama had made me a right nice scarecrow costume, but I was losing straw with every step. The sun had set and the road got darker and darker. The harvest moon hung on the edge of the trees and lit my way with smoky gray light. I sure hated that dark. I moved one foot in front of the other up that shadowy road, purely hating Jim for leaving me behind. Then I saw the old bend in the road." She looked out at the kids. "You know the one with all those thick trees. It's sure a nice place to go through when the hot sun is out, but it's another story when it's dark. I knew by looking at those thick trees that they were going to block out that moon. I thought on ways to go around, but you know there ain't another way since there's a swampy place all around it." The kids all nodded together.

"That's when I heard a giggle. I swung around and there stood a girl my age. She was right pretty with long dark curly hair. Fresh rosebuds hung from pink ribbons. I found that a bit strange for October, but I'd seen Granny's roses bloom as late as November when it was warm. The girl wore a long old-fashioned slip like my granny would have worn in her younger days."

I took a deep breath. This sounded like the girl I saw in the woods.

"I asked that girl her name." Granny looked out at all the kids. "She said her name was Katleen. Katleen Morgan."

"That's my great-grandmother," one of the boys yelled.

A girl nearby laughed. "Tyler, you're kin to everyone on this mountain."

"I told her she had a right nice costume, better than mine. I was an envious little girl at the time. Katleen giggled and told me they was her burying clothes. I wasn't the smartest child either cause I thought she was making it all up to scare me, but I was so relieved to have company, I would have walked with the devil himself had he been there. I asked her if she was on the way to the party, but she only shook her head. She told me how she dearly loved parties." Granny sipped her apple cider. "When we walked into the shelter of them trees, the first thing I noticed was Katleen's eyes. They was the color of cornflowers and showed up right nice in the dark. She told me how she used to be afraid of the dark.

"I asked her why she wasn't scared no more. Her answer was as simple: because there wasn't nothing to be afraid of. By this time, I was thinking that girl was pretty stupid. I sure didn't confess to my fear, cause you see, I was proud.

"She went on and told me how I should put no store in the darkness. Whatever could get me in the dark could sure enough get me in the day. We walked on.

"Now, this is the important part and it's exactly why I have to differ with the part of the Bible where it says pride cometh before a fall. She offered me her hand, but I couldn't get past my pride. I told her I wasn't no baby. She took her a big deep sigh like she was right disappointed.

"I pointed to lights ahead and told her we had to cross the branch and we'd be there. She stopped dead in her tracks. I yelled at her to come on, but she hung back as I crossed that old bridge. Now I was feeling like the boss. When I turned back to warn her I was leaving her behind, she was gone, vanished.

"You can imagine how good I felt when I got to that party. I felt even better after I whopped my brother up the side of his head. And I guess that's all." Granny held her hands out in front of her.

"It can't be!" the kids yelled.

"Well, I guess I left out one little part."

"Tell us!" Even I yelled with the kids that time. Jack stood behind me now, touching my shoulder like something had changed.

"When I got home that night my granny was rocking in her chair by the fire. Now, I couldn't get the whole thing out of my head, so I told her that I'd seen some strange girl on the road. She asked me if anyone at the party knew of her. I told her she turned back when we got to the bridge.

"Granny's face got still like she always did when she was mad at Jim and wanted to smack him. She asked if that girl had a name. I told her.

"She leaned way back in her chair and grabbed her heart. She told me what I'd seen weren't human, but a haint. It seems haints can't cross water. Then she asked me the strangest thing. She asked me if the haint touched me. I told her no. She said had Katleen Morgan touched me, I would have been the next soul to die. I was glad I never touched her.

"It seems Katleen Morgan had left out from a friend's house after dark one night a long time before—it was right around Halloween—and she got all twisted up. She was scared of the dark. It broke my granny's heart when they found Katleen with her lips purple. It was the first dead person my granny ever laid eyes on. Now me, I learned something from that night."

"What did you learn?" the kids yelled.

"I learned never, ever walk alone on these old roads after dark, cause I'd lived my own Halloween story, and I didn't care a bit about testing my luck again. So if you see Miss Katleen, she's here for a fear that you got."

The kids roared. Jack squeezed my shoulder.

"Do you remember the little girl I saw this afternoon?"

He nodded. "What is your fear, Rose?" I knew his question was more than plain joking. It was about much more than that.

Forty-five

Something at the party turned me around when it came to Jack. If possible I watched him closer than before. He had this way of walking as if his every action had a true purpose. I began to think about his past, about him. Could he really be so good?

"What did you think when your mama brought you up to Black Mountain so she could get married?" I had cooked a big dinner of beef stew and homemade bread.

He held a piece of the bread in his hand, butter dripping down his knuckles. After a long breath, he spoke in his quiet manner. "I probably took to the situation as much as Hobbs did. I just went about my dislikes in a whole other way than him." He waited to see if that was enough information or if I'd push for more. The look on my face must have told him to keep going. "I thought Mama had lost her mind marrying a man from Black Mountain without hardly knowing him. But she insisted it wasn't about loving someone. She didn't have no time for love. Instead, she saw it as a way to give me a better life, a instant family. She was plain silly thinking both of Henry James's kids would welcome me into the family." He looked over at me and took a big bite of bread, chewing slowly.

"So how did she die?"

"The doctor said natural causes, probably her heart. And I always accepted that right along with Henry James and AzLeigh, but then you found that necklace. See, Henry James put that burying box in the casket. I watched him. The necklace was a gift from me and AzLeigh for her birthday. He said it was the best gift he'd ever seen given. I knew him too well. He didn't take that necklace out. That leaves AzLeigh or Hobbs. No way AzLeigh would have gone near a dead body in those days." He leveled his stare right on me as if I weren't the real person sitting in front of him. "So it could only have been Hobbs."

A flicker of light flashed in my mind.

Jack nodded. "And Hobbs knew the necklace was worthless. So why would a boy who hated his stepmother as bad as Hobbs hated his take her necklace?" Jack sat up straight. "When Hobbs was younger, he used to take me hunting. I never much wanted to go but Mama made me. She said it would be good and that Hobbs was making a effort. That's before she figured him for who he was. One time he nailed a doe. Killed her in one clean shot. When we got to the deer, he took out his hunting knife and sliced off the doe's ear. He stuck it in the pocket of his jacket. Then he looked at me and said, 'I always take me a souvenir when I hit my target.' Those words have been playing themselves through my mind over and over since I saw the necklace." He watched for my reaction. "Somehow I don't think the necklace was in that drawer the whole time. Did you find anything else that went with it?"

My head was filled with a roaring sound, but I knew this was more than just a question. It was a test. "I found a diary that belonged to Nellie. It wasn't nothing special. I thought it was old. It looked too old for her to own it. But it only talked about Hobbs being Hobbs. I burned it because I just couldn't have any part of Nellie around me."

He slapped the table, making me jump. "I knew it. One day I surprised Nellie while she was exploring the attic. I could tell by her face she was lying when she told me nothing important was there. She was looking at Hobbs's mama's books. I recognized them. Of course she wouldn't have known the necklace was Mama's." He shivered like someone was walking over his grave. "Or maybe she did. Sometimes I wondered if Nellie wasn't somebody different than I knew." The curl to each word made me flinch. I never wanted to be on the receiving end of this tone.

"I should have given you the diary. I'm sorry."

"Unless she wrote in there that she killed Hobbs, the book wouldn't have done anyone no good."

I didn't tell him about the last paragraph. I couldn't. He reached out and touched my hand. "You are a real good person, Rose Gardner." His fingers were warm on my skin. A change floated in the window and sat down at the table with us. While I still hurt for Hobbs, the stirring in my chest was caused by this man sitting across from me. And I wasn't so sure I liked it.

"I hope Hobbs never killed anyone." The words sat in front of him.

"He killed, Rose. He killed. I wish I could tell you something different, something sweet and nice that you could rest in, but Hobbs Pritchard killed at least one man. I know this because I was there. And maybe he killed more than that. No way of knowing for sure." The words were soft but full of hidden anger.

"I'm sorry."

He nodded. "I'm sorry too."

I finally understood who Hobbs could be.

Someone chopped Hobbs's head off and stuffed it in a tree. The action was filled with angry violence, the kind that could only be committed by someone who both loved and hated him. The sheriff came up the mountain on Monday afternoon. Everything about him was slow. He huffed and puffed as he studied the skull in his hands. "It's human, all right." A wrinkle formed on his forehead. "It's the real thing." He flicked his thumbnail over the smooth bony surface as if he handled human remains every day.

"It probably belonged to Hobbs."

The sheriff kind of smiled. "Yeah, I figured it might. Unless someone else up here has come up missing."

"Just Nellie, but you knew about her."

He nodded. "I remember it well. Caused quite a stir."

"Who do you think killed Hobbs?" Jack took off his hat and ran his fingers through his hair. I was learning he did this when he was deep in thought.

The sheriff turned the skull upside down. "Ain't no telling who put an end to this man's life. He had enemies all over. I heard that he had a man out of Atlanta looking for him."

Atlanta. Hobbs had men from as far away as Vicksburg, Mississippi, looking for him, but I kept my mouth shut. What good would speaking out do? I knew who killed him.

"His wife disappeared about the time he did, right?" The sheriff looked at Jack, but I could have sworn he was watching me out of the corner of his eye.

"Folks searched a good bit for her but didn't find nothing."

The sheriff held the skull out to Jack.

"Yep, nothing was ever found." Jack's voice was a touch sad, or maybe just tired.

"Well, if his wife killed him, she was damn good at what she did. That truck of his had nothing in it."

For a second Jack was still and then he stuck his hand in his pocket and pulled out the wedding band. "This was found in the truck a week or so ago." He looked at me and back at the sheriff. "I know for a fact it belonged to Nellie."

The sheriff looked at it. "Looks like a man's ring to me."

Jack shrugged his shoulders. "Hobbs was just like that. He'd win something in a card game and pass it off as a gift."

The sheriff laughed. "No wonder she killed him."

"If she killed him, it was because no one would help her." Jack didn't look at me.

The sheriff tilted his head to the side. "What you getting at?"

"He beat her bad. I didn't know that, but it seemed everybody else on this mountain knew. No one would help her cause they was all afraid." His look was cool.

"Sounds like self-defense to me. But you know a sheriff can't do a whole lot about a husband beating on his wife. That's a private affair. It would never have held up in a court." He held his hands out. "She did herself and the whole mountain a favor by putting a end to him. I'd just like to know how she did it. How in the world did she cut his head off, Jack? Pritchard would never have stood by and let that happen to him."

"Maybe he was drunk." Jack said this in his quiet manner.

"Yep, but then that is plain-out premeditated cold blood."

"You're right about that." Jack looked at me.

"Well, as far as I'm concerned the case is closed. We'll never know and I ain't going searching for a woman who may or may not be dead." He nodded at the skull. "Put him to rest."

Could Hobbs rest? I really doubted it.

That night after Lonnie was asleep, I lit a lantern and went to the hollow tree. Now was the time to close what had been between us.

There wasn't a star shining. The air was crisp and the wind

still. "Hobbs?" My voice echoed off the forest. Only the river answered. "I came out here to tell you to leave Lonnie and me alone. It's over. I'm better. I can see what you did to Nellie. I know you killed Jack's mother. Jack says you killed another man. I think you had something to do with Jack's girlfriend dying so long ago. Remember, I'm smart. I know you. I don't blame you for my pain, because I didn't listen. You told me once you were bad."

A cold wind popped a branch in the tree.

"I'm a grown woman now. I know you took advantage of me that day I met you. Can you hear me?" I listened. "Well, that's all I have to say. I'm starting a new life. I think I might really like your stepbrother."

Again the cold wind whipped the tops of the trees.

"I know you don't like it, but honestly it doesn't matter what you think. She killed you, Hobbs, because you beat her so bad. I bet you didn't see that one coming. That little girl you picked over me, the one you had no intentions of ever leaving, killed you. She was smarter than me. Just leave Lonnie alone. Let him have the life you never had. I'm going now." I walked toward the house but turned back for one last look. There stood the shadow. "I brought you back to Asheville. My spell brought you back. Bet you didn't know that either. You probably never would have come back looking for me if not for that hoodoo spell." I walked back to the house without looking at the tree again. Let him stand out there for eternity. I was finally finished.

Forty-six

From that day forward I found it easy to care for Jack. He was plain and would always lead a quiet life, but my idea of excitement had changed. We ate supper together most nights, and he put Lonnie to bed with a story. We'd sit and talk for the longest. I told him all about me, everything, even the hoodoo part. He never laughed when I pulled out my book and bottles.

"You'll have to compete with Amanda if you keep practicing."

"Isn't she Pastor Dobbins's maid?"

Jack grinned. "Yep."

Hoodoo had served its purpose and now I was finished. A person had no real control over the powers of magic.

Jack told me about how he was tied to the mountain out of love and respect; how it would always be his home; how he thought he would live out his life in a quiet way.

Lonnie told Jack one night that he heard music in his head all the time. So Jack brought him a guitar. My little boy picked it up and began strumming it like he'd been playing it his whole life. After that he carried his guitar, nearly as big as him, around with him everywhere. I loved Jack for giving him something of his own, a way to make him feel special. Things were good with the three of us. It was fine with me if life stayed just like it was forever. But sometimes I caught Jack studying my face. I couldn't tell what he was thinking.

Then one day Jack came into the kitchen, took off his hat, and looked at the floor as if there was a piece of lead on his shoulders. "Could you have a seat, Rose?"

I had let my guard down and begun to enjoy my days. That was the stupidest thing I could have done. My throat closed. I sat in one of the kitchen chairs.

"I got to talk to you."

"What's happened?" I stilled my voice. "You're scaring me, Jack."

He looked startled. "Oh, I didn't mean . . . Well, you see, Rose, I was thinking and . . ."

My head roared. He was going to ask me to leave. How had I relaxed into him?

"Well, would you think about being my wife?" He even squatted down on one knee in front of me. "We've been spending so much time together and I think you feel the same way I do. I don't know if it's love but I like being with you. Lonnie could take my last name too, if that's okay."

He wanted me to marry him. Jack Allen wanted me to marry him.

He pulled something out of his pocket. "Here, this was Mama's. If it's big, I'm sorry. She wasn't a little woman. Maybe we can take it down to Asheville and have it made smaller."

Did I love him? I knew what I felt wasn't like my feelings for Hobbs, but that wasn't such a bad thing. Maybe my love for Jack was quiet, steady, calm like him.

"Will you marry me, Rose?"

I looked into his green eyes and lost my mind. "Yes, Jack, I will."

He kissed me for the first time; finally I had my fairy-tale ending.

We married on Christmas Eve at the foot of the waterfall. A light snow fell. I wore a white lace dress the women of the mountain made for me. Mama even came up to the wedding. She brought the judge to perform the ceremony. I was the happiest woman in the world.

I never told Jack what the last paragraph of Nellie's diary said. What was the point? The sheriff had closed the case. No one was looking for her. For all I knew she was dead somewhere. But there were times way later I wished I had told Jack the whole story, that I wished he had hunted Nellie until he found her and brought her back to the sheriff. Had she paid for her actions, my life would have been a happily-ever-after.

That spring the government urged us to plant victory gardens. America was at war with Japan and Germany. Jack insisted on enlisting in the army. I won't lie, I was scared. He didn't have to be a hero for the country. He kept our little family safe. We needed him. How could he leave? But for him it was about being an honorable man with a sense of responsibility. And wasn't that why I married him?

I turned a larger plot of ground out front. The thought of digging up the rest of Hobbs's bones somewhere went through my mind, but I only laughed at myself. And then the hoe hit a hard object. I knelt down and saw the sun reflect off of something. It couldn't be a bone. A canning jar completely intact was half out of the ground. Goose bumps formed on my arms. I brushed the dirt away. Inside was more money than I'd ever seen. Hobbs's treasure.

"Jack! Jack!"

He came running from the barn and stopped. "What's wrong?"

I held up the jar.

His eyes lit up. "Lordy be, the treasure."

"What do we do with it?" The money could make a lot of difference to the people on the mountain.

"I think we got to spread our good fortune around." He was thinking the same as I was.

I laughed and looked at the woods. A man stood there. He wore a cap and round spectacles. He watched me with a steady stare.

"I think we should go buy you a new dress."

I looked at him. "A new dress sounds nice."

Jack smiled. "You'll be okay while I'm gone to war."

I buried my face in his chest. "I want you to be okay."

"I will. I'll come home. I promise."

The man vanished. I wish I could say I gave him a lot of thought, but the truth was I was praying that Jack wouldn't die. I prayed that he wouldn't even have to go.

Years later I would think of that man staring at me, but by then it would be too late. Not that I could have changed anything that happened. Some things are out of our hands.

Part Five

Iona Harbor

Forty-seven

My mama told me the same bedtime story each night all through my childhood. She told it with such detail I was sure Hobbs and Nellie Pritchard were real people. I wished they were part of my boring family's history. But they were just characters in a tale spun to keep me in line, to show me the correct path to take in life. They were my moral compass.

Like all mamas, mine had her ways that drove me nearly crazy. And like all daughters, I fought every suggestion she gave me. I wanted to stand on my own two feet without her as a crutch. I was afraid if I stayed too close and became too comfortable, I would evaporate. This made for a testy relationship, to say the least. It would take me years before I came to understand that every thought that came out of my head had rolled downhill from something she tried to instill in me. For better or worse.

Daddy was the pastor of the First Episcopal Church of Darien just like Grandpa was before him. How boring was that? We were a regular happy family without any secrets to speak of. We lived in a big house by the marshes, and beyond that was the ocean. Growing up I never thought much about having the smell of salt in my hair all the time or much less a gator scooting across our backyard, waving his tail side to side. Darien, Georgia, was home.

Mama was everything a pastor's wife was supposed to be. She even wrote little articles for the newspaper. People liked reading her work because it was like a big soft feather pillow.

I can't say how many women would ask, "Don't you want to be just like your mama when you grow up?"

God help me, but that was the last thing I wanted.

We lived in the house that Daddy grew up in. Maw Maw lived with us and had been there since before I was born. I loved Maw Maw the best. I had to be careful not to let Grandma Harbor know this. She would have been heartbroken. Of course everything made her heartbroken since Grandpa died of a heart attack the year I was thirteen. I loved Maw Maw because she was the best ghost-story teller in the world, and she could even read tea leaves. She read them for me all the time. *Iona, you'll go through a rough patch but you'll be a fine young woman.* This was a lot more fun than Daddy's God with His stern face, reminding me of all the trespasses I made. If Daddy had known I questioned God's existence, he would have thrown a fit, and this man never threw fits. I couldn't see where Mama believed any better than I did. Something deep inside told me my mama didn't hold a candle to the Annie Harbor from the past. Every once in a while she'd slip up and start telling me a story from her life, catch herself—at the best part—and stop in midsentence, laughing it off as if she were giving me some important tip before I was ready. I hungered after those things she didn't want me to learn. Maybe it was part of being a teenager and wishing for a more mysterious life that kept me hounding Mama for the truth. Maybe there were no secrets in our family, but I had a feeling the truths were ten times better than anything I could cook up myself.

I loved music from an early age. Where this love came from was beyond me. Mama didn't listen to the radio. Daddy never sang anything but gospel. He was a straitlaced pastor, never breaking the rules. The only time I saw him angry was the day my two-week-old baby brother died. I was four. Grandma Harbor told me she thought he would lose his calling. He was so wild-eyed with grief she worried he might walk a straight line out of Darien and never look back. Instead, he took up the harmonica and played the most mournful songs. By the time Mama came out of the attic where she closed herself off for a week, he had thrown it away and was carrying his Bible again. That was the extent of the musical inclination in our house.

So I, Iona Harbor, became a treasure floating between Mama and Daddy. My parents loved me way more than they should—too much love smothers the daylights out of a girl—and the older I got the more they held on. Mama was worse than Daddy. She watched my every move.

Each girl has defining moments in her life. Mine was a little more defined than most teenagers'. The summer of 1955 started off like any other school break. All the days ran together. It was a Monday morning in late June and already it was hotter than a late August afternoon. I ran my fingers across an imaginary keyboard, eyes closed; music played in my mind, beautiful and sweet, taking me to a place where people applauded my effort. I hummed into the air, keying the magic notes on the old wooden table where my family ate each meal.

"Iona! Are you daydreaming again?"

My musical notes banged to a sudden stop, sour. "I'm thinking, Mama." True to some degree.

"You think way too much. All those silly daydreams eating

away at time you could be using for better things." Mama cracked eggs into a cast-iron frying pan.

"I learned so much from Miss Stewart. I know if I had my own piano, I could prove to you how good I am." I faced Mama eye to eye. At the age of fifteen years, three months, and twenty days, I was as tall as many of the boys my age. Tall like Uncle Charles, Daddy's brother that died in World War II. Because Daddy had flat feet, he never went. So Uncle Charles became the hero of his family, or so Grandma Harbor believed. That must have been tough for Daddy.

"The only thing in your head is fluff, cotton candy fluff. It will bring you to no good, Iona. You have to trust me on this. I know." Mama was so pretty and delicate it almost fooled me into listening to her. I would have given anything to have her looks, but I had her father's height and bone structure. Jees, I hated that she couldn't just love me without improving my every move. She handed me a basket. "Go gather some apples for a pie tonight while I cook breakfast. That'll be nice. Don't you think?" Mama had this little apple tree Daddy planted out back when they first met. It was a June apple tree with apples smaller and sweeter than the fall fruit. Mama said it made her think of home. Somewhere in the mountains. But neither Mama or Maw Maw gave an exact location.

"Why can't you just leave me alone?" I screamed at the blue sky when I was well out of hearing range. Some girls my age were already pinned and planning their weddings after graduation. The apple tree reminded me of an old twisted woman. The fruit was pinkish red. People were a lot like apples, each shaped similar, but different at the same time, marked with distinguishing traits. One day I would prove to Mama how talented I was. She thought she could plan my whole life. I was leaving Darien for college, where I would study music. She wouldn't stop me.

Forty-eight

Those long summer days I would walk the town that was set up in little squares like a small version of Savannah, located north of us. The hot wind wrapped me up in my thoughts, and I walked and walked. The sea birds would dip in and out of the Altamaha River. I would stop to watch the shrimp boats work their way to the dock with a day's catch. This was the part I loved about Darien. There was no doubt the place was in my bones. One afternoon the music in my head turned real, spilling through the wind, mingling with the birdcalls. I followed the tune to Mrs. Walters's house. It was well known for its ghost, who was a woman who killed herself. The house was painted the brightest blue and sat right in the curve of the river. Maw Maw thought it was the tackiest house in Darien and should be bulldozed down. The house was supposed to be empty. The owner, Mrs. Walters, had moved to Atlanta to live with her brother. Through one of the large windows, I saw a bare-chested man playing a baby grand piano. His dark horn-rimmed glasses made him handsome in an intelligent sort of way. He had to be the new music teacher. Darien High School had prided itself on adding music to the school schedule in the coming fall. I, for one, was beside myself. Looking at this man pouring music across the marsh reminded me how far I had to go. I stood there eavesdropping in plain view. He kept playing in his own world, and I so envied that place. Finally I left and headed home.

Mama worked the dough for biscuits at her wooden chopping-block table Daddy built. Her biscuits had to be the best in Georgia.

I washed the potatoes. "Do you want me to peel all of these?"

"I can do it, honey." Maw Maw's hands were gnarled with arthritis.

"I'm okay, but thanks."

"You sit and relax." When Mama smiled at Maw Maw it was real, not fake like the smile she pasted on her face for church or Grandma Harbor. The two of them had some special silent language that drew them closer together. I couldn't remember Mama ever being grouchy with Maw Maw like she was with Daddy and me. Mama wasn't always trying to boss Maw Maw around like she did us.

"Why are we making so much food?" I had five pounds of potatoes.

"We have company coming."

"Who?" Probably some boring church officer.

"Your father hasn't seen fit to inform me who his guest might be." Mama frowned as she cut out biscuits.

Daddy brought guests for supper like people brought home stray animals.

My stomach fluttered for no reason and the air crackled

with unexplained excitement like heat lightning chasing across the ocean sky at night.

"Your mama fusses, but she was just as bad when she was a young girl. I never knew who she might bring home. She loved helping people. After her daddy died not one chair at our table was empty. She spent three years working in a soup kitchen during the Depression. That was a hard place, wasn't it, Annie?"

Wouldn't you know it? Mama the perfect teenager.

"I don't want to talk about that." Mama gave Maw Maw the eye.

I tried to keep from making a sound, hoping they'd forgotten me.

"I don't know why. I'd be proud of that work if it was me." Maw Maw clicked her tongue.

Mama looked at me.

"Did you wear your white gloves, Mama?" I didn't dare look back.

"Leave the rest of the potatoes and go upstairs and dress. I don't want shorts at the dinner table tonight."

I shrugged and left the pile of potatoes.

When Mama thought I was out of hearing, she puffed loud. "You've got to be careful of what you say. Iona doesn't need those old memories to think about. You could slip."

"I can't help things went like they went." Maw Maw's voice was quiet but stern.

"I live with it every day of my life. I want better for Iona."

Now there was a big secret wrapped tight in Mama's warning. I couldn't imagine it was anything too bad. She ran our family like a well-oiled machine. Daddy always shot me a smile when Mama wasn't looking, like she wasn't our boss at all, but I knew neither of us could stand up to her.

*   *   *

Daddy's car pulled into the drive forty-five minutes later. I was
hanging out my bedroom window, fiddling with my transistor
radio—a Christmas present designed to make me forget my
longed-for piano and lessons. By holding the radio north, I
caught snatches of a melody from a station in Savannah. On a
clear night I could pick up WQXI in Atlanta. Static rattled from
the single speaker and then a whisper of Elvis came through.
Daddy emerged from the car followed by . . . were my eyes
fooling me? The music teacher. I switched off the radio and
pulled myself back into my bedroom. Thank goodness he hadn't
seen me.

I pulled on my pink sundress with the full skirt and
buckled my white strap sandals—the ones Mama insisted were
too old for me. Gosh, I was almost sixteen, a woman, but she
didn't see me that way.

The music teacher sat at the table laughing at something
Daddy said; even Mama was smiling. The mantel clock struck
six, and everyone looked at me poised on the back stairs. Heavy
humid air wafted in the windows; little curls escaped my
ponytail.

"Iona, we've been waiting on you." Mama raised her eye-
brows at my clothes. "Now, this one here only thinks about
music, music, music. I never know what to do with her. She's
had some piano lessons and the talent is there, but I want her
to concentrate on something practical."

Daddy cleared his throat as I pulled out my chair wishing I
could die on the spot. "Let's not plan Iona's life here at the
table, Annie." He winked at me. "You look nice, pumpkin. This
is your new music teacher, in case you haven't figured that out
by now." He chuckled.

I dearly loved my daddy best of all, but sometimes I could
have shoved a shoe in his mouth. Pumpkin? Did I look like
a pumpkin?

"This is Mr. Mackey." Mama's tone was short, hurt.

The music teacher held out his hand. "Call me JT. My father is called Mr. Mackey. So you love music?" His voice reminded me of the notes running in my head.

"Yes sir."

He made a little frown. "What kind of music do you like?"

I was expected to say gospel. "I love music that punches me right in the stomach, that makes me want to move. Sometimes the song is rock, sometimes country. I even love some of the old hymns at church." I added the last part for Daddy.

Mama passed the mashed potatoes to Mr. Mackey. "See, I told you she can't think straight when it comes to music. Songs don't punch you in the stomach, Iona." But I saw the truth in Mama's expression. She knew exactly what I was describing.

"I know what your daughter is talking about. I love all kinds of music." Mr. Mackey gave Mama a wide smile. "But some songs are special. The melody takes you away from where you are and what you're doing."

"I think music is God's art," Daddy added.

"Yes." Mr. Mackey winked at me as if we had some sort of secret.

"Well, I stick to the good old church songs." Maw Maw spoke around a stiff smile. If I didn't know her better, I would have thought she was being short with Mr. Mackey.

Mr. Mackey turned a beautiful clear smile on Maw Maw, but she didn't thaw one bit. So he looked over at me. "Iona, I hope you're going to take my class this fall."

"Don't worry. I wouldn't miss it."

Mama frowned.

"I've been waiting for a real music class all my life. I'll be a junior, which gives me a better chance to make it in." I gave him my sweetest smile. Something shifted in the air but no one seemed to notice but me.

"Oh, I'll make sure you get into my class." We stared at each other as if no one was around.

Mama cleared her throat. She wanted me to find a nice boy who would shrimp the rest of his life. That way I could live close by. God.

"I'll tell you what, come around at two tomorrow. We'll get a head start on our lessons. I only work with serious musicians."

My body tingled all over.

He turned his charm on Mama as if he knew she was the boss, the one who would decide for me. "Of course you would have to approve, Mrs. Harbor. I wouldn't want to go against your plans for Iona."

I held my breath.

Mama busied herself covering the breadbasket like a storekeeper closing up shop. "Well." She didn't look up. "I don't approve of Iona wasting time."

"She has a lot of work here," Maw Maw chimed in.

I looked at her with utter surprise. She was always on my side.

"Please, Mama. I'll finish the sewing for the ladies' circle. I promise not to get behind."

Mama was quiet. I counted to ten in my head.

"I guess this once, since you'll be taking music in school, but you have to keep up with the sewing." Mama eyed me across the table.

Daddy let out a breath.

Maw Maw frowned at me, and I saw where Mama got her attitude.

"Thank you, Mama." I moved around the table and hugged her neck. Her shoulders turned rigid.

"Don't disappoint me."

"I promise."

Later after Mr. Mackey left, I heard Maw Maw talking to Mama in the kitchen. "I'm telling you I got the same feeling. He's just like him."

"What do you mean?" Mama sounded perplexed.

"I bet if I had my tea leaves, I could show you he's no good."

Mama looked up and saw me standing on the stairs. "Iona, are you still downstairs?"

"I just wanted to thank you for letting me have this extra time for music. It means a whole lot." I smiled my best gooddaughter smile.

Mama clicked her tongue. "You best be careful."

I left the two women in my life sitting at the table in our kitchen. Nothing could spoil this chance. Nothing.

Forty-nine

The next afternoon couldn't get here fast enough. I barely slept for thinking of those ivory keys under my fingers. Finally someone would take me seriously. The same music I heard the day before led me right back to the bright-blue house, where I rang the old-fashioned pull bell mounted to the doorjamb. The melody came to a gradual stop, trailing into the air as if sad to end, clinging to objects in protest. I looked away from the glass panel next to the door so as not to appear rude.

"Hello." Mr. Mackey wore faded jeans, a pale-blue oxford shirt opened up the front, and no shoes. He buttoned his shirt. "I'm glad you made it, Iona. I need a break."

"What were you playing?"

He ushered me into the house with a sweep of his hand. "A piece I'm writing."

"You're a composer too?"

He laughed. "I teach to support my music habit. The bills have to be paid." He shrugged. "My father doesn't think much of my music or my teaching." His smile was knowing.

"You're nothing like the teachers I've known."

"Really? Why am I so different?"

"Most teachers are stuffy and frown all the time. They're a million years old and would make the class learn classical music, not the new stuff." I looked around the big room. "And they're always Republicans." His world held a baby grand piano in the middle of the high-ceilinged room. Sheet music with penciled notes was scattered around the floor, and an empty bowl with the remains of his lunch sat on a short side table beside the bench. A whole wall was dedicated to bookshelves, where his portable record player sat. A large leather sofa took up the floor space at the far end of the room, under the tall window that looked out on the marsh.

"Don't knock the classics."

"A lady killed herself here."

He nodded. "I know. I saw her in the bedroom upstairs. I think that must have been the place she hung herself."

I watched to see if he was pulling my leg but he seemed serious enough. "This is beautiful." I touched the shiny wood of the piano.

Mr. Mackey sat on the bench. "So, Iona, shall we find out what you're made of? You say you hear music in your head. Prove it to me." He raised a dark eyebrow.

My breath came quick. God, what had I gotten myself into?

He ran his fingers over the keys. "It's scary the first time you stare your dream square in the face. But there are two choices you can make: one, walk over here and show me what you can do, or two, you walk out the door and forget music. It's one of those moments, Iona." A tune worked around the room. "Come and try to make the notes in your head come alive." He motioned to the keys.

"I haven't played in a while, but I . . ." I looked at my feet.

"I drew a keyboard on a piece of cardboard box. I practice my scales on this every night, and I sneak to the church to play there."

He looked solemn. "Shame on a mother who makes a girl use a paper keyboard. What passion you have, little girl." He patted the bench. "Either you try or you become the daughter your mother wants."

I sat down.

He leaned in close. "Play, Iona," he whispered.

My fingers worked like rusty hinges on an unused gate.

"Go to that place in your head where the music lives. Trust yourself."

I closed my eyes as Mr. Mackey's warm breath touched my cheek and ear. The hot wind blew through the windows. The music spread through my body and released into my fingers, across the keys; a sour note here, a bad chord there, but beauty and peace worked into my soul. Mr. Mackey joined me with his own accompaniment, covering my bad places, creating a new song, refining me, a little wild, but not just my song, ours. The music left me and entered him while I watched, my hands shaking in my lap. He played in another world; I rode the magic carpet his notes wove. I loved him. The kind of love that comes out of nowhere and hits a girl in the gut. A jealous love that took hold of me with both hands. When he finished, we sat on the bench, waiting for the music to rest. Birds sang outside. The wind rustled the marsh grass. A gator splashed off the bank into the deep brown water of the Altamaha, my very blood.

He took one of my hands and placed my fingers in position on the keys. "This is the chord you missed. You have the music, Iona." He was silent.

I couldn't trust looking him full in the face.

"Can you practice here every day?"

"I have to." My knee jiggled.

He stilled it with a touch of his fingers. "Yes, you must."

And so it started, innocent and from true passion like all love should. I told Mama I was walking, and she never questioned me. Why would she? I was her good girl. When I played the piano, JT smiled. I saw all the love he held for me. My passion for music and JT twisted around each other like a tightly braided rope. I found myself imagining what it would be like to kiss him. I'd kissed boys before; I wasn't completely sheltered. But something told me that kissing JT Mackey would be a whole new experience.

One afternoon when I finished a difficult piece, he bent over and kissed me full on the lips, holding my chin with two slender fingers in the most gentle of ways, as if I were something precious. One kiss led to a kiss each day, then two. One afternoon I surprised him by acing a challenging assignment better than he could have guessed, better than he had played it. He ran his hand over my breast and down into my shirt. Electricity spread through my joints. My skin stuck to the leather sofa as the summer heat closed in on us. He was twenty-four. Eight years wasn't so terrible. When I turned thirty, he would be thirty-eight. Perfect. My lessons became broader and included what all my girlfriends saved for their wedding night. Who cared? I had no intention of marrying, but I did want to be with JT the rest of my life.

Our summer continued on this way. The heat that year was unbearable. We got brave and walked the town together in the evenings. We fell into each other's arms as soon as I walked into his door and then sat naked on the piano bench to practice. At home I worked harder than ever on stuff like church socials, sewing, and of course math. Mama never noticed the change in me. But Maw Maw watched me like a hawk.

When the first day of school came, my stomach fluttered.

Something was over. Music was my last class of the day. JT would smile at me when I came in the door, but nothing more. I didn't dare tell my girlfriends. For one thing, they held a poor view of a girl who did what I did, and the other was they would tell Daddy for sure. Darien would run JT out of town tarred and feathered and strip Daddy of his pulpit. Each evening I went to his house and he cooked big bowls of chili and sometimes homemade bread. I pretended we would live this way forever.

Then one night, JT met me at the door. "People are talking, Iona. We're going to have to take a break. I can't afford to lose my job, and you don't need to lose your reputation."

"What about my lessons? How will I practice?"

"You're good enough for a vacation."

"You said every day."

"It'll only be for two weeks. Then we can start back." He smiled.

"Just two weeks."

He bent over and kissed me. "Come here." We went to the sofa.

Our arrangement lasted all of two days, when I decided I couldn't take it anymore. I was in the kitchen ready to slip out for my nightly walk when Daddy came in carrying a paper bag. "Look what I found in the attic."

Inside was a brown toy piano. "I'm almost sixteen, Daddy."

"I know. I bought it for you when you were four. I'm so proud of all your hard work, Iona. Would you play at church this week?"

Shame ran through me.

"You let me know. Are you going for your walk?" The way he looked at me told me he knew about JT and me.

"Yes." I pushed out the back door.

When I reached JT's house, I prayed he'd be happy to see me. Then I caught a flash of something moving in the big front room. I was looking through the glass panel beside the door. His body that I knew so well was tangled around Kathy Morris, a freshman who was fourteen. He was doing to her what we had done all summer so well together. He rolled to one side, and his stare locked with mine. Kathy landed on the floor. I walked away.

The door opened. "Hey!"

I walked faster.

"Come back here, Iona. We need to talk."

"Fuck you." I laughed so hard my breath left my lungs. I trotted along the road, tears rolling down my face. I could bring his world crashing down. Mama was right. My head was full of cotton candy fluff.

The toy piano sat on the kitchen table. My fingers were drawn to the small keys, where I found a tune. I was better than JT. The sound of applause made me jump.

"Bravo, Iona!" Daddy stood in the door.

My life was beginning; something hard and tender at the same time was taking over. I stuck out my tongue at Daddy. He laughed.

"I'll play for you at church."

He put his arm around me. "I'm glad you're back, Iona."

Fifty

Men like JT Mackey always get what's coming to them. I saw what became of JT when I turned seventeen. He was forced into marriage with one of my classmates, a quiet, skittish girl. I smiled when I heard the news but moved on to my next class. See, I learned a lot from Mr. Mackey about what not to look for in a man. I also learned I was a good musician. JT's baby was born six months later. He lost his job and took his wife to Savannah. His dreams were gone. And that was too bad, since he was gifted.

Me, I made excellent grades. I practiced piano at the church every afternoon. My anger toward JT turned into a melody and my dreams wove through the very air I breathed. Music was my life. JT hadn't stolen that.

Two months before I finished high school, I announced to my parents that the college in Chapel Hill, North Carolina, had accepted me. I had wanted to apply to Juilliard, but I couldn't be that far away from my parents. At least I would be studying music.

Mama turned as white as a sheet flapping on the line out back. "Why do you have to go way up there, Iona?" Mama held a bowl of oatmeal in her hands. Daddy drank his coffee, hidden behind his newspaper.

"That's the best news, baby girl." Maw Maw smiled. She had turned fragile over the year, reminding me life runs out. I had to go away. I had to have a chance at my life.

"It's too far." Mama frowned.

"Don't ruin it for her." Maw Maw frowned at Mama.

I grabbed toast from the toaster. "Chapel Hill is a great college. Don't you think, Daddy?"

"We'll miss you." He folded his newspaper.

"You know it's a great college. Don't let Mama win."

"Win what, Iona?" Mama held her hand to her chest as if I had shot her.

"See what I'm talking about?"

Daddy looked at both of us. "Annie, she's a grown woman. We have to allow her to decide some things for herself. It's time."

"Now I'm not allowing our daughter a life? Really, Iona, is that how you feel?"

I took a deep breath and tried to remember she was scared. "Mama, it's 1957. You don't have to hover over me all the time."

"What's that got to do with anything?"

"Annie, she won't act like you. Don't worry." Maw Maw patted Mama's shoulder.

Mama shrugged her hand away. "Leave this between Iona and me."

Maw Maw didn't look a bit put out. What had Mama done when she was young?

"Why can't you find a nice boy?" Mama didn't look me in the face.

"Are you kidding? I have bigger plans than to become a fisherman's wife."

"You could do worse." The words were bullets in my chest.

"Girls." Daddy sounded a bit stern. "I like a calm home."

"I'm going to North Carolina. Maybe I'll meet a nice boy there." I frowned at Mama.

Mama looked like a trapped animal. "I want to protect you."

This made my stomach flip. "I don't need protecting. I promise."

"You think you know everything." Mama looked out at the marsh.

"Mama, I'm not you. I'm Iona Harbor, a musician. I'd die in this town."

Mama looked away, but before she did, I saw her mask of calmness fall. "You have no idea what's out there, Iona."

And she was right about that. It would take a few years and some truths before I understood.

That night I heard my parents talking in their room. The truth was I mashed my ear to their door.

"Let her go to college in peace, Annie, because she's going no matter what."

"You don't understand, Harold."

"I think there are lots of things about you, Annie, I don't understand. But I do know my daughter. Maybe one day you will tell me what happened to you the spring before you came to live here in Darien."

"There's nothing to tell, Howard. You always think there's more to me."

Fifty-one

By the time I left for college Maw Maw was failing fast. Mama had her hands full. I even started feeling guilty about leaving. "Do you want me to wait until winter quarter?"

Mama was washing dishes and stopped with a plate in midair. "I don't believe I'm going to say this, but I won't be the reason you stay home. I won't be the reason you didn't go after your dream. I'll be fine with Maw Maw."

I couldn't open my mouth.

"I would give my whole life up for you, Iona. You're my heart. Do you understand?"

But how could a spoiled precious only child understand anything about selfless love? "Sure, Mama."

She gave me a sideways look and went back to washing dishes.

"I love you too." I threw my arms around her.

I left for college right before Labor Day. The first month I cried myself to sleep every night. One afternoon I called home collect.

Mama answered, accepting the charges. "What's wrong, Iona?"

"Nothing, Mama. Can't I just call?" My words were much sharper than I intended. I'd planned to tell her how much I loved her, Daddy, and Maw Maw; what a terrible mistake it was for me to go off to college; how the professors saw me as a little hick girl from Georgia.

"Are you homesick?" Mama asked.

Anger swelled inside because she saw through me, hundreds of miles away. "No. I just wanted to talk, but you have to turn it into a major deal."

"You know, Iona, if you called me to give you permission to quit college and come home, you called the wrong person."

"You're the one who wants me home under your wing."

"I won't tell you to quit."

"I don't need your permission!"

"No, Iona, you don't. That is exactly my point." Her breathing was heavy.

"What are you talking about?"

"I won't have you be thirty, married to some shrimper, with three kids, hating me for ruining your life! You're not doing that to me, young lady."

"I'm hanging up now, Mama. I don't know why I called you."

"Yes you do."

"Why then?"

"You needed me to tell you to stay in school and quit whining."

"Good-bye, Mama."

"Good-bye, Iona."

She hung up first and I cried. It turned out Mama was on my side. I'd be home for Thanksgiving. That wasn't so far off.

* * *

The first year of college whizzed by. Before I knew it, I was going home for the summer. Mama had made the decision to move Maw Maw to a nursing home in Savannah. Why would she send Maw Maw away? We were supposed to look after each other, right?

Then one night just after I came home, I woke to find Maw Maw standing over my bed.

"Nellie."

"It's me, Maw Maw, Iona."

Her eyes were vacant. "I need to find Nellie. You know where she is, don't you? I need to help her."

"Who's Nellie?"

She clamped her fingers around my wrist. "Help me find her before the bad thing happens."

"Come back to bed." Mama stood in the door. "See, there's not enough hands to keep her down at night. Twice she's gone out to the marsh looking for Daddy."

"There you are, Nellie. You got to get this notion of marrying Hobbs out of your head, girl." She touched Mama's face.

"I'm Annie, your daughter."

"I think I know my daughter when I see her. I'm not crazy."

"Okay." Mama winked at me. "Go back to sleep, Iona. I'll stay up with her."

I helped move my sweet little grandmother to a home in Savannah. That's how I met Anthony.

It was the end of June and so humid the air could be cut by a knife. Mama and Daddy were checking Maw Maw into the home, and I couldn't bear to watch. The place was nice enough, with gardens and benches facing the river, but a prison couldn't be hidden behind a bunch of flowers and smiles. The old people sat in their wheelchairs or hobbled along with their walkers. They smelled funny and reminded me that someday

I'd be old. I noticed Anthony first. Had we been at school, he could have walked by without me seeing him. But that day I noticed him on the bench looking at a newspaper because he was the youngest person around, not counting me.

"What do you think of Martin Luther King Jr.?"

"Excuse me?" I was standing under a large oak tree, thinking he hadn't noticed me.

He looked up from the newspaper. "The civil rights movement. Don't you keep up with current events?"

"I've been a little busy with school and now my grandmother. I don't have time to read about some people riding buses."

"Some people? Don't you know what could happen to them? Don't you care?"

Irritation welled inside me. "Of course I care, but you know they're bringing it on themselves. They know people are going to get upset. They know the bigots are going to come after them for stirring up trouble. Look what happened at Little Rock."

He shook his head. "These people can't eat or sleep where they want. They can't even use the bathrooms they want to. They have to fight a mob to attend a decent school. What if that was you? I bet you'd pay attention then."

My head was spinning. "I don't need this."

"What would you say if I told you my father was a Negro? Would you keep talking to me?"

His skin was white like mine and I absolutely didn't like him. "You're full of yourself."

"What if I told you that girls didn't need to go to college? I think you should be home, married, and pregnant with your third child."

Blinding anger started in my toes and rushed up my body. "I'd tell you to go to hell. I have no intentions of marrying."

He laughed at me. "See, you can get involved."

I both liked and hated him. "I'm a musician. I play music. That's how I plan on changing the world."

"I took you for an art major." He smiled a big toothy grin. "I go to the art college. I paint. I paint big. Like wall size. My mother is a nurse here. We're going to have lunch in a few minutes. Another lecture on finding a real future, like being a doctor."

"How about your father?"

He gave me a stern look. "That part is true. He was black. He died in a car accident when I was five. Does he change us being friends?"

"No."

"My name is Anthony." He held out his hand. "What's yours?"

"Iona."

"You're pretty."

"Thanks."

"Do you live in Savannah?"

"No, Darien is home."

He nodded. "Are you coming back to visit your grand-mother?"

"Next week. I have to go back to school at the end of the summer."

He pulled a pencil from his shirt pocket and a scrap of paper from his pants. "Call me when you come back. I'll meet you here. We can go have coffee."

"Okay."

"I'll show you the city. Lots of good stuff."

Fifty-two

I saw Anthony every week for the rest of the summer. On most visits while Mama sat with Maw Maw, I went off with Anthony, not feeling one bit bad. Mama was so consumed with guilt she made up for my lack of attention. She never asked me what I did with my time.

Anthony took me down to River Street and then to the old cemetery. He rattled off the history of the city. One afternoon a terrible storm blew up while we were reading the headstones. Anthony pulled me under a tree and kissed me for what seemed like forever. After that it was easier to imagine sleeping with him. Two weeks before I was to go back to school, he took me to his mother's row house close to the river and made love to me in his bed up in the attic.

When he dropped me back at the nursing home, Mama was waiting. "I was beginning to worry, Iona. What do you do with your time?" She searched my face as if she were looking at me for the first time.

"I'm sorry."

She waited with her hands on her narrow hips.

"I was having lunch and a good talk. The time got away from me. How is Maw Maw?"

"The same. Iona, why don't you invite your boy to supper next week, please."

Did I have a choice? "Okay." I rolled my eyes at the back of her head.

Anthony came to supper the night before I left for my second year at college. Behind us was a magical summer, a kind of limbo, where the world didn't exist. In front of us was a question. What do we do now? And I was taking him home to meet my parents. How crazy was that?

"Wow, Iona, you didn't tell me you lived on the marsh."

"Here it is, my life." We stood on the porch watching the grass rustle in the wind. Mama's haunting spirit was always a presence in my mind when I was home.

Anthony handed me a bottle of wine. "I brought it for dinner. I hope that's okay."

"It'll have to be okay. It's a gift." I smiled. "I forgot to tell you my father is a minister, but the good thing is we're Episcopalian. We don't mind a little nip now and then." I giggled.

"Jees, that's a big thing to forget." He laughed, but I knew he was nervous.

"It's not my dad you have to watch. My mother is the person who will pick you apart."

Did I hear him dragging his feet as we walked into the house?

Mama appeared like an apparition from nowhere. "Well, is this your friend?" She looked at me with a sly expression. "You're everything Iona said." She held out her hand.

Anthony took it. "I'm so glad to finally meet you, ma'am."

"You know Iona is our pride and joy." Mama looked at me.

"And how did you two meet again?" The question hung around the three of us.

"My mother is a nurse at the home where Iona's grandmother stays." Anthony looked directly into Mama's eyes.

"And here I was thinking Iona was wasting her summer away. It's nice to know she was entertained." Mama ran her fingers through her short blond curls. "What's your last name, Anthony?"

"Taylor, ma'am."

She nodded. "Now we can proceed."

"He brought wine for supper." I held out the bottle.

Mama's eyes literally twinkled. "What would the congregation say?" A giggle escaped her. She took the bottle. "Your father can pretend it's communion wine." She winked.

"Would you like some help in the kitchen?" Anthony offered.

Mama shot a look at him. "Are you kidding? Can you cut vegetables?"

"Yes ma'am. I'm good in the kitchen. Mama taught me to fend for myself."

"Oh young man, I do believe you are winning me over." She turned a dazzling smile on me. "Take him to walk on the marsh. Dinner will be ready soon."

And that's how Mama fell head over heels in love with Anthony.

We walked hand in hand. "I don't think I can stand you to go back to school, Iona. What if you forget me?"

"I have to go back. Music is my life."

"I know." He smiled.

The wind blew as the tide moved into the marsh grass. An egret stood not far from us. "I'll be back for the holidays."

"You'll find someone else up there in North Carolina."

"No one like you." I touched his cheek. "Come on." I pulled him along.

"Where are we going?"

"It's a surprise."

When we stood in front of Daddy's church, Anthony looked at me. "So you're going to marry me. That's it."

I pushed at him. "You silly. No."

"Tell my broken heart why you brought me here."

I pulled him into the church. "Have a seat."

He sat down in the front pew while I sat at the piano. The music flowed through me as I thought of us making love. In that moment, I could have married him and tossed school out the window. We were complete. Maybe in the long run that would have been best. But he listened. I played.

The next morning Mama smiled as I came into the kitchen. She was taking me to the bus station. Daddy had some kind of church meeting.

"He's a good boy," she sang from the stove. Her apron was a spotless white.

"Well, did you think he wouldn't be? Jees, Mama."

"Do you want to stop and tell Maw Maw bye before I drop you?"

"Sure."

Maw Maw sat in a chair near the window. I placed my hand on her shoulder. "I have to go back to school."

She looked at me.

"I'm going to check with the nurse about her medicine. I'll be right back." Mama's heels clicked down the quiet hall.

"I told you not to marry that boy, Nellie." Maw Maw looked at me.

"It's me, Iona, Maw Maw."

"He was bad. I knew he was bad. That Hobbs was the meanest man to ever come off Black Mountain."

The old ghost story had entered her mind and she thought it was real. Poor thing. "That's just a silly story. Remember Mama told me that one all the time."

She grabbed my wrist. "He tried to kill her. Do you understand? She didn't have a choice for what she did. Do you understand me?" Her eyes were wild and crazy.

She wasn't there with me but in the story. "Settle down, Maw Maw. It's me, Iona."

"He beat her so bad. I told Nellie that he would do something bad, but she wouldn't listen to me. Stay away from Hobbs Pritchard. You understand?"

"Yes ma'am. I understand."

Her grip relaxed. "You were always my good girl, Iona. Your mama worked hard not to let you get hurt like she did."

"How did she get hurt?" I swallowed hard.

"Well, you know already. She's been telling you the story for years."

"Mama, Iona is leaving for school today. She's come to say good-bye." Mama stood in the door.

Maw Maw looked at her hands as if she were a bad child.

The crazy thing was I got the feeling I now knew something about Mama's secret. But I couldn't. A crazy ghost story told to a child to keep her thoughts in the right direction. Come on. My feeling didn't make sense.

Mama kissed and hugged me at the bus station. The overhead fans spun slowly, clicking away the minutes I had left.

"She's getting worse, Iona. Don't let it upset you. You go learn your music."

"Yes ma'am," I answered like a small child.

Fifty-three

The first time I saw Lonnie, he wore this sultry smile that wiped Anthony from my mind. He sat on the handrail outside the math building and the current he generated reached out and grabbed me. Like so many boys of the time, he wore his hair in an Everly Brothers–style haircut. But something was different about this boy. Maybe it was the fact he wore no socks with some old leather sandals. Or maybe it was the way he raised his eyebrow slightly when he caught me looking.

I rushed through the big double doors, my cheeks burning. The heat off his beautiful cornflower-blue eyes burnt holes in my back. It was quite possible I would have forgotten him had I never seen him again, but later that evening, when I went to the music room to practice, my life opened like a rare rose in late fall.

I was lost in my music; I became aware of a new presence slowly, like a fog, a mountain fog, denser than normal, drifting in from the west. Lonnie sat in one of the chairs. It would be many years before I realized he played me like the fine-tuned guitar he always wore on his back. When I looked into his eyes,

I stopped playing and went to stand in front of him. Magic unfolded. I never gave it a second thought when I followed him to his car. This was a few years before the age of love, peace, and drugs, but I found all three in him. He took me on long hikes into the mountains, where I itched to capture nature in my music.

We made love on a blanket spread over a large flat rock that jutted over a fast-moving creek. The hard surface was alive with the warmth of the sun. Lonnie told me the Cherokees believed rocks could guide a person in the right direction. Anthony slid fluidly from my life.

Lonnie could always be found driving his convertible with the top down. He taught me to smoke something he called marijuana from a cigarette he rolled. This involved inhaling the smoke deep into my chest and holding it for as long as I could. Lonnie was a free spirit, a composer of music, lyrics that wove long intricate stories into haunting melodies. He was way ahead of his time. I had fallen in love.

On one of our drives into the mountains, I asked him where he grew up, thinking it would be someplace like New York City or L.A.

"A hick town." He smiled at me. "I want you to write the music for some of my new lyrics."

I ran my fingers through his hair. "A hick town."

"Where did you come from?"

"The coast of Georgia."

"Damn, I didn't even think Georgia had a coast," he hooted.

"It does and I grew up there. It is one of the most beautiful places in the world."

Lonnie looked over at me. "I wish I could like where my home is. I mean, I'm famous there and all. My real dad was murdered."

"That's horrible."

"Someone cut off his head."

I choked on the smoke I pulled into my lungs.

"Really. I mean it."

Laughter was building in my mind.

"I found his skull in the old hollow tree out by our house. I was just a little boy, but I knew."

I noticed the car was drifting onto the shoulder of the road.

He grinned. "We're too out of it to talk bout this now. But it's something I think about every day."

"I'm sorry."

He shrugged and righted the car. "I'm going home. The whole town has a big party at our house the Saturday before Halloween. It's kind of a tradition with my mom and dad. You want to come and meet my family?"

"Sure." We had crossed some invisible line.

"It's all too crazy," he hooted.

The weekend came and I didn't bother to tell Mama and Daddy about my plan to go with Lonnie. Mama's letters always mentioned Anthony, and I couldn't stand the thought of answering her list of questions.

Lonnie and I set out early Saturday morning. Lonnie grabbed his guitar and threw it in the back of his car. He smelled of whiskey.

"Now remember, moms will be moms, but mine is a piece of work. She's crazy overprotective. My dad's a little easier."

"I thought you said—"

"My stepdad."

I got into the passenger side.

"You want to smoke? You'll want to be high before you meet my parents."

I shook my head. "I'm not going to smoke for a while. It's messing with my music."

He threw his head back and laughed. "You're so damn dedicated. The folks will love you. Dad will be looking for me to give you a ring or something. Maybe even our ghost will appear for you. We have the most famous ghost story in North Carolina."

I ignored how fast he was taking the curves. "I know a pretty good story too."

"Ours is the best. See, ours is about my daddy's death and his wife, who more than likely killed him before she killed herself."

I got a chill. "Your mother is alive."

"Yeah." He looked over at me, taking another curve fast.

"Do you want me to drive?"

"I'm fine."

"So who is the woman your father was married to? You got me all turned around."

He grinned. "My mama never married my daddy. She married his stepbrother. How's that for family history?"

"Wow."

"People wonder why I have problems." He sounded angry. "They all say I'm turning out to be just like my real father, the great almighty Hobbs Pritchard. He's the villain of Black Mountain, the man who drove Nellie Pritchard to murder and then to throw herself off the mountain."

I thought of Maw Maw's fingers gripped around my wrist. How could my story be mixed up with Lonnie's father?

"You're awful quiet."

A chill walked right through my hair.

Fifty-four

Lonnie's mother was friendly enough. Her dark hair curled around her face in the universal mom hairdo of the sixties. But she had the most beautiful eyes. The view in front of the simple house stopped me in my tracks. Layers and layers of mountains as far as I could see reminded me of waves in the ocean. All I needed was the smell of salt and I'd be home.

"Pretty, huh?" Lonnie whispered. He hugged his mother. "This is Iona Harbor. She comes from the coast of Georgia. Her music is beautiful." He pulled me close. "I told her we have ghosts lurking around."

Mrs. Allen smiled and slapped him with a dish towel. "Lonnie, don't scare her away." She looked at me. "Don't you listen to him. He's the only person around this house who ever saw a ghost."

As we walked into the front room, my vision blurred, but the feeling was gone in an instant. A fire burned in the fireplace, and I had a hard time taking my stare away from the flames. I held out my hand. "It's nice to meet you, Mrs. Allen, and he didn't scare me."

"It's a pleasure, honey." She winked her approval at Lonnie and took my hand. "You found one with manners. Your dad is down at Aunt Ida's old house. We finally rented it out."

"Why don't he just sell the place?" Lonnie leaned his guitar case against a chair.

"We thought you might want to live there when you finish school."

"No way. I've told you guys over and over I'm not coming back to this mountain to live."

"Well, you never know, Lonnie. People do change their minds."

A truck pulled into the drive. A tall man with graying hair emerged. He smiled when he saw Lonnie's convertible.

"There's Dad now." He held out his hand for me to follow him.

"He'll be so tickled you brought a friend," Mrs. Allen called after us.

Lonnie pulled me out the door.

"Dad."

Lonnie's dad smiled and stopped in place when he saw me. A small frown worked at his mouth. He struggled on whether to like me or not.

"This is Iona Harbor. She's from down on the coast of Georgia. Her daddy's a preacher. Go figure. I'm dating a preacher's daughter."

Mr. Allen held out his hand. His face slowly became calm. "I thought you looked like someone I used to know. My eyes are getting bad." He laughed. "You can call me Jack."

No way. I couldn't call him anything but Mr. Allen.

"Over here is Mom's flower garden." Lonnie was proud.

Fall flowers—chrysanthemums and a few daisies—were blooming. "It's beautiful." A wave of familiarity washed over me and then was gone, as if I had stood in that very spot before.

"My wife loves her garden." Mr. Allen looked at his son with undisguised love.

"So where will the party be held?" I looked around the yard.

"Out here. We'll help set up the games—bobbing for apples, pumpkin carving—and the teenagers always have a haunted house in the barn. We even tell ghost stories around the bonfire." Lonnie pointed to a fire pit loaded with wood.

"My family is so boring compared to yours."

"You know, Lonnie, I'm glad you came home for Halloween." Mr. Allen patted Lonnie on the shoulder.

"This is a great place," I said.

Lonnie's face hardened. "This place has its dark corners."

Mr. Allen took off his hat. "Lonnie, we have a lot to do. I'll meet you in the barn." He walked away.

Lonnie watched him. "Dad doesn't like me talking about the past."

The night promised to be fun as the yard began to fill with guests. The decorations and the sight of Lonnie goofing off with some of the other guys put me into the partying spirit.

Mr. Allen stuck a match to the wood and a whoosh of flames shot into the air. The party began. The black oily smoke spiraled up as the heat wafted toward me. I found a chair as Lonnie ran off to work in the haunted house. Mr. Allen carved intricate patterns on pumpkins for the little ones, while Mrs. Allen ran the apple-bobbing game. The more I watched, the more I knew I should be a part of this family. I watched the flames leaping into the air for a while before I noticed a man leaning against a big tree. His arms were folded across his chest and his head was cocked to one side. He watched me as if he knew me. A puff of smoke made my eyes water. I rubbed them and looked. The man was gone.

A loud commotion came from the barn. A crowd of boys burst out of the door. Lonnie's mom looked up from where she sat. A young boy ran from the crowd.

"I saw him! I saw him!"

"Who?" Mrs. Allen asked in a calm voice.

"Hobbs Pritchard. I know it was him. He was standing in the corner of the barn grinning; then his face turned into a skull." The boy looked to be around ten.

"Don't be silly. That story is old and it's losing its punch," one of the other adults said.

"But I did see him."

I felt sure the boy saw something.

Lonnie came walking into the firelight. He was quiet.

"Are you finished so soon?" I asked him.

"I don't have the stomach for it this year."

"What's wrong?" I tried to get a reading on him.

"Nothing to worry about." He put his arm around me. "Let's go walk in the woods."

I thought of the man. "No, thanks. I saw this creepy man over there by that tree." I pointed.

His grip turned tight. "What did he look like?"

"Just a man. It was how he looked at me that bothered me so much."

"Iona saw Hobbs too." His words silenced the crowd, and everyone turned to stare at me. "Iona doesn't even know the whole story." He raised his arm in salute to me.

All of a sudden I just wanted to go back to school and leave that awful place. The crowd was watching me as if I had something important to say.

"I saw a man by that tree."

The people began to whisper.

"That's enough of this talk. Iona is our guest. There are no ghosts." Mr. Allen moved toward me. "I think we should have some fun."

Slowly everyone went back to what they had been doing before the scare.

I pulled Lonnie's arm. "Let's go to the house."

Lonnie grinned and shrugged.

The house was warm and bright. "Have you been drinking?"

Lonnie laughed. "A little, but I know what I saw, Iona. I'm not crazy."

"Why don't you go sleep it off?"

He came close. "Why don't you go with me?"

"Stop. This is your parents' house."

He pulled back. "Yeah, all three of them." He stared at the stairs. "I want to go back to school. Let's go. Will you drive?"

"It's late. What will your parents think?"

"We won't tell them. I just want out of here, Iona."

He reminded me of a lost little boy.

His car was parked close to the road to make room for the guests. No one noticed us leave. "I don't understand why you just don't tell them good-bye, Lonnie. I feel bad about that."

"They'll make a big deal, Iona. I don't want a big deal."

Lonnie lit a joint as I maneuvered the mountain road.

"Did you get your guitar?"

"No. I don't give a damn. I'll get Mom to send it. I'm not going back, ever."

"What happened?" I realized he was a lot more shaken up than he let on. "Is it what I said about seeing the man?"

"You saw my real father, Hobbs Pritchard."

"That's the name of the man in the story Mama used to tell me."

"Then she must have been on this mountain, because there was only one Hobbs."

I shook the thought of Mama being on this mountain out of my mind. "What did you see, Lonnie?"

"I saw him, Hobbs. I saw him in the barn. He was sitting on a bale of hay up in the loft. That little boy saw him too. Hobbs grinned at me and said, 'It won't be long, son.'"

"Long for what, Lonnie?" My voice cracked as I caught a sideways glance at him. At that moment a man stepped into the road. He seemed caught in the headlights. He wore little round spectacles, an old-fashioned suit, and a funny little driving hat. He never flinched as I slammed on the brakes.

"Whoa there, now," Lonnie yelled.

Part Six

Annie Harbor

Fifty-five

Mama passed away in her sleep on October 25, 1958, at the nursing home in Savannah nineteen years after giving up everything she owned to find me and finally succeed in saving me from myself. With her death, my life as a daughter was over. I was an orphan. Mama was my one and only shining star. She kept me on track when no one else could. My mama was made of much tougher stuff than me.

The makings for a roast beef sandwich was scattered across the kitchen counter when the phone rang.

"Hello."

"Mrs. Harbor?"

"Yes."

"This is Louise Mars from Pellem Rest Home. Mrs. Clay passed away quietly just an hour or so ago. The nurse on duty found her when she came to bring her medicine."

No words would come out of my mouth.

"Mrs. Harbor, did you hear me?"

"Yes. Thank you." That's all I said, thank you. Thank you

my mama has died. I replaced the receiver in the cradle while the woman was still talking. No one was home. I picked up the phone again and dialed Iona's number. I waited as the girl who answered went to track her down. She returned out of breath only to tell me my daughter was off with her boyfriend for the weekend.

"How can that be? He's here in Savannah."

"I'm sorry, that's all I know. She's gone for the weekend." *Click*, and the girl was gone.

The house vibrated with silence. Mama was dead. No longer did she have to fight to keep all my lies straight in a mind moving in and out of reality. All my silly secrets. Were they worth the sacrifice of having her die alone?

Mama came rolling into Darien two days after me. From behind the windshield of her old truck, she smiled at me like she'd won a contest. "You said I'd be living here too, Nellie."

I placed my finger on her lips. "I'm Annie Tucker now. You can never tell anyone who I really am. I'll be lost if you do."

"You done killed him." The sentence hung between us like a heavy thundercloud.

"I got us a place close to the river." We didn't bring up the subject again.

I met Harold two weeks later and things between us moved fast. Of course Mama had another warning for me, and just like with Hobbs, I didn't listen.

"You can't let that man—him being a preacher—not know your whole story. You can't let him think this baby is his. It will end in disaster."

Not once had I mentioned I was pregnant. I married Harold two weeks later, in spite of his own mother's misgivings.

My plan was to once again live happily ever after. Mama fell harder for my husband than I ever did. Don't get me wrong. I loved Harold Harbor until the day he died. But Hobbs had stolen something precious from deep inside my soul. There wasn't a shred of trust or belief in the common good of humans left. And without those things, a soul gets old and tired even when she is young. Without those things, I couldn't use good judgment. Without those things, I thought I would never be in control of my own life again.

Harold insisted Mama move in with us, and that's the best gift he ever gave me. I never planned to let her out of my sight again. My new life fit me like an expensive dress. Mama called me Annie without a problem. Nellie had died. Sometimes I thought of making her a gravestone and placing it next to Daddy in the graveyard out by the church.

Mama's eyes nearly popped out of her head when she saw the house where we would live. "We're here just like you said. Your daddy must be grinning."

"It's a safe place. No one will ever look for me here."

She nodded. "I pray every night you have a girl. I don't want to be reminded of that man ever again."

"Don't talk like that, Mama. This baby will be Harold's. He's a good man. It deserves one good parent."

"Never forget you did what you had to do, nothing more. You're not bad."

I didn't tell her how I planned the murder of my husband, how it was a wisp of a thought on some of those empty days. In the first weeks of my second marriage, I got up in the dead of the night and sat at the kitchen table. In those long hours before the sun came up over the marsh, I thought of ways I could have left Hobbs without killing him. There were plenty. Funny how hindsight is so clear and perfect.

Iona was born on a cold day right before Thanksgiving. Everyone was amazed at how healthy she was to be born two *months early. Harold was all over himself to have a girl. He never paid a bit of attention to anyone who did raise an eyebrow. He trusted me and I never felt guilty.*

"Look at her, Annie. She looks just like you. She's our angel." He smiled at me.

And I knew this to be totally true.

Iona and Mama were my life. Harold loved us all. It didn't matter that sometimes I couldn't stand for him to touch me. I moved past the feeling quick enough. Somehow I got the idea in my head I had to pay for what I did to Hobbs. That payment came in the form of losing our son to crib death, and that's all I have to say about that part of our life. I paid a high price for my deed.

So there I stood in my living room, searching for Iona. I needed my only child. My heart was broken. After trying to call Iona three more times and making every girl in her dorm house mad, I called Harold. He came straight home from his office at church.

"We should move her body to the funeral home." Harold stood in the kitchen with one hand on my shoulder. He had turned gray around the temples and new lines had formed around his eyes. What would I do if I didn't have him? He was my safety net, my one sure thing. But I held back like I always did.

"Yes. I'm still looking for Iona. I've called her dorm house so much the girls hang up on me." I smiled weakly. "How can she be off with Anthony?"

"Maybe the girl got her wires crossed. Iona's good about talking to us. She would have called us if Anthony was visiting." He patted my shoulder.

"I hope she's okay."

"She's a grown woman, Annie."

"She's not grown, Harold."

He laughed in his quiet way. "Yes, she grew up without you even seeing her."

He was right.

Harold gave me a big hug. "Do you want to go see your mother?"

I took a deep breath. "I want to wait for Iona to call." I pictured Mama in that bed in the tiny room of the nursing home. She never had to go there. I made her so I could cover my tracks, my lie from so long ago. When would the past quit following me?

That night, after Harold was snoring, I went down to the kitchen table. Every time I closed my eyes, I saw Mama. Poor Mama. Where was Iona? Why hadn't she called? The clock ticked in the front room, *tick, tick, tick.* The moon was big in the sky, and that February night in 1939 played out in my mind. I learned to just go with the pictures because they weren't going away. Those terrible choices set Annie's life in motion. The long-ago flames still parched my heart.

The phone made me jump. "Hello?" The clock showed two in the morning.

"I'm calling the parents of Iona Harbor." The voice was clean and crisp, professional.

"This is her mother. What's wrong?" Because I knew something was wrong. Finally I would pay the price for my sin.

"This is the county hospital in Asheville. There has been a serious accident and your daughter has been badly injured. We need you to come as soon as possible."

My head roared. "My daughter is not in Asheville."

"We have an Iona Harbor here. Her contact information at school was your number."

Harold stood in the door. "Here." He took the phone from me.

Anger boiled up inside me. "She's my daughter. I need to know what happened." *Mama!* I screamed in my head. I forgot she wasn't here anymore. *Please!* I managed one word to Harold's God.

"Yes. Yes. We'll be there in a few hours. We're coming from the Georgia coast. Can you give me a number?" He scribbled on the pad that sat by the phone. "Please do everything you can."

I sank onto the floor. "Don't you tell me she's dying. Don't do it!"

He dropped to his knees. "We have to go. She's not good, Annie. But we raised a fighter. She was in a car accident. She was driving a boy's car. He was in the car with her. That's all I know." He pulled me up with him. "We have to be strong for her, Annie."

"I want my mama."

He hugged me. "I know you do." I could hear the tears in his words.

Iona had to live. But I couldn't grasp this in my heart. We ran to the car. The air was heavy with salt. I had been in Darien for nineteen years and never once went farther than Savannah or Brunswick. I saw Iona's face in my mind. *Live. You have to live, my sweet, sweet darling.*

"I don't know where the hospital is in Asheville."

"I know where it is. Just drive."

Harold looked at me but stayed quiet.

"Drive, Harold. Don't let my baby die."

"We have to pray."

"I'm praying to your God, Harold. You drive."

Fifty-six

When I went into labor with Iona, the pains came hard every two and a half minutes, fooling me into believing birth would come easy for me. The midwife checked me and frowned, telling me I had a long way to go before my baby was born. She suggested I walk around the house, but the pains were horrible. Instead, I sat in the old rocker in our upstairs bedroom. I rocked back and forth, watching the red maple out the window. By the time I moved through the horrible pains into a place only I could enter, twelve hours had gone by. I wasn't aware of the passage of time, and yet I was inside each moment, waiting, working to move forward. The trip to Asheville was like this. Each second glowed around the edges. Inside my head, I saw her face. Silent prayers for her to live moved in and out of me like the air I was breathing. *Let my child live. Let her live.*

When we pulled into the hospital's parking lot, it was before lunch. Inside of me Iona's heart beat, a rhythm not unlike when a mother holds her baby on her chest. I ran to the emergency room doors as if all the time pent up in the car had ruptured something inside me, pushing me into a chaotic world.

A woman looked up from the desk. "Are you Lonnie Allen's parent?"

"No!" I screamed over the *thud, thud, thud* resounding inside me. "My daughter is Iona Harbor."

The woman's face relaxed. Did I imagine that? "Wonderful, Mrs. Harbor. Let me get someone to take you back."

The double doors pushed open and a doctor appeared wearing a blue surgery suit, a mask pulled down around his chin. "Mr. and Mrs. Harbor?"

I noticed Harold was standing close. His breath hit my neck. "How's our girl?" He took the doctor's outstretched hand.

"She's much better than we thought. She's going to make it. Come with me."

Those sweet words filled my heart, spilling into each breath of air. A woman entered through the big outside double doors. Something about her stopped me in my tracks. Her face was marked with tears. Out of a reflex, I held out a hand to the woman.

"Annie, are you coming?" Harold was with the doctor. Both were waiting on me.

Behind the woman a man walked through the doors. Tall, rattled around the edges. Because of this, I almost missed who he was: Jack. In his face I saw the death of his son. The boy in the car with my Iona. I don't know how I knew this. I just did. My daughter lived and his son died. For a minute I thought he was reaching for my hand, but he gathered the woman in his arms. The gray around his temples made him more handsome than ever.

"Doctor, Lonnie Allen's parents are here," the woman at the desk called to the doctor with Harold.

There Harold and I were, paused at the double doors

leading to my Iona. The whole world stood still. I looked away, but not before I knew Jack saw me. He knew me. The past and the present twisted together.

"Step through the doors. I'll join you in a minute." The doctor held one door open.

Harold and I passed through it together. I held the arm I had outstretched to the woman close to me, protective, as if it were burnt, damaged in some horrible way. The woman's long shadow stretched through the small church's door, the church where I married my first husband.

"It can't be," I whispered. The doors shut.

"What did you say?" Harold tried to touch my shoulder but I moved away, leaning on the cement-block wall.

I hugged myself as if I were part of the woman's misery. What was her name?

"Did you know that woman?" Harold searched my face with an innocent stare.

"I think they're the parents of the boy Iona was with." My voice was calmer than I expected. "I'm not sure how I know. I just do."

He nodded.

We heard what sounded like sobs through the doors.

A doctor walked up to us. "You're the Harbors?"

"Yes," Harold answered.

He motioned us to follow. "Your daughter has a lot of recovery to go through. We lost her once at the accident. We have to wait for her to wake up." He looked at us. "How long it takes her to wake up is crucial." He placed a hand on a curtain and swept it back.

Iona was covered with cuts and bruises. Tubes ran everywhere. Her eyes were closed. Bandages covered her hands. *Dear God, I don't deserve you to listen but please let her have her music. Don't take that away.*

"The car caught fire. She is lucky to be alive."

Nothing about luck figured into this miracle.

"She plays piano."

The doctor's face grew impassive. "We don't know right now how her hands will heal. It will depend on her determination."

How many times had I yelled at her for thinking about music? A large stone sat on my chest. I touched one of her bandaged hands. "You fight, Iona," I whispered above the whining machines.

"Talk to her, Mrs. Harbor. She can hear you."

"Can I speak to someone about the accident?" Harold looked at me and I nodded. "We'd like to know just what happened."

"Come with me. The young man who owned the car didn't make it. The state police are speaking with his parents. I'm sure they would like to speak to you." The doctor pulled the curtain closed.

Harold turned and winked at me. What would I do without him?

I sat beside Iona. I refused to give Jack and his wife any more thought for the time being. I couldn't think of their son or why Iona was driving his car. I had hovered over her so much—I was only trying to protect her—that she kept secrets from me. Was Jack's wife who I thought she was? I just wouldn't speculate. It was too dangerous. I was back in North Carolina—Nellie's final resting place. How could I be back here? Nellie wasn't dead; she lived in Jack. She lived on Black Mountain. She was a prisoner. For that matter, she lived in my heart this whole time. She kept me awake at night, worrying. She made me shelter Iona. It was her who put Mama in the nursing home. Maybe if I became Annie all the way through, or better yet told the whole truth . . .

Harold stuck his head around the curtain and motioned me into the hall. A state trooper was there to tell us what happened. He held his big hat in front of him. My hands shook so bad I hid them behind my back.

"It seems your daughter was driving the car when a deer jumped off an embankment. This kind of thing has been happening more and more these days. We never found the deer, but we're sure that's what caused your daughter to swerve over the embankment. We found alcohol in the car, but all indications point to the young man drinking, not your daughter. Her blood test was clean. This may have been why she was driving."

"Iona would never drink." Harold spoke with confidence.

"How are the boy's parents?" My daughter had another life I didn't know about.

"They are not doing too good, as you can imagine. You see, your daughter and Lonnie Allen had just left his parents' house. They were having some kind of Halloween party."

"Where did the accident happen?" My head roared.

"A place called Black Mountain. It's probably a good forty-five minutes from here."

My legs went weak. I held out my hand to Harold, but it was the trooper who caught me going down. "Let's find you a chair, ma'am."

Harold pulled a chair from the wall.

"Mr. and Mrs. Allen would like to speak with you before they leave the hospital with their son."

I nodded.

"Only if you're up to it, Annie."

There was my open doorway, my clean way out, my way to keep running like I had been since I killed Hobbs. "I'll be fine."

"I know they'll be beholding, ma'am." The trooper placed his hat back on his head.

Harold touched my shoulder, and I sank into him. My mind shattered. "We'll do this together."

I heard Jack before I had the nerve to look at him. Heavy footfalls with soft ones right beside him. I looked directly at the woman, who held out her hand. Her eyes were ringed red and her curly dark hair escaped a scarf she must have grabbed when word came. I took her hand and a shift in my soul pushed us together, tangling our thoughts. Her son died. My daughter lived.

"My name is Rose Allen."

My fingers trembled. Her name put my teeth on edge. "I'm so sorry." *Stand tall. You're Annie Harbor.* It came in a tiny whisper, Mama's whisper.

"He was my life."

I couldn't look her in the eyes.

"It's a terrible thing." Harold spoke from beside me.

Rose clutched my hand. "When Iona is better, I need to see her. I need to know why he wanted to leave early without saying good-bye. Your daughter is so kind and sweet. You've raised her well. Lonnie always had trouble. There were problems that night because he thought he saw his real father, who's been dead since before his birth."

I pulled at my hand, but she held tight.

"I just need to know why they left."

"Come on, Rose, come on." Jack gently pulled his wife's hand away from mine.

Rose? That was the name of the girl Hobbs was going to see in Asheville, the girl he loved better than me.

Had Jack married Hobbs's girl? The boy—Iona's friend— could he have belonged to Hobbs? What kind of mess was this? The thoughts rushed around my head while I tried to listen to Harold speak his condolences. Jack looked away when I tried to meet his stare. Yes? Yes. He knew it was the face of Nellie he looked into. He knew my secrets. He knew my unspoken questions. He knew everything.

Jack led Rose away without looking at me again. Harold nodded toward the couple and followed. He was in full character, the good minister.

Iona's doctor walked down the hall toward me. "I need to speak to you and your husband." He looked so stern and serious I thought it was the worst news ever.

"My husband stepped away. You can tell me."

He cleared his throat. "Your daughter's bloodwork came back."

He was going to tell me she had been drinking after all.

"Your daughter is pregnant."

For one innocent second relief washed through me. "A baby." That was all. We could work with a baby.

Jack's back was straight, giving him more height. He held his wife's elbow and moved down the hall like a brave knight. I looked at the doctor. "What can we do about this situation?"

Fifty-seven

"Are you suggesting what I think, Mrs. Harbor?" The doctor took a step back.

I couldn't believe it myself, but allowing Iona to carry that baby was unthinkable. "Don't you see my daughter's condition? What if this causes some kind of harm?"

The doctor's Adam's apple moved up and then down. "What you are suggesting is against the law. I take my medical oath seriously."

"Not in every case. There must be reasons that allow the procedure."

"Let's see what happens with your daughter before we jump into this way of thinking." My horrible choices reflected in his eyes. He nodded and walked off.

To hell with him. If he knew the truth he would be all too glad to accommodate me. Iona was still. The machines beeped and gurgled. *It's simple, just tell the truth. For once tell the truth.* I laughed aloud. Once again I was plotting against someone's life for what I thought was a justifiable reason. I bent over Iona and whispered in her ear. "You've gone and got yourself in a mess. We're one in the same. I couldn't save you."

"She'll play again." Harold stood just inside the curtain.

A good wife would have told Harold everything. The time was perfect for clearing the air. But I had to see my mess through to the end alone. No one else deserved to be saddled with it. I looked at him, this man I married for better or worse. What would happen to us if I told him my secret?

"We'll make it through this together, Annie. We have each other." Harold took my hand.

I wanted to pull it back, but instead, I sobbed.

My hours at the hospital blurred together. They moved Iona to the intensive care floor. I spent most of my time looking in the window, watching her chest move up and down, her face dead still. The baby growing inside her kept appearing in my mind. When I fell asleep in the chairs lined against the wall, I saw this boy sitting next to my daughter. He had no face. I couldn't allow any features to develop. This Lonnie, Hobbs's son with Rose, was my Iona's half-brother.

Then at the end of the second day, I sat at her bed and took her bandaged hands. "You loved to play your music. I always told you it was fluff, cotton candy fluff. I was wrong, Iona. You need to wake up and hear your mama say she was wrong." The room with all its whirring sounds was like being inside a bubble away from the world. "I messed up, Iona. Wake up, and I'll find a way to do right." I closed my eyes and wondered if I told the truth, would God allow her to live? Movement. I looked at Iona. Her eyelids fluttered and her fingers moved. "Harold!" Again the fingers moved. "Harold!"

"What?" He was standing by the bed.

"Get a nurse."

Iona's eyes were open.

"Can you hear me, baby?"

Three blinks and she turned her head in my direction. "What, Mama?"

Harold wept as the nurse rushed by to the bed.

"I love you." I squeezed her hand.

The nurse buzzed for a doctor. "We've been waiting for a couple days on you, young lady." She smiled at Iona, who gave her a puzzled look.

Iona smiled, squeezed my hand, and closed her eyes.

"Daddy's here."

Harold came to stand beside the bed.

"Daddy," she whispered with her eyes closed.

Whatever happened from this moment forward, we would be united. I didn't have to ever tell my story. A baby wasn't so bad. I didn't know for sure Rose was Rose. She could be anyone. Did I really have to tell any of this?

"Mama, why am I here?"

I looked at Harold. "You had an accident."

"How?"

"In a car."

Harold shifted next to me.

"Where's Lonnie?"

The question hung over the bed. I looked at the nurse.

"Okay, Mama and Daddy. We need the doctor to take a look at Iona. You may talk after that."

Bless her.

"You were in his car." Harold spoke in a quiet voice. Damn him for being so honest.

Iona looked at him. "Was he driving?"

"No," he whispered.

Tears formed in her eyes.

"We have to step out, Harold." My voice was sharp.

"Did he get hurt, Daddy?"

I looked straight into her eyes. For some reason, I couldn't allow Harold to answer. "He died from his injuries."

She squeezed her eyes shut and took a deep breath. "Because of me."

"No, sweetie, a deer jumped in front of you. You swerved to miss it."

She cried and I stood by her bed, helpless.

Iona was moved out of ICU and into a regular room. Harold went home to make arrangements to have Mama cremated. We would have a memorial service when Iona could go home.

On her fifth day in the hospital, Iona actually smiled a real smile. Her face transformed. The bandages were taken off her hands. She hadn't asked about her music. I was thankful for this.

"I dreamed about Lonnie." Her voice was quiet but not sad.

I looked out the window.

"He was whole, healed."

Still I didn't respond.

"See, he had a lot of problems, Mama. He was everything you've tried to save me from. I was starting to understand that when this happened." She reached over to me. "I'm sorry I've hurt you."

"You've hurt yourself, not me." I took her hand but my words didn't sound inviting or caring.

"I want to see Lonnie's parents. I need to tell them what I remember."

"That's too much for you, Iona. Let it go. Let them grieve."

"It's my decision," she said softly.

Something had changed between us. She wasn't the little girl who needed my guidance.

"We'll talk to Daddy."

"I did this morning. He thinks it's a good idea."

Anger flashed through me. Who did Harold think he was?

As if we had summoned him, Harold slid through the door. "My girls."

"I've told Mama I'm going to meet with Lonnie's parents." She smiled at me. "I need this, Mama. I need to say I'm sorry."

"For what? You didn't do anything." I tucked my trembling hand under my legs.

"I think it's a fine idea, baby." Life was so simple for people like Harold. They told the truth and reaped the benefits.

"If you feel it will help you, Iona. You have to move forward. I'm sure this Lonnie wouldn't have it any other way."

Harold squeezed my arm. "I'm going to call Mr. and Mrs. Allen."

I almost argued with him but I smiled instead. When he was gone, I scooted my chair closer to Iona. "I need to talk to you."

"I'm sorry, Mama."

"Stop saying that. We all have done things that hurt others. I've failed you in so many ways."

"No you haven't. Mama, you tried to tell me that life can get away from you within a second. I didn't listen. This happened because of my choices."

"Iona, we need to talk about choices."

Harold pushed through the door. He was still handsome, and he didn't deserve my hidden life. "We'll see them tonight, and as soon as you get out we're going there. Mrs. Allen thought you might like to see Lonnie's grave."

A horrible shadow passed over my baby's face. "Did anyone ask Iona if she wanted to go to that place again?" I caught myself before "Black Mountain" slipped out. "Iona, do you remember that story I used to tell you before bed each night?"

"That was the worst kind of story, so sad." Harold frowned.

"Where did you get the story, Mama?" She was opening the door for me to walk through and confess.

"I'm not sure. I heard it told when I was young."

"Did Maw Maw tell you the story?"

"I'm not sure if it's that old. I don't know. Maybe she did. Maybe she saw it in her tea leaves." I laughed.

"When I get out of here, I want to see Maw Maw. I want to ask her about the names."

For nineteen years I lived with the story in my heart, my fairy-tale ending. "I have to tell you something that I've kept from you." My heart beat so loud I was sure both Harold and Iona could hear.

"Your grandmother passed away." Harold's words smoothed out the crazy thought I had of telling the whole truth.

Iona stared at her father and then at me.

"She didn't even know who she was on most days. A lot of the time she thought she was part of that silly story." I lied, lied, lied.

"Dead?" Iona's voice broke.

"She died on the morning of your accident. I tried to find you." I made the words as easy as I could. "They say she passed away quietly. That's the best way, or so they say." I looked at her. "I'd like to make a little noise when I leave this world."

Iona smiled. "Me too, Mama. I'll miss her. She kept so much of herself out of view."

"Your grandmother was a wise woman. I didn't listen to her enough."

"I think I'm going to steal your mama for a while." Harold put his hand on my arm.

Iona smiled. "Okay. Go, Mama. I'll be right here."

We walked to the cafeteria side by side. Passion was never in my vocabulary when it came to Harold. He was steady, safe. No, deep lust didn't factor into our marriage.

"Annie, is there anything you need to tell me?" Harold took a Snickers bar off the rack.

"Not a thing." I didn't miss a beat.

"After nineteen years of marriage, I think you can tell me about the past. I know there is something. And honestly I think it has something to do with that story you always told Iona."

I looked him dead in the eye. "Are you kidding? What would that have to do with anything? I'm tired, Harold. I've lost my mother and nearly lost my daughter. I'm sorry I'm not myself." I fought the fear in my gut.

He handed me an Almond Joy. "Okay. But you can tell me anything. You're my girl, Annie. Nothing you ever did or will do could change that."

"That's good to know." But I knew he couldn't possibly forgive what Nellie had done.

Fifty-eight

Some parts of a person never leave you. I heard his soft, steady voice in the hall. It was more of a tone than the actual words, more like a melody. My heart fluttered and a giggle sat in my chest. Iona sat propped against her pillow. Harold had gone to make phone calls home.

"They're here," Iona whispered.

I nodded. The small tap on the door made me jump anyway. "Come in." I tried to sound calm.

Rose had her hair pulled back and her face was bare, open, a plate-glass window into her heart. Jack stood tall, holding her together with one hand placed on her shoulder.

"I hope this isn't too much trouble."

"It's no bother, Mr. Allen." Iona's face crumpled and tears sprang in her eyes.

Rose moved to my daughter's side. "We know it was a horrible accident. Deer come out of nowhere. There's a lot on Black Mountain."

Jack looked straight at me.

"I should have made him wait," Iona whispered.

"We all know Lonnie didn't wait when he wanted something. You did the best you could." Jack smiled at Iona.

A wild look passed through Rose's eyes. "But if you had made him wait . . ."

Jack squeezed her shoulder. "We've been through this. There was nothing different to be done."

"Why did you leave, Iona?" Rose's voice broke.

I tried not to imagine her young and in Hobbs's arms. No wonder he wanted her instead of me. She was beautiful.

Iona took a breath and wiped at her tears. "He was leaving whether I went or not. I drove because, well, he had been drinking."

"He was having such a good time at the party. Why did he want to leave?" Rose took one of Iona's hands in hers.

Iona looked at me and I nodded as if I had a clue to what she was about to say.

"He saw his real father in the barn."

"Hobbs. He saw Hobbs?" Rose cut a look at me. Did she see who I was?

My chest tightened. Why couldn't Harold be there at that very moment? Here stood Rose and me, the women in Hobbs Pritchard's life, standing in the same room together. I looked at Iona and then I looked at Jack. He stared back with our story written in his expression. He married Rose and took in her son. Harold pushed open the door and for a minute the two men blended together and became one. I looked away and studied my daughter's face. She was solid, whole, my star to navigate by.

"I should have come to find you." Iona was beating herself up.

Nellie emerged from her grave and her hate for this woman who stepped into her marriage pushed her into the open. Hate for Jack because he married Rose and didn't help her that night swirled in my brain. Hate for Lonnie for walking into my daughter's life made me ball my fingers into fists. Hate for myself, for Annie, who pushed me toward the bed. I hadn't saved my precious daughter. All Nellie's actions led to this moment.

I hugged Iona to me. "You did what you had to do, Iona. Sometimes you're backed up against the wall and have to make the right choice." Everyone was watching me. "You couldn't let him drive in his condition," I added. "You are a good person."

I looked at Jack and his wife. "Please go. Leave my family alone."

"No." Iona pulled away. "Don't leave." She held her hands, her beautiful marred hands, out to Rose again. "I'm sorry. I loved him."

Rose moved to Iona and sobbed.

"You can come see Lonnie's grave when you get out of here," Jack said.

"She doesn't need to go back there." I clasped my hands together to keep them from shaking.

"We talked about her going, Annie. It will be fine." Harold stood beside me.

"He's in the church cemetery, buried beside Hobbs." Jack stared at me.

They had found Hobbs's head. A shiver ran down my backbone.

Two days later Iona was ready to leave the hospital. "I think we have to talk to her," Harold said.

I thought of the baby, which the doctor and I had never spoken of again. "About what?"

"About her hands. About her music."

"We have time." My head spun. "I think I'll skip going to this grave. I'll stay here and wait. I just can't go."

"Annie, you can't let Iona go without you. She's closer to you."

I wanted to laugh in his face. "Are you kidding?"

He looked shocked. "You really don't understand how hard she struggles to please you?"

I held up my hand. "I can't take one of your sermons. I just can't. Why do you have to be so darn perfect?" We stood outside on the sidewalk.

"You have to go whether you're angry with me or not." He took a step forward and then turned around. "Annie, do you know Mr. Allen?"

"What?"

"It's just that he looks at you like he knows you from somewhere."

"Harold, I'm so exhausted." Real tears filled my eyes.

He came to me with a hug. "I'm sorry. I know you've had it hard. But you have to come with Iona."

I nodded, having dodged telling him a bold-faced lie. "I almost lost her."

"We almost lost her, Annie." He released me and we went into the hospital.

Iona wore new clothes I had bought at a little shop Mama always visited downtown. "I love this color blue, Mama."

I smiled. "I'm glad." The dress was shorter than I would have liked but it was all the rage.

"I know you don't want to go to Black Mountain." Her arms were cold and she hugged herself. November in North Carolina was different than home.

"I don't think I'll ever love anyone else like I loved Lonnie."

"You know, Iona, I know you don't think I understand. You will love someone again, but in a way you're right. You will never love anyone like you did him."

She hugged me.

"Look, Iona, we have to talk."

She looked at me funny. "What?"

"I know something that even your father doesn't know. He was gone when the doctor came to tell us. I haven't said anything because I wanted to wait until you were strong enough to take the news. Then when I saw you were, I just didn't." The words tumbled from me. "First—your father knows this—the doctors say you may never play professionally."

"I figured that out, but I think I'll prove them wrong. I'm like you."

"We have to think about this part before we tell your father. It could ruin him."

How unfair was that? I knew this wasn't about him.

"What's wrong?" Iona frowned.

"You're going to have a baby."

Outside the hospital window, people were going for lunch. Life was moving.

"I know you're thinking it's some kind of gift from God, but you're wrong. You can't bring a baby into this world from that relationship. You said yourself Lonnie wasn't stable. What if his problems are passed on to this child?" I had to make her understand.

"What do you mean, Mama?" Her voice was quiet and calm.

"Think about it, Iona. Your father loves you. He'd never tell you to do something about this baby. But the truth is he'll be ruined. You know it. He's a minister. He's an example. He'll lose his whole life."

What kind of mother was I?

"Are you suggesting I get rid of this baby? That's illegal. Plus I can't kill this baby or anything else. No. I killed Lonnie. No."

I killed your real father. "Iona! You did not kill him. You know that. This is not a baby yet. It's too small. We can find someone who will do the procedure. Women have it done. I bet Atlanta has someone. Shoot, we'll go to New York if we have to. What about school? What about fighting and making yourself play?"

Iona stepped away from me. "Now you care about my music? Make up your mind." Years of her anger came at me. "I could give it up for adoption."

"Do you want that? Bring it into the world to give it away?"

"Who knows if I'll play professionally." She looked at her hands.

"Iona, since when have you listened to reason?"

She half smiled.

"Think about it. We have to do something quick. We won't tell your father. He's a man and will never understand. It's so easy for them to pass judgment."

"Daddy wouldn't judge me."

I rushed ahead. "Oh no, but why worry him? Why make him choose? We can do this on our own."

She was pale but calm. "I want to go see Lonnie's grave."

"Okay."

"You are going, aren't you, Mama?"

My daughter stood before me alive when she should have been dead. All my choices brought me to this place, whether good or bad. I had to move forward. "Of course I'm going."

Fifty-nine

Harold crept up the mountain road in our station wagon, nothing like my first ride in a rattletrap of a truck. I caught myself imagining Hobbs as a forty-five-year-old man driving us up the mountain. The destruction would have been so much worse had he lived that long. But Hobbs was all I ever wanted that warm fall day in 1938.

"It's a pretty place." Leave it to Harold to be so positive.

The Connor cabin looked older but solid. The yard was empty. All the boys would be grown now. What happened to Maynard? Did he have a good life? What about his mother?

"Where did he say the cemetery was?"

"Up toward the top. In the sharp curve, you'll see the church first. It's to the side."

Harold looked at me. "Mr. Allen told you all that?"

"He must have." I looked out the window as we passed Aunt Ida's house. A child's bike sat in the drive. If Harold only knew; this was my nightmare come to life.

"I don't remember him saying anything about a sharp curve."

"He must have." I was so good at a lot of things now. I

could work my way around the lie with great skill. In the side mirror, I caught the reflection of Hobbs and then realized it was only Iona.

A mailbox marked the drive to our old house. Imagine, a mail route. I tucked my hands under my legs. The ax was over my head, heavy. Some mornings I woke to the dead weight in my arm muscles. Not many people walked away from murder. And I sure didn't. I had been imprisoned for nineteen years inside my head.

The church was so much smaller than I remembered. There was a real paved parking lot. I wondered if that boring pastor still preached. Harold parked in one of the spaces, and Iona lugged a big pot of mums from the car.

I fought the urge to show them the way to the family plot, but it didn't take Iona long to find Lonnie's grave. It was the only fresh grave in the place.

She dropped to her knees and dug a hole with her fingers. "No white flowers for you, Lonnie," she whispered.

I stood close to her while Harold stood at a gravestone next to us.

"Annie, isn't that the name of the man in that silly story you told Iona every night?" He knew. Somehow he knew enough to begin questioning me.

I shrugged. "I guess so. But it's just a name."

"An unusual name."

An older woman stood down the hill behind Harold. I would have known her anywhere. "I'm going to walk over here and give you some time, Iona."

Harold watched me walk by him before he spoke. "Annie, someday I want you to tell me the whole story about what happened. Will you do that before I die?"

"Darling, you're not going to die for a long time. I'll have lots of stories by then."

He frowned and went to stand by Iona.

Mrs. Connor stood in her family plot. I cast a shadow over the grave of her husband. "I always wondered if you'd come back to this old mountain, Nellie."

Tears blurred my vision. "I haven't heard my real name in someone's mouth in a long, long time. Even Mama couldn't use it. My name is Annie now."

She turned to look at me. "You're a good soul. That's never changed. I can feel it."

"I don't much feel like a good soul these days." I looked over the top of her head at Iona.

"Look at you. You're town folk now. You even talk fancy."

I smiled. "How's Maynard?"

"Smart as a whistle. Lives over in Knoxville with his family. Oshie is a doctor."

"Wow."

She smiled. "Yes ma'am. I raised good boys."

"How about Shelly?"

Mrs. Connor nodded. "She had a few rough patches but she's still around here now and then. You ought to hear her story yourself. She made good use of that money."

"I can't this time." I nodded at Iona. "That's my girl."

"She looks like you, Nellie. Was she hooked up with that Lonnie?"

I nodded.

"Lord, Nellie, you know he was Hobbs's son?"

"I found out when he died."

"Good thing she wasn't Hobbs's girl cause . . ." She looked at me. "Oh my. What a mess."

"Yes, it's a mess. It's a fine mess."

"I seen his ghost the other night, standing in the road where the car skidded off."

"Does this mountain ever lose any of its spirits?"

"I reckon the troubled ones just hang on here. They're welcome to stay. It's one of those places."

"I wonder if I'll come back here and wander over this mountain when I die."

Mrs. Connor laughed. "It'll all depend on what you get off your chest, Nellie. Don't no one care about that business with Hobbs but you and him. But you're the one holding the story so close; protecting it has caused you a lot of pain."

Iona walked in my direction.

"But I couldn't tell her." I pointed my chin at Iona.

"Tell it all now before it's too late."

Sixty

Darien never felt so much like home. We held Mama's memorial service. Harold was a wonderful speaker. He captured Mama's spirit. Iona, pale and quiet, stood close to me as I sprinkled Mama's ashes into the ocean. She never wanted to be buried by Daddy. We took the ferry to Sapelo Island. The wind blew as I let the dust out of the urn. Mama's remains. Peace filled my heart.

The next day Iona came down the steps with her bags.

"What are you doing?" I was cooking her favorite breakfast, oatmeal with brown sugar.

"I'm going back to school. I'm recovered."

Harold closed his newspaper. "I think you're right, Iona. Get back on that horse."

"I thought we decided to talk about your future." I held the spoon in midair.

"I'm grown, Mama. I have to make a life for myself." Her calmness echoed in the room.

"You could stay a couple more weeks."

"Mama . . ."

"Annie, let her be for now."

This wasn't how it was supposed to turn out.

"I'll take you to the bus station." I untied my apron.

"Anthony is picking me up."

"You can't leave, Iona. You've been through too much. So much is still going on." I willed her to look me in the eyes.

"I'm not planning on trapping him into a loveless marriage, Mama. He's giving me a ride to school. I've got to get out of here." Her face remained smooth.

I wanted to take her by the shoulders and shake her. "We need to talk."

"We've talked and talked. Now I've got to decide what I'm going to do. Not you."

And there it was. Her life rolled into two sentences.

"I'll be fine. I won't give up my music. What else can happen to me? It only gets better from here."

"A lot, young lady." The words came out harsher than I intended. She was being stupid. I knew if I let her walk out that door something bad was going to happen.

"Annie, let Iona go back to school. The holidays will be here in a couple of weeks. We can talk future then."

Harold's face was thinner. All this had taken a toll on him. I pulled out a chair and sank into it.

Iona kissed the top of her father's head. She made no move to come close to me. This had all become my fault. Wasn't that the first truth to surface in a long time?

In less than an hour, Iona was gone. If I had been on Black Mountain, I would have seen Merlin Hocket. I knew that in the bottom of my heart. Only doom could be on the horizon, no matter what Iona chose.

With my little girl gone, it was easy to push all the pressing thoughts to the back of my mind. There was no plan to save

her. I was exhausted. I wondered if this was how Mama felt
when I left with Hobbs. What had she done to cause me to run
up that hill with him to waiting doom? Nothing. Mamas can't
protect their daughters. Not really. They're helpless to watch
and wait.

Harold was busy at the church. We ate quiet suppers
together. A couple of times I almost told him the whole story,
all of it. One night I served his favorite pot roast. I pulled the
chair close to him and sat down. He only opened the
newspaper and began to read. He didn't want to know my past.
A part of me would always love Harold in a special way, but not
like I should, not like a decent wife loves her husband. What
was love anyway? Maybe people got tired of searching for it and
settled for someone, settled into a way of life, and made it
work. But that wasn't love.

Two nights later, I sat up straight in my bed. Harold was
sleeping in the den. Neither one of us had brought this
arrangement up for discussion. Mama stood in the corner of
the room. At first I thought I might be sleeping, but I wasn't.
She was there, beautiful like when I was a child before I met
Hobbs, before Daddy died. Her hair was swept up on her head
like she was going to a party and I couldn't help but think of
the story she told of her own mama visiting her after death.

"Nellie."

What a beautiful sound my name made. "Mama," I whispered, trying not to break the spell.

"You've been through so much in your life. Much of it you
brought on yourself. Your daughter has made a terrible choice.
She needs you now. Go now, Nellie. I'm not sure she'll live
through this." She looked so sad. "Go now, tonight. Drive.
Don't wait. Go like I should have chased you."

My feet hit the floor without thinking. For once in my life I
would listen to Mama. I thought of waking Harold but I knew

he would talk me out of going. I didn't have time to explain a dream to him.

The sun was sitting on top of the trees when I pulled into the parking lot of the school. I knocked on the big door several times before a woman wrapped in a pink robe answered.

"Can I help you?" She spit the words at me.

I must have looked a sight. "I'm Iona Harbor's mother. There's an emergency."

The woman pushed the door open. "She's on the second floor, room three."

"I know." I took the stairs two at a time. When I reached room three, I gave the door a hard push and the lock gave. The twin bed was covered with blood. Iona was crumpled in a heap between the bed and the wall.

"Call the ambulance now!" I pulled Iona closer to me.

She looked at me with glassy eyes. "Mama?"

"Iona, what have you done?"

"What's going on in here?" The woman stood in the door.

"Call an ambulance. Now. My daughter is going to die if you don't."

The woman ran away.

"I got rid of it, Mama. I did it on my own. Now I want to die."

"Don't you dare die, Iona! You can't do that to me. You don't know the whole story. You don't know and I have to tell you. I never told you the real story."

She looked at me and nodded. "Okay."

She was as limp as a washcloth. "Iona, you keep talking to me."

She looked at me. "Mama?"

"Why, Iona? What were you thinking?"

"I want to go to Lonnie."

"You can't until you hear the whole story. Then you'll understand." I cried.

Her breath was heavy.

"You stay with me, Iona! I mean it! I can't lose you now."

Then the ambulance drivers were there, pushing me away. I rode in the ambulance with her, holding her hand. "I need you."

A nurse motioned me back through the double doors. "Doctor Morgan would like to speak with you." Her face was stern, and I thought of the other hospital, only weeks before. *Not today either, Lord. Please not today. God, I'm so sorry I ever said anything. Forgive me for all I have done. Please!*

The doctor was young enough to be my son. He held a clipboard and I couldn't tell from his face whether bad news was headed my way or not. "Mrs. Harbor?"

"Yes. I'm Iona's mother."

"Are you aware of her situation?"

"I found her. I rode in the ambulance with her."

He nodded. "Had you not found her when you did, she wouldn't be alive. She's lost a lot of blood. Are you aware of what she was trying to accomplish?"

"I have a good idea." I didn't say I'd put the idea in her mind.

He touched my arm. "I know this is tough. Your daughter is still pregnant. Of course we'll have to do a procedure. The baby doesn't have a chance of survival now. Iona will survive, but there's a good chance she will never have children."

I looked at him. "I don't know what to say. I don't know what to say."

He nodded. His eyes reflected pity. He put all the blame on Iona, but the blame should have been placed on me.

"When can I see my daughter?"

"I need you to sign a consent form for the procedure, then you can go back for a minute. I doubt she'll be awake."

The form required my signature. In the loopy letters of my

name, or my assumed name, I signed away a life. What made me any different than Hobbs Pritchard? When did I ever think I had the right to play God?

Doctor Morgan tugged on the clipboard that I held. "Go through those doors and to the right. She's going to be okay, but you might want to consider finding her someone to talk to, a doctor."

I nodded and pushed away from him through the doors. Iona was pale, her eyes closed, as if she might not wake back up. "Sweetie, I'm here. Oh Iona, I didn't mean for you to take things into your hands. I would have done anything to help you. This is my fault. Do you understand? All of this is my fault. It started so long ago. I caused this. I was wrong, Iona." She never moved. I stood holding her hand until the nurse came to get her.

"She'll be in the operating room about forty-five minutes." The nurse pulled on the bed. "Doctor Morgan will see you after it's over."

I called Harold.

"Hello." He sounded sleepy, and I was sure he had no idea I had left the house.

"Harold."

"What?" Now I had his attention. "Where are you?"

"I'm here at the hospital with Iona. I had a terrible dream during the night. I woke up and knew I was supposed to come here. If I had awakened you, you would have talked me out of it."

"What's happened, Annie?"

"I'm not sure," I lied. "But I think Iona has lost a baby. I think she's in bad condition, Harold. Can you borrow a car?"

"What hospital are you at?"

"I'm not sure. It's close to the school. I rode in the ambulance. She was almost gone when I got there. No one would have believed me, Harold."

"Annie, you should have told me. We could have gotten someone to go check on her. Got her help sooner."

"You wouldn't have believed me, Harold," but I was talking to a dial tone.

By the time Harold reached the hospital, I was sitting in Iona's room waiting on her to regain consciousness. When he entered the room, I could see he was not the man I married. I had destroyed him too.

"She was pregnant. She tried to get rid of the baby on her own. She almost bled to death. If I hadn't gotten there when I did, she would have died. She'll be okay, but the baby is lost." My tone was flat. His judgment was written in his eyes.

"Did you know about this?"

I only looked at him.

"What can we do for her?" He stood close to the bed, to his only child, who was not his child, but was his child in every way.

"Help her want to live. Love her." I stroked her hand. The scars from the car wreck weren't so angry, but her skin was tinged orange from her own blood. I rubbed at the places with a warm washcloth. "The stains won't go away, Harold." In that moment I cried. I sobbed and sobbed. Harold touched my shoulder.

"She'll live a good life. I'll make sure." I looked at him as fear and hatred blended into one. "I'd give my whole life for her. I have given my whole life for her. Do you understand what I have, what we have?"

"I know you don't know me. I know that scares the hell out of you. There's no reason in this world for you to hang on with me, none, but Iona needs us both. I'm willing to give that to her. How about you, Harold? Can you live with me? Can you mend our daughter?"

The anger in his eyes flashed. "I won't give up on her,

Annie. She's my child too. I have more to give than you know. Why would you ask such a question? We're a family for better or worse. This is the worst, Annie."

Iona, pale as death, was the glue that stuck us together. He was my husband. I would remain with him until death did part us.

Sixty-one

A good marriage can withstand many things, but my marriage wasn't good. It wasn't bad, but it wasn't the kind books are written about. Harold was a preacher, and the church had a say in our lives whether either of us wanted to admit this or not. Harold wouldn't leave me, and I wouldn't leave him. Both of us had our reasons. Harold would lose his job. No church in those days wanted a preacher who left his wife. I owed him too much to hurt him that way. Iona needed both of us as her solid rock, even if we were truly sand beneath her feet. Maybe if I had told Harold the truth, spilled my guts, he would have understood, warmed to me again. But in my heart, I knew he wasn't this kind of man. Not many men could be.

Often in those days after Iona came home, I thought of Jack. It made no sense whatsoever. I knew I'd never see him again, but part of me knew he was the only person I could ever talk to about my past.

Iona stayed home a year. She was quiet, withdrawn. Anthony came around. We had to give him credit for not giving up on our daughter. It was in the summer when I noticed a change in her. She came from upstairs one morning and told me she was going back to school. This was the best news I'd heard.

"I'm not going back to Chapel Hill. I'm going to the University of Georgia. Anthony goes there, and they have a good music department."

"That sounds wonderful."

Her shoulders relaxed, and she uncurled her fingers. "I think you mean that."

"I do."

She smiled a smile, the first I'd seen in ages. "I need you to help me with one thing." The words were testing words.

"What?"

"I want to go back to Black Mountain one more time." My face must have revealed my true feelings. "Mama, don't be afraid. I want to say good-bye to Lonnie, proper. I talked to Anthony and he thinks it's a good idea. He offered to take me and wanted to be there, but I didn't think it would be good for us as a couple, you know."

My face must have shown amazement because Iona laughed.

"It wasn't easy, but I told him everything, all of it, Mama. He knows I might never have children. He knows I might never play music professionally. On both counts he thinks I'm wrong." She took my hand. "He believes in me, Mama."

Tears rolled down my face. I'm not sure if they were for me or her, probably both. "I will go with you." I could make one more trip up that mountain.

"Good. I'll tell Anthony."

"I'll tell your father."

Iona looked surprised.

"He won't like it, but he'll live with it."

* * *

Harold was hard at work in his office at the church. I stood in the door and watched how the light showed the bare spots on his scalp. Part of me wanted to run and kiss that tender part of his head, but we were past those kinds of feelings.

He glanced up and a frown formed on his forehead. "Is something wrong?"

I came in the door. "I don't think it's wrong, but I wanted to tell you Iona's plans."

He folded his hands in front of him. "So you two have been planning without me again."

"You could say she planned this one all on her own. She's much better at this than me. I could learn a lesson from her."

He smiled. "So what is her plan?"

"She's going back to school."

He flinched.

"Not to Chapel Hill, but in Athens, where Anthony goes."

"He's a good young man."

"I have to agree. You don't run into men like him often."

He searched my face. "I hope I'm one of those men, Annie."

I laughed. "Of course you are, Harold. You're a saint."

He smiled. "No I'm not."

"This is the part you won't care for. She wants to go back to Black Mountain to give Lonnie a 'proper good-bye.' It seems she's told Anthony the whole story, and I mean the whole story. He agrees with her plan. She's asked me to go with her."

"What did you say?" He watched me carefully.

"I said yes of course."

He folded his fingers together on his desk. I had become a member of his congregation. "You seemed so against the place before."

"I suppose I did."

"Why the change of heart?"

I shrugged. "My daughter has found the guts to tell her whole story to this man. I have to help her put the past behind her."

He nodded. "It will be very cleansing for her."

"Yes. I'm proud of her. She has a lot of guts."

"A lot like her mother."

I looked away. "I'm nowhere near as brave as her, Harold."

"You are. You just don't know it."

We set out for Black Mountain the next Monday. I no longer feared what would happen to me if someone recognized me. It was hot and sunny when we pulled into the parking lot of the church. Iona was driving. Aunt Ida's house had been torn down and replaced by two new houses made to look old. So many people were looking for that kind of thing. I thought of Hobbs's sister. Did anyone ever find her? Where were Jack and Rose? Did they leave? So many questions were left unanswered. When we got out of the car, Iona smiled at me.

"You don't have to go up there, Mama."

"I'm going."

The graves were on a hill that was completely green, dotted here and there with granite stones. I knew him before he even turned around. His shoulders weren't as straight, and he leaned forward more, but it was him.

"Mama, I think that's—"

"Yes, it's Lonnie's dad."

"Or stepdad."

I touched her arm. "He was more a father than his real father could ever have been."

"Yeah, I guess you're right." She looked around. "Maybe I should wait."

"He won't mind." I didn't look at her. I couldn't let her know my feelings.

"Come with me."

"You know I will." We climbed that hill together.

He turned and watched us, straightening his shoulders. There was a fresh grave. My stomach ached.

"Iona." He held out his hand. "I'm so glad to see you."

"I wanted to visit Lonnie's grave one more time." She held a small book in her hand. "I have something I want to leave."

Jack nodded. "Good." Then he looked at me. "It's good to see you again, Mrs. Harbor."

I looked away with a lump in my throat. "I think I'll give you some time alone, Iona."

Iona looked over at me. "Who died?"

"My wife passed away a month ago today."

"Oh no." Iona fought tears, and I wondered how good all this truth stuff was for her.

"She had what the doctor called a rare form of cancer."

I touched his arm. "I'm sorry."

He looked at me with tears in his eyes. "I loved her more than I could ever tell her."

"But she knew." I looked over at Iona. "You take your time. I'll walk with Mr. Allen."

He smiled. "I know who you are," he whispered.

"We knew each other too well." We walked through the graves out of earshot. "She doesn't know, Jack." It felt good to say his name.

"I know."

"It's a mess. I figured it all out, you know. What my lies have caused."

He patted my shoulder. "Things are better now?"

I smiled. "They are. Iona is better. She's going back to school."

"Good."

We were silent.

"So, how in the world did you end up with his girlfriend, Jack?" There it was, one of the questions that burned in my heart.

"She was my heart, Nellie."

The words made my legs weak, and I stopped walking.

"I wish I knew how that felt."

He looked at me. "What about your husband?"

"I've not been good at marriages."

"Rose and I had a fine marriage. It was only Lonnie who tried our patience at times. He had Hobbs's knack of seeking out trouble wherever he could. Iona is like you, Nellie. She has none of her father in her."

So he knew.

"I saw you in her the first time she came up that mountain. I thought I was crazy, but then, well, you know . . ."

"Yes."

"Her life will be blessed."

"Not because of anything I've done." I could see the top of Iona's head as she sat by Lonnie's grave.

"I think it's because of what you did do."

I loved him more as an older man. "You're too kind, trying to make me feel better, but the truth is, my daughter is smart all on her own. Nothing I did in the past has helped her. It only hurt her."

"That's not fair to yourself, Nellie." His green eyes flashed. "You had to do more than survive."

We were talking about the past and clearing the air.

"Playing God only causes a person grief and heartache."

He nodded.

"I've had to pay for my sins, and others have paid too."

"It's all over. It's been over for a long time."

"Not for me." I looked at him and felt like that dumb young girl.

"You're a grown woman. Look at you. You're not that dumb little girl that came riding up the mountain in Hobbs's truck."

"Sometimes I think I'm still her."

He looked around. "This old mountain has been good to me. You know I found Mama's necklace. Until I saw it, I never believed Hobbs killed anyone other than Clyde Parker. I always thought the mountain gave him way too much credit for his meanness. But I know he killed her. You found the necklace and brought it from his hiding place." He touched my arm. "You took a cold-blooded murderer out of this world. Nellie, there ain't no telling how many people you saved beside yourself."

Was I in a dream? "I'd like to put it behind me."

"There's a way. You have to be honest."

Iona moved toward us.

"You look me up sometime, Nellie. I'd love to talk again." His old smile twinkled in his eyes.

"You have a good life, Jack."

"I have and now it's time to start on chapter two."

I drove us down the mountain, Iona deep in her thoughts and me on the verge of screaming with joy. My talk with Jack released a pent-up fear, the power Hobbs had over me. Was it really over? Not yet.

When we sat down to supper that night, I thought of Jack's words. I had to be honest. I looked at Harold and Iona and took a big deep breath. "I want to tell you the truth about that story."

"What story?" Harold was looking through his newspaper, but Iona was alert, watching my face.

"'Ghost on Black Mountain'?" Iona folded her fingers on the table.

"Yes."

Harold closed the paper and folded it neat, meeting my stare with interest.

"Now what I'm going to tell you by no means lets me off the hook. You see, it's like this: Once there was Nellie and Hobbs Pritchard." Harold watched me close and Iona's fingers shook. "I was Nellie and I married Hobbs Pritchard even though Mama warned me against him. She saw death in her tea leaves. But I didn't listen. I thought I knew everything . . ."

Epilogue

Iona married Anthony after she finished school. He went off to Vietnam and she fretted at home until his return. They were married in her daddy's church by her daddy. Iona became a professor at Chapel Hill, where she taught music and played for her family each and every night. Anthony became a well-known wildlife artist. They had three boys, Harold, Tony, and Lonnie.

It took a little time, but Harold finally accepted that Annie was actually Nellie. He never judged her like she so often imagined. Instead, they spent about a year talking endlessly about how she survived such a tough time. Harold loved Annie or Nellie, whoever she was, and there was no doubting that. He loved his daughter, Iona, and never regretted the day he met his wife, even if she wasn't totally honest. Forgiving her this trespass was the easiest thing he ever did.

Harold died right after preaching one of his favorite sermons, on the prodigal son. He was sixty-eight. Nellie was right by his side, holding him, begging him to breathe. She couldn't let him go. He was her heart.

She buried him in the cemetery near her daddy. There was one plot left open for her, and even though in that first year she often thought of dying too, she never gave up. She didn't leave their house for another twelve years. His clothes hung in the closet for as long as she lived there.

Jack Allen lived to be a hundred years old and remained in the old homeplace. He watched more and more folks move to the mountain, even met AzLeigh's granddaughter, whom he willed the house to. There were many times in his life he often thought he might leave the mountain, but to the end Black Mountain was his home.

In the last years of Nellie's life, she insisted on moving into an assisted-living home, rather than Iona and Anthony's house. "A mother has no business living with her daughter. I might tell some important secret when I start to lose my mind." She grinned at Iona, who only shook her head. Nellie had long ago learned to forgive herself for her sins, since God had forgiven her so many years earlier.

The home where Nellie moved was located right outside of Asheville, not four hours away from Iona, on a small piece of property where the house Hobbs rented for him and Rose once stood. It was here she met Maynard Connor all over again and in a more proper way. He was fine-looking for a man of eighty-three. He'd lived a life full of surprises like Nellie. Of course he remembered her right off and even called her Mrs. Pritchard the first time they spoke.

"I'm not Mrs. Pritchard, you old fool. I'm Nellie to you."

Maynard only laughed. "You killed him, didn't you?"

Nellie smiled. "That's not a story I tell to anyone nowadays, Maynard."

They were friends the rest of her life, eating supper together and watching movies.

On the day Nellie passed away, before Maynard had one of those little attendees unlock her door, she was sitting in her recliner looking out the window, enjoying the warmth of the sun as it beat through the glass. She had a perfect view of Black Mountain on a clear day. And that day was clear as a bell.

That mountain was like a picture her son-in-law might paint, every detail defined. She could make out where developers were building a new community. Life went on and on back on Black Mountain. Nellie had come to realize the place was a character within itself, alive and vital like any talking, walking, breathing person. The mountain would never die out, and the thought plain comforted her.

Acknowledgments

There are so many people who helped bring *Ghost on Black Mountain* full circle: Holly's belief in my work kept me in the seat. Jeanie dug in and pushed this book until it landed in the perfect publishing house. You are a blessing sent from God. Kara Cesare brought out the best in my writing through her fabulous editing. I'm grateful to my Jack for encouraging me when a lot of husbands would have stopped believing. I couldn't have written a word without Ella. You always have the best ideas. Thank you to my lovely grown children, Melissa, Cassey, Beth, and Stephen, for listening to their mother rattle on and on about Black Mountain. Thank you to my enduring fan Myrtis Doyle. You never gave up on this writer. We haven't made it to Hollywood yet, but I got a feeling we will. Thanks to Darlene and Dianne for reading the book so many times their vision grew worse. If not for my brother, who was forced as a young child to listen to my stories, Hobbs and Nellie might not have come into existence. And a special thanks to Maria for being my voice of reason on this journey.

Ghost on Black Mountain

ANN HITE

Introduction

On Black Mountain, ghosts roam almost as freely as the living, carrying dark pasts and warnings of what's to come. In her haunting debut, Ann Hite weaves together the stories of five Southern women whose lives are irrevocably changed by one man and the act that kills him. These women navigate through tragedy and darkness, battling their own demons and confronting others' as they struggle toward new beginnings and a chance at happiness. Each perspective offers a shocking revelation that reshapes the truth, leaving readers to wonder if anyone is really the person she seems to be.

Topics and Questions for Discussion

1. *Ghost on Black Mountain* is told by multiple narrators and out of chronological order. How does this affect your understanding of the events that take place in the novel and your opinions of the main characters? How do you think the story would be different if it were told chronologically and/or from one perspective?

2. Which narrator do you sympathize with or connect to the most? Why?

3. If you could have read more from one character's perspective in this novel, whose would it be?

4. In many ways the ghosts are their own characters and help dictate the course of action in the story. Compare the different reactions the witnesses have to seeing ghosts.

Consider how the ghosts directly influence a character's actions.

5. What do you think attracts Nellie to Hobbs in the first place? Did she ever love him? When does she see him for who he really is?

6. Examine Shelly's role in the story. How does her role as a narrator differ from the others'? What makes her essential to the story?

7. On page 195, Aunt Ida says, "I let Nellie down. I didn't help her when Hobbs near beat her to death." Would Nellie have found another way out if someone had simply answered her cries for help? Do you think she was justified in her actions?

8. Nellie's decision brings consequences that reach far into the future and alter the lives of several people. How important is the time period in which this story is set? How would this story work in the present?

9. Aunt Ida and Rose seem to be the only characters who were able to see any good in Hobbs. Whose version of Hobbs do you think was closest to who he really was? Could he have been a good father to Lonnie if he'd had the chance? Or was he purely mean and violent, as most people thought he was?

10. Mother-and-daughter relationships are prevalent throughout *Ghost on Black Mountain*. In some cases, readers see a character as both a mother and a daughter. Discuss the influence of these special relationships on each of the narrators.

11. On page 313, Nellie admits that "Mamas can't protect their daughters. Not really. They're helpless to watch and wait." Do you think this is true? How is it proved or disproved in the course of the story?

12. In the first part of Nellie's story, there are moments of tenderness between her and Jack. Had things been different, do you think Jack and Nellie could have loved each other?

13. Iona and Lonnie both grew up with loving parents, though Iona knew nothing of her real father for most of her life. Do you think Lonnie would have turned out differently had he never known about Hobbs or found his father's skull?

14. There are many romances in *Ghost on Black Mountain*— some end happily and others don't. Discuss the different dynamics in the relationships between Nellie and Hobbs, Rose and Hobbs, Rose and Jack, Nellie and Harold, Iona and Lonnie, and Iona and Anthony. Which of these, if any, do you think were rooted in true love?

Enhance Your Book Club

1. Have you ever had a paranormal encounter? Share your own ghost stories at your book club meeting!

2. Visit www.realhaunts.com to find a local haunted house in your hometown. Plan a visit with your book club for your next meeting and come up with your own ghost story!

3. Check out the *Ghost on Black Mountain* podcast download available on iTunes! It's a recording of the original short story by Ann Hite that inspired the novel.

A Conversation with Ann Hite

Congratulations on your first novel! What has been the most exciting part of the process so far?

When I began writing about Nellie and Hobbs, I never dreamed it would actually become a novel. I was writing for fun, allowing the characters space on the page. Up until that point, I had written only short stories. So, when my fun writing exercises turned into a novel-size manuscript, I was somewhat in awe. I had fallen in love with Nellie, Josie, Shelly, Rose, and Iona. When I signed my book contract, I remember thinking, Is this actually happening? But I must say the day I received the image of the book cover was the most thrilling. I actually had to go for a nice long walk and allow reality to sink into my brain. I was a novelist. That was truly a dream come true.

How did you come to be a writer? What other authors are you inspired by?

Every year my grandmother would visit for two weeks with my family in whatever state or country we were living in. I remember looking forward to this like a child looks forward to a visit from Santa. She was the book lover and storyteller of our clan. Each evening she would gather me on her lap and tell me episodes from her childhood. As I grew older, the tales became more revealing. After years of moving around the country and five years in Europe, I finally returned to the South. I was ten and it was the midsixties. This was enough to make a writer out of most book-loving girls. My mother had brought my brother and me to live with our grandmother in Atlanta. It was then I began to absorb the both wonderful and eerie tales told by my extended family. Every weekend we piled into my grandmother's Oldsmobile and drove to "the country" to visit with my great-aunts. I would sit among what I considered very exotic women. One aunt was always on the verge of a nervous breakdown, wringing her lace hankie in her fingers. Another wore a scarf around brush curlers wound tightly into bleach-blond hair, a cigarette hanging from her fingers. And of course there was the cousin who went and married out of the faith. Her husband was Catholic. If I was quiet, they forgot I was there and began to tell the old mountain tales. These were not for the faint of heart. Believe me. I loved each story and memorized them all. This atmosphere of tall tales, spells, and spirits gave birth to Black Mountain, even though I didn't have a name for the community back then. I spent many hours writing and forcing my little brother to sit on the back stoop of my grandmother's home and listen to my stories of ghosts and goblins. I can't tell you how many times I got in trouble for scaring him silly. Ah, but children do grow up. Or do they? I became a writer.

Books came long before writing. So I have a love for many different authors. But the genres have always remained the same: Southern literature and contemporary fiction. William Faulkner's "A Rose for Emily" and Flannery O'Connor's "A Good Man Is Hard to Find" gave me the desire to show the more complex side of the South. In the late eighties, I fell in love with Ellen Gilchrist's books. I've read them all over and over. Her stories of Rhoda Manning are my favorite. Her work taught me how to write in my own voice. The first time I read *The Secret Life of Bees* by Sue Monk Kidd, I knew somehow I would succeed as a writer. The image of Lily watching the bees flying around her room gave me goose bumps and remains with me today. Julia Glass's novels, especially *I See You Everywhere*, taught me that language should sing off the page. I own every book Louise Erdrich has written. I can't get enough of her work. I also love Anne Lamott. Michael Cunningham's *The Hours* taught me that structure could be rearranged and turned into art. And of course I can't leave out *To Kill a Mockingbird*. It's what I aspire to each time I sit down at my desk.

Before it was a novel, you had written many short stories about Black Mountain. How did you manage to weave these stories together into a novel?

"Ghost on Black Mountain" was the first Black Mountain story I wrote. As new stories came to me, I noticed that Hobbs or Nellie made appearances. Nellie was a chatty character and came to me just as I was falling off to sleep most nights. She would tell me about her life. Then Shelly showed up on the page. But it wasn't until my agent suggested some of my short stories were actually outlines of novels that the aha moment occurred. When I sat down to tell the "whole extended" story of Nellie and Hobbs, the scenes just poured out of me with little effort. I'm a blank-page, character-driven writer, so truly I had no idea where Nellie would find herself at the end of the book.

Though the novel tells many stories, Nellie seems to be the central figure. How did you make the decision to create multiple narrators? Could you imagine the story being told from only one point of view? How different would that book have been from *Ghost on Black Mountain*?

I actually began the first draft of this novel in third person from only Nellie's point of view. About sixty pages into the story I had lost Nellie's original voice. What I had was a cardboard cutout character at best. I went back and began writing her in first person. This brought the book back to life. While I was on one of my long walks, Rose came to me fully formed. I knew she had to tell her story in her own voice. The original manuscript had only four narrators: Nellie, Rose, Iona, and Annie. My wonderful editor at Gallery Books suggested that if I gave Nellie's mother, Josie, and Shelly voices in the book, the story would become richer. The suggestion was perfect. Shelly's narrating provided me with details about Hobbs that tightened the plot. Josie revealed Nellie's history. This experience was exciting.

Had I kept the first sixty pages and told this story only in Nellie's voice, the novel would have lost its richness and depth. When I was studying under Emily Ellison [an Atlanta author] many moons ago, she told me something that I use in all my writing today. Every good piece of work, whether it is a story, essay, or novel, has a light that shines throughout the narrative. The way in which *Ghost on Black Mountain* is narrated provides that satisfying illumination.

Did you always know how the book would end, or did it come together as you were writing?

Because *Ghost on Black Mountain* began as a short story, I knew some of what would take place, but I did not know how Nellie's story would end. Had I known, I would never have written the book. All my work begins with at least one question. In this book's case, I wanted to know what happened to a person after he or she makes the decision to take someone's life. How does this mark the person's future, even if he or she had every right to take such a drastic, harsh action? And what if this person gets away with the deed? Those questions drove me until I found the answers.

What was your inspiration for *Ghost on Black Mountain*? Are any of your characters inspired by real people? Is there one character that you relate to the most?

I never know what will inspire me to write. Sometimes it is a song. Sometimes an old photo. It can be something as simple as a snippet of an old family story. Nellie crept into my head after my husband read an article aloud about a woman who lived in the Smoky Mountains during the twenties. She killed her husband and then attempted to hide his body. She was hanged for her crime.

Both Rose Gardner and Nellie Pritchard are loosely based on my grandmother when she was young. She never killed anyone, but she did lead a double life in many ways, like Nellie. The strengths and weaknesses of both women reflect the grandmother I knew.

Iona Harbor is one of my favorite characters. She was raised by two powerful women. They were so powerful that they overshadowed Iona's father. While I believe at some level I have to relate to each of my characters, whether they are good or bad, I really understand the frustration Iona experienced while trying to find her own way. She wanted to be herself, a musician, in a family that had other ideas.

Ghost on Black Mountain is set in the South, and you yourself live in Atlanta, Georgia. Could this novel have been set anywhere else? How did your personal ties to the setting influence your writing?

I'm a Southern girl who was raised everywhere but the South for a good part of her childhood. It's this very contradiction that gives me the ability to appreciate my Southern history, to see all the warts and not become sentimental about the place or people when I write. My passion for the South fuels my writing. I can't imagine setting any of my work anywhere but my beloved

South. My characters are simple/complex mountain people, whose families have lived in the same place for generations.

My husband's family had a tradition of vacationing in the Smoky Mountains each year. The first time I visited this beautiful place, I thought of the area where my grandmother grew up. So when these characters began to show themselves, it only seemed natural to place them in the mountains of North Carolina.

The end of Shelly's story is left as somewhat of a mystery. Does her story continue beyond the pages of the book for you, or does each character exist solely in what is written?

Shelly is a character I often claim I must have channeled. She came to me with her own set of traits, gifts, and history. I could see the clothes she would wear and her smirk of a smile. She tells me when I have one of her scenes wrong and bugs me in my dreams. I knew the first time she showed up on the page she was someone special. Her story does continue beyond these pages. At this point, I even know what she becomes in her adult life.

Do you believe in ghosts?

My logical mind says no, but I have had experiences that can't be explained away. In June of 2010, while on a writing retreat, I went to take photos of the church that inspired the First Episcopal Church of Black Mountain. I had to hike a good half mile off the road into the woods. I was alone. When I found the perfect shot, a black shadow scurried across my screen. I searched around the area for the source and never found one. I took the photo without any more events. I couldn't help but think of Nellie and how she saw Merlin on the way to the pastor's house near the church. But to answer your question, I mostly enjoy a good ghost story without worrying about the real sprits.

What is your next project? Will there be more Black Mountain books?

The answer to this question goes with the question about Shelly. I'm currently working on a novel about Shelly Parker in which I find out what happens to her after Nellie leaves the mountain. What does she do with the money Nellie gives her? What's her history? What does Shelly want more than anything else in her life? Yes, there are plenty of ghosts. And I'm coming to know Pastor Dobbins and his family better. Also there are a few new characters, like Maude Tuggle, the granny woman.

The rough draft of the third book is finished. This novel tells the story of Hobbs and his sister as children. This book was actually written right after I finished the first draft of *Ghost on Black Mountain*. I wanted to know what made Hobbs who he became.